W9-BOC-912

NO LONGER THE PROPERTY OF
BALDWIN PUBLIC LIBRARY

Praise for *Coldsleep Lullaby*

'A beautifully assured whodunit ... The narrative segues between present-day and 17th-century Stellenbosch, until Brown bends the strands together like two electrical wires that flare up in revelation.'
— Michele Magwood, *Sunday Times*

'A cracker of a thriller ... engagingly written with a real sense of drama and narrative tension.' — Jennifer Crocker, *Cape Times*

'An excellent and gripping novel ... This is not simply a murder mystery – it is an excellently presented chronicle of the complexities of the human experience.' — Conrad Linström, *Pretoria News*

'This is a book to curl up with and devour way past bedtime, the rhythm of the plot well weighted, and always moving at a steady clip ... this is a confident and thrilling second novel from an exciting literary talent.' — Tom Gray, iafrica.com

'A first-rate thriller.'
— Brian Joss, Community Newspapers, Cape Town

'A finely crafted novel with an unstoppable plot.'
— Jenny Crwys-Williams, *Top Billing*

Praise for *Inyenzi*

'One of the best novellas to come out of Africa in ages.'
— *Financial Mail*

'An extraordinary, well-researched book ... *Inyenzi* is a brave, bold, confident and compassionate work.' — *Cape Times*

'An intelligent, finely drawn evocation of a beautiful suffering country.' — *Leadership*

Praise for *Street Blues*

'*Street Blues* ... is a must-read ... At times hilarious, at others shocking, this compassionate and beautifully crafted book will draw you in and give you a unique portrait of South Africa.'

– Margie Orford, *Psychologies*

Praise for *Refuge*

'If you want to know what the hottest issue is right now in our writing, then read this book. If you want to remember that feeling of amazement at the triumph of literature over the blindness of the establishment, get hold of this novel.'

– Leon de Kock, *Sunday Independent*

'Andrew Brown is probably one of the best of the new generation of South African writers ... What is most pleasing about Brown is that he sacrifices neither a good plot nor social commentary. With writers like him, the South African crime novel is both coming of age and becoming a serious contender on the global literary stage.'

– Anthony Egan, *Mail & Guardian*

'Andrew Brown is that rare breed of crime writer who can make you question society while still remaining riveted in the pages of his story ... *Refuge* is fast, sometimes witty, sometimes tragic, and always very, very good.'

– Bianca Capazorio, *Cape Argus*

'As an expose of cruel and disdainful human nature, *Refuge* is an emotionally gut-wrenching and gripping fictional tale of crisis and betrayal.'

– Joanne Hichens, *Cape Times*

'I loved this book and will read it again and again ... It is a riveting read from one of South Africa's most compelling authors.'

– Lindi Obose, *Sowetan*

Coldsleep Lullaby

Coldsleep Lullaby

A Mystery

Andrew Brown

Minotaur Books

A Thomas Dunne Book

New York

BALDWIN PUBLIC LIBRARY

This is a work of fiction. All of the characters, organizations, and events portrayed in this novel are either products of the author's imagination or are used fictitiously.

A THOMAS DUNNE BOOK FOR MINOTAUR BOOKS.
An imprint of St. Martin's Publishing Group.

COLDSLEEP LULLABY. Copyright © 2012 by Andrew Brown. All rights reserved. Printed in the United States of America. For information, address St. Martin's Press, 175 Fifth Avenue, New York, N.Y. 10010.

www.thomasdunnebooks.com
www.minotaurbooks.com

Library of Congress Cataloging-in-Publication Data

Brown, Andrew (Andrew David)
   Coldsleep lullaby : a mystery / Andrew Brown. — First U.S. Edition.
      p. cm.
   ISBN 978-1-250-03599-8 (hardback)
   ISBN 978-1-250-03600-1 (e-book)
   1. South African fiction. 2. Detective and mystery stories, South
African (English). I. Title.
   PR9369.3.B715C65 2014
   823'.92—dc23

2014003893

Minotaur books may be purchased for educational, business, or promotional use. For information on bulk purchases, please contact Macmillan Corporate and Premium Sales Department at 1-800-221-7945, extension 5442, or write specialmarkets@macmillan.com.

First published in South Africa by Zebra Press, an imprint of Random House Struik (Pty) Ltd

First U.S. Edition: June 2014

10 9 8 7 6 5 4 3 2 1

BALDWIN PUBLIC LIBRARY

For my father

O skoonheid van die lyf, jy slaat
óp uit die aarde soos die rooi vonk
uit die vuursteen spring; wild en jonk
is nog die skoonheid van die lyf op die swaar aarde
waaruit hy rank, hy ken sy waarde
nog half maar en die ver blom nog nie
waarheen hy groei en reik; maar dié
wat skoonheid en hoogheid dra as las
en ver verlange, is 'n vreemde ras
van mense en bloot aan veel gevaar.

— NP van Wyk Louw, Raka

ONE

S HE drifted in the water's slow current, her toes caressed by the grasses and blanket-weed lining the muddy bank. Although it was early morning, the water was warm. The February sun was bright, already scorching the thin clouds that passed beneath it. None of the pleasant moisture of dawn filled the air; instead the prickly dryness of summer breathed down the valleys and over the thatched roofs of the farmhouses. Drops of water on the vines, sprayed finely from automatic sprinklers before sunrise, had already been absorbed by the breeze, leaving only a dusting of sulphur patterned across the leaves. The gravel strips in front of the labourers' cottages were baked hard. In the distance, tarred roads shimmered in the strengthening heat, the mirage broken now and then by the first trucks leaving Stellenbosch for Cape Town. The early morning whirr of Christmas beetles and cicadas had stilled. Doves cooed quietly on the telephone lines, the singing birds buried deep in the thorny shade of the berry bushes.

Three centuries earlier, the newly appointed Governor at the Cape had set out in such heat, perhaps less intense then – being November – but as overwhelming to the foreigner. He had brought his horses to the same water to drink, cool and brackish. This was the first river beyond the tiny colony; he and his companions had stopped on its banks and taken long draws of water, gratefully naming it the Eerste River. The river had witnessed the passing of history. For centuries, it had replenished ostrich eggs used by the San for storing water; it had quenched the thirst of the new colony's leaders and their horses; it had watered the first vines; witnessed the growth of the small settlement. And it had decided the fate of the town's inhabitants – the Dutch and English masters and their slaves, thrown together from across the world. The river had felt their dreams, their desperate hopes, cast like twigs into its course, flowing away from the town and into the sea.

Now the Eerste River pushed lazily along its bunkered course, grasses and boulders strewn across its path, sometimes blocking its way. Alien trees – pines, eucalyptus and plains – lined both sides, their roots snaking into the water. The grey crags of the Simonsberg, Jonkershoek and Pieke ranges gazed down onto the valley, holding it in a tight embrace and steering the river cautiously along at their feet. The town, 'Van der Stel se Bosch', nestled among the lower hills and slopes, protected and seemingly serene.

Now the main streets of the university town were traversed by young women with red cheeks and loose cotton dresses, and young men with goatee beards and sandals – men too big for their boyish bodies, pushing bicycles – making their way to the first classes of the day. All displayed a lack of haste, the lazy ease of students. Some paused beneath the shade of elderly oak trees – the foreigner's blighted gift to the Eikestad – stubbing a cigarette into the run-off whitewash collected at the bottom of garden walls, or rearranging a rucksack, before setting off through the early morning glare.

Oak trees dominated the centre of the town, their asymmetrical trunks bulging and narrowing along their lengths. Thick boughs emerged unexpectedly, branching at irregular intervals, heavy and with little foliage. The older trees sported protrusions at their bases, giving them the surreal appearance of having melted into the pavement. Some had massive hollows at their centres, where the wood had been gnawed by grey squirrels and beetles, or rotted away, leaving ledges of white and orange fungus. The patterned symmetry of the occasional cypress or pine only emphasised the confident majesty of the oaks.

Leiwater trickled alongside the paths, running under rounded pedestrian bridges and disappearing into drains, in places flanked by ornate whitewashed walls. The water oozed from beneath tarred roads over beds of moss and bright green algae. Fallen oak leaves, curled and browned by the sun like shrivelled dead chameleons, lined the sides of the deep channels, providing a moist cover for small black river crabs, shiny millipedes and isopods. Cellophane crisp packets and crushed cigarette boxes poked out from the beds of leaves, glinting in the sun. The smell of guavas mixed with the exhaust fumes of tour buses and taxis.

She floated, oblivious to the growing heat. The strong light illuminated the brackish water around her, the rays piercing deeply into the orange-brown hue. A platanna swam hurriedly past her, kicking its webbed feet backwards like a speed skater with its arms held out in front. She drifted face down in the water. Thin tentacles of hair framed her scalp, hovering like a jellyfish over the dragonfly larvae moving about on the murky surface of the mud below. Her breasts, pale in contrast to the darkened colours surrounding her, moved almost imperceptibly with the slight current, her nipples smoothed against the areola in the tepid water.

A glossy hadeda watched, waiting for her to pass by. Red and blue iridescence shimmered across its wings in the sunlight. The platanna buried into the mud next to a beer bottle. The green glass was coated with slime, the label eaten away by small black freshwater snails and the rasping mouths of tadpoles. She had collected these tadpoles when she was a little girl; she had caught them in the same canal, only further down where the water poured over the weir and swirled in deeper eddies before continuing on to the farmlands. She had picked them off the shallow rocks on the side, where they lay recovering from the shock of being sucked over the stony platform. She had taken them home in jam jars and poured them into a small square aquarium.

There, the water had soon turned murky and filled her bedroom with a putrid smell. She'd leave it unchanged until it was thick with algae, producing stale bubbles that clumped together unbroken on the surface. Then she would pour the liquid out, catching the developing tadpoles in a net as they plunged in a helpless stream towards the drain. A squirming mass of black, the individual bodies were only discernible when she filled the tank with fresh water and tipped them out. She would sit and marvel at the changes that had taken place, hidden from her until then. It was her favourite part – comparing the unseen changes in each of her wards: the small buds of limbs, the tails diminishing as their nutrients were absorbed into the growing body, the round pouted lips of tadpoles and the slashed mouths of frogs.

She was floating towards the weir now, the rushing sound of the water filtering towards her. A large tadpole swam confidently up from the bottom, coming up close to her swaying hair before darting back to safety. Someone poked her hard on her thigh with a black baton, pushing her hips under water and making her upper torso arch. The platanna left a swirling muddy cloud as it swam away.

A young policeman hovered on the bank, the toes of his black boots pressing into the mud at the water's edge. The naked woman in the water seemed both peaceful and taut, as if she was waiting to leap up and spray him with generous slaps of water, laughing and pointing at him. He did not touch her again. He looked behind him to see who was watching, but the couple who had been walking their dog was standing at a respectable distance, holding each other's arms and talking in hushed tones. He turned back to the woman in the river.

Her body was lithe, despite the slackness induced by the water. He wondered how old she was. Her heels were smooth and showed none of the rough, cracked skin of the poor or the homeless. Her rounded buttocks bobbed up out of the water, showing an uncreased line of skin from the small of her back over the soft mound and across her upper thigh. He could see only one of her arms, and the forearm was obscured by her head. Her other arm descended beneath her body, trailing in the mud and snagging on the remnants of newspaper and plastic packets collected on the bottom. Her hair spread out from her head, decorated with broken twigs and fallen leaves. A small black beetle sought refuge from the water, climbing delicately up one of the strands.

The policeman's attention turned once more to her back and legs. Thin strips of white skin contrasted against the tan of her lower back and thighs; a small white V trailing into the strings of a bikini bottom, wrapping around her waist and disappearing evocatively between her buttocks, slinking unseen towards her anus.

There was no similar marking on her back – no narrowing line of a bikini top or bra, he noticed. Smooth brown skin stretched invitingly from her shoulders down to the line around her lower waist.

His throat felt dry and he wiped his hands against his trousers, digging his boots deeper into the mud. The water ran over the polished leather, wetting the black cotton laces. Her arm dragged against the side of the bank, halting the gentle movement of her body with the current.

The young constable moved forward as the water pressed against her thighs, the pressure pushing her closer towards him. He felt himself looming over her naked body, tipping towards her. He flushed with boyish excitement as he edged closer. Then one boot slipped, sliding into the mud. He thrashed against the water, sending the hadeda into the air, protesting raucously. Scrambling to regain his balance, he bumped his leg against her hip. The solidness of her weight against him, the unexpected contact, bolted through him and he clenched his teeth, trying not to swear. A grunt forced its way out of his mouth as he fell back onto the bank, crabwalking away from her body.

He sat panting on the grass, embarrassed and alarmed. The man behind him shouted something – a questioning call which the policeman ignored. Instead, he slid down towards the water again. She awaited him, lying sleepily as he approached. Holding his baton firmly in his hand, he leaned towards her. The rounded tip of the baton pushed against her skin but did not move her. He positioned himself closer to her, close enough to reach out and touch her, to slide his hand underneath her and lift her towards him. Close enough to run his hand across her back. But he did not touch her. Instead, he pushed harder with his baton. She started to turn towards him in the water. The sun burned on his neck. He felt sweaty and grimy.

He first saw her arm folded limply across her stomach – loose muscles floating in brown water. She turned towards him in slow motion, showing her body to him in minute degrees. Still she hid her face from him. Her legs paused at the peak of their turn, then finally slid over one another with a small splash. The turn of her thighs brought her torso towards the sun, her feet disappearing into the water. Her bikini line showed brightly, wrapped around from her back and running just above the tight dots of shaven pubic hair. The change in her position was causing her body to sink, he realised. He reached forward, holding his breath, and grabbed her arm. Her skin was malleable, like soft plastic. He shuddered involuntarily, drawing her body up to his leg. A flaccid breast brushed against his trouser leg.

Still he could not see her face. Her hair was matted in wet clumps across her cheek. He let her head drop beneath the surface, still holding her arm. The water dragged her hair back, away from her eyes. Her face, still cloaked with hair, broke the surface again, and the woman stared straight up at the young policeman.

'*Fok!*' he cried out in shock, as if he had been hurt. Backing up the bank, he mouthed obscenities at the ground. The couple retreated towards the road, holding onto each other in alarm.

Her dark-brown eyes were wide and unforgiving. She was pretty and seemed very young. He did not recognise her. Her head dropped below the surface and rose again. This time her hair flowed beneath her, revealing her full face. An open wound – a deep, purple slash with raised edges – crossed her forehead. Clear water dribbled out of the side of her smashed skull.

'*Nee, nee, nee!*' The words rushed up into his throat, burning his tongue like vomit. He could not keep them in his mouth and his speech was reduced to a garbled string of fierce sounds.

'You okay?' the man shouted from the road, unsure whether to come to his aid. The policeman felt humiliated. He wished they would leave. He wished the man would take the body of the young woman away. He wished the man's wife would hold him tightly. He wanted to cry – from the horror, for the young woman in the river, for himself.

'You need a hand?' the man shouted again, making no effort to come forward.

'*Nee* ... no,' the policeman managed, looking back. 'It's okay. I've got ... her.' He turned back to the river and spat into the ground.

The constable leaned over against the bonnet of the van. The metal was hot, but the ungiving surface and hint of diesel were comforting. The radio crackled loudly with a complaint from a neighbouring suburb. The couple was trying to get their Labrador into the car. The young constable tried to calm himself down. He thought of his training at the barracks. He thought of his uniform. He felt the 9mm firearm strapped to his side. He touched the smooth roundness of his baton. He thought of the body moving in the river and felt the heaving breaths rising once again.

The radio came on. 'Call sign Philander. Constable Philander. *Kom in op daai Kode Agt.* Code Eight on that complaint. Response? Over.'

Constable Philander took a deep breath and stood up. His face was wet with sweat and tears. He wiped his mouth with the back of his arm, leaving a crusty mark on the skin. A dirty arc of mud stained his boot, and grass seeds stuck onto his socks. He opened the passenger door of the vehicle and slumped down into the worn seat, his firearm digging roughly into his side. The radio gave its customary beep as he pressed the button.

'Control, Stellenbosch call sign Philander,' he heaved. *'Jy kan dit ... positief.* Positive, control. Positive.'

'Positief!' the radio crackled back at him. *'Wat bedoel jy positief? Wat gaan daar aan, man?'* But the policeman ignored it.

The ibis returned to the bank of the river. The young woman stared up into the blue sky, unblinking and unconcerned as the gnats swarmed about her face.

HUSH, LITTLE BABY

Hush, little baby, don't say a word.
Papa's gonna buy you a mockingbird

And if that mockingbird won't sing,
Papa's gonna buy you a diamond ring

And if that diamond ring turns brass,
Papa's gonna buy you a looking glass

And if that looking glass gets broke,
Papa's gonna buy you a billy goat

And if that billy goat won't pull,
Papa's gonna buy you a cart and bull

And if that cart and bull fall down,
You'll still be the sweetest little baby in town.

TWO

DETECTIVE Inspector Eberard Februarie stood in front of a mirror, his light-blue cotton shirt unbuttoned. Water dripped off his face and splashed onto the tiled floor – grey-white squares with chipped and yellowed grouting. The bathroom smelt of wholesale disinfectant, the same bite of cheap chemicals that pervaded the entire building. The detective's waking hours were defined by the odour; it followed him wherever he went, wafting from cracks and corners, encircling his body and permeating his uniform. It was the only smell he could detect now that his senses had constricted. He thought it had been the cocaine that had damaged his nasal passages, searing the delicate membrane and burning his sense of smell away, but the truth was that his senses were abandoning his body. As his emotions numbed, so his points of contact with the outside world retreated. Food became tasteless; sounds seemed muffled and distant; everything he touched was smooth and sticky. But it was the loss of smell that he noticed most. Now, all the offices, in every station he visited, emitted the astringent smell. The corridors of the courts were washed with it, and, when he delivered suspects to the awaiting-trial cells, or interviewed prisoners in the prison itself, he walked past amorphous dark-green figures on their hands and knees, slopping the same substance on tired linoleum floors. It was the smell of the state, the smell of his captured life, and it followed him everywhere, impersonal, harsh and pervasive.

The soap on the basin was an unhealthy pink colour, soggy from standing in pools of water. It disintegrated into slug-like chunks as he tried to pick it up. The taps were discoloured from fingerprinting ink, and someone had tried to write their name in thick black lines on the wall. Messages in blue ballpoint pen were scrawled among the black stains. *'Jonny Boy was hier.'* *'Fok die boere.'* *'Nog jare wat kom.'* The towel hanging next to the basin was unusable – threadbare and streaked with stains. It hung over the rail, moist, like the fresh skin of an animal. A window grated on its hinges, caught by the breeze. The rank, foetid smell of a blocked drain blew into the room. This is my world, Eberard thought.

He sighed and cupped his hands under the gushing water again. It at least was cool and clean, running over his fingers in loops. The sensation calmed him, and he splashed his face once more before standing up. His unbuttoned shirt parted and he stared at his brown chest. In his imagination, he saw a jagged bullet wound. Its centre was black, a circle of nothingness behind which the damage to his body lurked. He had seen enough bullet wounds to know. The edges were a dark red, the colour of old blood, with small flaps of skin and flesh protruding into the void. He fingered the flaps of his cotton shirt and imagined the threads, pulled out by the force of the bullet, sticking to the skin around the wound. It was strange, he thought, mesmerised by the morbid vision, nothing leaks out of the hole. Surely something should ooze out of the wound, a trickle of blood or moisture? The wad of lead, crafted and turned on some machine, would tear into his body, but his body let nothing out. Someone – who? – would do this one day, would fire a shot into him, but he would have no response, nothing to give back. He tried to imagine the pain his body would feel. Would it be a blunt pain, like when someone punches you hard in the stomach, like a bruise on your hip? Or would it be a sharp pain, definable and identifiable? The pain of a knife or a burn? I should feel not only the pain of broken skin and flesh, he thought, but also the indeterminate pain of organs, of broken bones, inside me.

The sound of the water slurping down the drain broke his reverie. He ran his palm over his smooth chest, hairless except for a few tight curls between his sagging pectoral muscles. The reality of being injured felt very close; he could put out his hand and touch the wound. He could create the scene with ease. He could stare at himself in the mirror and see the damage. But he could not take hold of the pain. The detective had stopped feeling emotion when he had been medically boarded for stress. Working in the narcotics unit, the access to hard drugs had been too easy and his need for escape too strong. Addiction had tightened its grip and squeezed his career and marriage dry. Now he longed to feel anything at all, even if only the physical pain of a blade or bullet.

'Februarie!' The door was pushed open with energy, knocking against the inside wall with a cracking bang. Eberard jumped involuntarily. He felt suddenly guilty, as if he had been caught doing something surreptitious. Reading someone's diary. Or masturbating.

'Sorry, Inspector,' the administration officer apologised, looking away, 'but there's a call for you. You can take it in my office.'

'Tell them to hold. I'm coming now.' Eberard turned off the tap and buttoned up his shirt. Although he had showered that morning, his hair was matted and looked unwashed. He ran his fingers across his head, turning away from the mirror without bothering to check his final appearance.

'Inspector.' The area commissioner's deep voice commanded respect. The receiver was warm from someone else's touch, repulsive rather than comforting. 'I need for you to take charge of a new investigation.' The speaker's accent was densely Afrikaans. 'Cape Town Violent Crimes Unit don't have the manpower to take a case in Stellenbosch. Captain Fourie will meet you at the morgue. He'll explain it to you so far. The body was removed this morning, but otherwise you'll start from the beginning.' The commissioner cleared his throat loudly, emitting the sound of phlegm mixed with nicotine. 'Ja, so if you can meet the captain.'

'Right away?' Eberard asked, restraining his irritation. His desk was already piled high with dockets waiting for his attention.

'If you don't think you're ready *vir hierdie soort* … for this kind of case,' the commissioner said slowly, meaningfully. A gulf of accusation stood between the two men. Both paused, breathing into the receivers. Waiting.

'No, Commissioner,' Eberard broke the silence, 'I'm only asking if I must meet Captain Fourie right away?'

'*Ja, nou dadelik. Dankie*, Inspector.' The commissioner hung up before Eberard could ask anything further. He put the receiver down slowly and stared out of the dusty window.

The back of the yard was filled with confiscated vehicles,

minibus taxis involved in collisions, twisted and deformed. An old bronze Mercedes rested in the corner, with thick, cylindrical holes punched along the driver's door and the side window smashed open. Glass pieces glinted like diamonds in the sun, scattered across the tarmac between the wrecks. A faded red Mazda, its front wheels missing and its axle pushing into the tar, squatted in a pool of old black oil. The oil had solidified and grasses and sweet papers had embedded themselves in the grime. Broken windows, torn metal, defaced lives. Each wreck had its own story, grimly waiting to be towed to the Kuilsriver yard, where it would be stripped and crushed. Squashed into unidentified blocks of scrap. No more a reminder of its tragedy. But out there, in someone's life, the tragedy remained, never to be forgotten. To the policemen, these wrecks were invisible; they arrived and left, but were no more noticeable than the bergies sleeping in doorways, or the dying prostitutes standing on street corners. Their stories were of no consequence.

Eberard Februarie had requested a post at a small station on his return to work, with the hope of reducing his workload. He had wanted to be close to Cape Town, to his daughter, to try to rekindle a meaningful relationship with her, despite his ex-wife's best efforts to isolate him. He was in need of a work environment with less expectations and fewer temptations. And perhaps colleagues who had no knowledge of, or interest in, his past. His request had been granted, but moving to the small town of Stellenbosch had been difficult. The community was insular and self-contained. They did not warm to newcomers easily, and he spent his spare time mostly alone. The racial tension between officers at the station was more pronounced than in the bigger units; perhaps it was only that it could not be avoided as easily. His male colleagues remained in their small groups, racially demarcated, laughing at private jokes and talking of shared events from their past. Towards the newcomer they were suspicious and unhelpful.

His female colleagues were more generous. He sensed that their attitude towards him was governed by maternal pity, and that it was his vulnerability that softened them. It made for unsatisfying interactions, however; they displayed a morbid interest in his emotional trauma, quietly tugging at the threads of his hurt, persistently teasing information from him. He longed to break free of the stigma that had attached to him, but he increasingly discovered that his history defined him – it wasn't a limb he could simply cut off. He was seen by the outside world as a patient, a person in need of care. The more he tried to fight against the definition, the more concerted were the efforts to uncover his turmoil.

The station commander, Superintendent Kotze, had called him into his office during his first week. 'Inspector, as you know, this isn't a large station and we have a shortage of manpower. I can't assign you a partner. You'll have to work on your own for now. But with your experience, I'm sure that won't be a problem.' The double meaning of the statement hung in the air. The superintendent shuffled some papers on his desk, clearing his throat. 'But we do have reservists who have applied to be moved from the shifts to come and help with the detectives. I'll assign one of them to you, once we've considered their applications. With your experience, they'll learn a lot.'

Eberard knew that having a reservist assigned to him was a sign of disrespect. But he did not protest. During the eighteen months that he had been at the station, he'd been assigned a variety of ill-trained and overenthusiastic reservists. Each brought their own peculiar problems. Inevitably, after a few months, they would complain of his surliness, his lack of communication, his failure to teach them anything about criminal investigation, and they would return to the shifts.

Recently, he had been assigned a young woman reservist. She was an undergraduate law student at the university and her availability was erratic. The lack of routine in her work as a reservist would normally have annoyed the detective, but to his surprise he found that he enjoyed working with her. Constable Xoliswa Nduku had only recently completed her reservist training and had spent her required six months working behind the charge office desk. The detective had noticed her there on occasion: a tall, powerfully built woman with striking facial features. She was young and, as a police officer, wholly inexperienced. Because of her youth, gender and race, she would normally have faced a barrage of snide comments and lewd passes in the charge office, but she carried herself with a grace and confidence that was almost intimidating.

In the beginning, Eberard had found her stillness threatening. She would sit alongside him for hours without saying a word. He had assumed that she was shy and perhaps unintelligent. He had tried talking to her about insignificant events, his speech strained and thin, but she had shown no interest and he had given up. But now her silence was a comfort to him; he liked her for not prying like the others. He knew that his first impression of her had been wrong; her silence was a sign of her confidence, not her lack of it. She did not feel the need to fill up time with small talk. She preferred to sit and observe. She would think and watch and, when the need arose, she would talk, looking straight at her listener, expecting their full attention. The words left her lips in an unhesitating stream; she was both coherent and succinct. When she was finished, she would consider the response, again giving the speaker her unflinching attention. Then she would be still once more. Perhaps fifteen years her senior, Eberard still felt unnerved by her at times.

She was waiting for him now in the yard at the station. Though her presence at the station was sporadic, she was always punctual.

'Good afternoon, Inspector,' she said, climbing into the passenger seat and smiling at Eberard warmly. A slight whiff of soap and spray-on deodorant entered the car, breaking through the layer of burning disinfectant about his nose. Eberard turned to her, a little surprised. She looked back at him, quizzically. 'Is something the matter, Inspector?'

'No, no,' he replied quickly. Too quickly. 'It's just that ... you smell so nice.' He felt the heat of a blush on his cheeks. 'I'm just not used to smelling ... such good smells.' She laughed and looked away, not wishing to prolong his embarrassment. He tried to cover his discomfort, dropping the keys on the floor and swearing quietly under his breath.

They drove through the busy streets of the town in silence. The gates of the pathology laboratory appeared on the left, and Eberard turned into the tarred car park, parking in the bay closest to the aluminium and glass entrance. It occurred to him that this could be his passenger's first visit. 'Xoli, have you been here before?' he asked. 'To the morgue?' Again he felt suddenly uncomfortable, although he could not discern why.

She turned to face him. 'Mmm, when I was eighteen,' she said, nodding. 'I had to identify my brother's body.'

'Oh.' Eberard suddenly wished he hadn't asked the question. 'Was he ... I mean, how did he ...' His voice trailed off as Xoliswa explained, matter-of-factly, how her brother's life had been ended by a falling crate on the apple farm where he had worked as a labourer. She had identified the body at the same morgue.

'I'm sorry,' Eberard managed.

'One of the guys tried to touch my breasts while I was saying goodbye to my brother.'

Eberard's eyes involuntarily dropped from her face to where her chest pressed out against the fabric of her uniform. A prickle of sweat broke out on his neck. 'But that was the only time I came here. I've never been here as a policewoman.' She waited briefly for a reply and, when none was forthcoming, opened her door and stepped out into the sunshine.

Captain Fourie was waiting for them. He was a small, compact man, dressed neatly in senior officer's uniform. A clipped moustache ran in a thin line exactly halfway between the bottom of his nose and his top lip. Eberard thought he heard him click his heels as he put out his hand. His handshake was tight and cold.

'Inspector.' His voice was shrill and the consonants grated.

Eberard turned to introduce Xoliswa, but the captain had already turned on his heels. 'Follow me,' he said curtly, walking swiftly down the corridor.

The walls were filled with torn posters, pictures from old campaigns against child abuse, Aids, sexually transmitted diseases. A new South African Police Union poster had been stuck up with large mounds of Prestik, half-covering the picture of a child with pleading eyes and a bruise on her cheek. An empty box rested on a small table, below a sign drawn in black koki pen: 'The Truth on Aids. Please take one'. The smell of disinfectant filled his nose again, although this time it was mixed with something even more pungent. Eberard sighed and followed the captain.

'In here.' The captain turned and pushed through two heavy swing doors. The smell became stronger. Xoliswa stood back and allowed her senior to enter first. The smell in the room was almost overpowering. Eberard expected the walls to be scorched with ammonia and the floors to be scoured. The state pathologist was hunched over his desk, concentrating on a small plastic container, a desk lamp peering over him.

'Dr Rademan,' the captain announced, 'the investigating officer is here to see you.' Fourie turned to Eberard. 'The doctor will explain everything you need to know. The paperwork is in the docket.' He pushed a thin file into Eberard's hands and walked past him and Xoliswa. He clearly had misgivings about handing the investigation over to the two of them. The swing doors swished angrily behind him as he left. Xoliswa looked around the room and then frowned towards the doctor.

'Come here, please.' Rademan's voice was warm and limp, and he waved to them vaguely, his attention still focused on the container in front of him.

Eberard walked across the laboratory towards him, avoiding the steel table in the middle of the room. Jars with tight lids, filled with greenish-yellow liquid and indiscernible body parts, lined the shelves above Rademan's desk. A stacked pile of dockets had collapsed, dropping papers onto the floor. Last year's calendar was hanging at an angle next to the desk above a jar of old ballpoints and koki pens without their caps, dried and unusable. The pathologist looked up at Eberard briefly.

'Dr Rademan. How do you do? And what is your name?'

Eberard looked over the man's shoulder into the plastic container; the doctor was pushing pieces of bright pink polony and lettuce between two thin slices of white bread. 'That's the trouble with bringing your lunch to work in your briefcase.' Rademan gave a nervous laugh. 'It gets thrown around, you see, and all the filling falls out. Won't take a minute. Sorry, what did you say your name was?'

'Inspector Februarie, Doctor,' Eberard replied, 'and this is Constable Nduku.'

'February and Duku. February and Duku,' Rademan repeated to himself. 'It's not Starsky and Hutch, now is it? No, not quite Starsky and Hutch.' The pathologist laughed to himself and looked up for appreciation. 'No, well, anyway, don't mind that,' he continued distractedly.

A kitchen cutting board lay next to Rademan's lunch box, with a lump of what looked like wet dough in the middle, neatly positioned next to a steel scalpel. Liquid had collected around the base of the dough and was trickling off the edge of the board. Rademan held up his sandwich triumphantly and took a large bite out of its centre. He noticed Eberard staring at the cutting board. 'Dessert!' he exclaimed with a twinkle in his eye, spraying crumbs of white bread and polony. Still laughing, he put the sandwich back into his lunch box and wiped his hands down the front of his coat. He picked up his scalpel and pressed the back of the instrument into the dough. A delicate stream of bubbles, and then a thicker froth, emerged out of the one end.

'Do you see that? That's water and mucus. Well, in truth it's a reaction to the presence of water. But either way, it's the water that's important, isn't it?' Eberard looked at him blankly. 'Well, she was alive when she went into the water, wasn't she? She was breathing when she went under. You see that? There, you see the froth. She was alive.'

Eberard started to feel dizzy. 'I'm sorry, Dr Rademan, I haven't really been told anything about this case yet,' he explained. 'I mean, all I know is that you've taken out someone's lung and found that they drowned. Other than that I'm not really sure what I'm dealing with here.' He flipped open the docket: brief details of a body found, the place, the time, the name of the first officer on the scene – a Constable Philander – nothing substantial. 'The captain was unfortunately too busy to fill me in properly,' he added. The pathologist raised his eyebrows knowingly.

'She's over here.' Rademan stood up and walked over to the steel table. Eberard saw to his surprise that Xoliswa had been standing alongside the table all the time, studying the body carefully. 'She's young, white, female, as you can see.' Rademan was more serious now, although still animated. 'I would say that she's about eighteen or nineteen years old. Probably a middle-class family – well manicured, you see.' He gestured towards her feet. 'Nails are clipped, the hair is cared for, although it has been subjected to various amounts of dyeing, and there are no signs of poor nutrition. Pretty child, in fact.'

The young woman lay on her back. Her body had been slit open from her throat to below her navel. Eberard took a step back. The body still retained the overall sense of a human being, the head, shoulders, the legs and feet. But the middle had been ripped out, cut up and dissected as if she were some exotic vegetable. The dark opening in her torso gaped at him.

Rademan looked at him quizzically. 'Don't worry, Inspector. We'll put her back together before her family sees her. Which reminds me, I understand that her identity has not yet been confirmed, so no family members have been contacted as yet.' Eberard flipped through the file for confirmation. 'Now, come closer and I'll show you the important bits.'

Eberard moved forward reluctantly, trying to blinker in on detail. 'As I've shown you,' the pathologist continued, 'the actual cause of death was drowning. She was still alive when she went into the water. But I very much doubt that she was conscious.' Rademan took out a small torch and moved to the head of the table. 'What we see here is a massive fracture of the left temporal portion of the skull.' He shone the torch into the gaping fracture; pieces of bone were embedded in the wound.

Eberard felt a dangerously familiar need to escape; the taste of tobacco and chemicals on his tongue made him feel nauseous. The pathologist's voice rattled on. He had not yet removed the brain; he wanted them to see the fracture first. The fracture was large and deep and would have caused immediate brain dysfunction. It appeared to have resulted from a single blow, a blow of great force, from a blunt object such as a rock.

'If you look carefully,' the doctor leaned in closely, his mouth almost brushing against her cheek, 'you'll see small grains of sand pushed into the fracture. It's not conclusive, but I'd suggest that she was hit with a rock, maybe a brick or something similar. While she was deeply unconscious, but still alive, she was placed somewhere in the stream where she was found.'

'So was the cause of death the blow to the head or drowning, Doctor?' Xoliswa was staring at Rademan, who seemed a little taken aback. He coughed nervously while appraising her more carefully. 'Would the person who hit her have killed her if she hadn't been put in the river?' Xoliswa clarified.

'Yes, yes, I see your point. What if someone else put her in the water? Yes, uhm ... well certainly, as I said, it's clear that she was still breathing when she went in. The blow was severe and may well have killed her without the intervention of the water. I'll need to conclude my investigation to be sure. But what is clear is that she died from of a lack of oxygen as a result of immersion in water. She drowned. Either way, whoever did this achieved what they set out to do ... assuming that the same person put her in the river.'

Xoliswa nodded. Her eyes were focused on the young body, her fingertips brushing against the cold steel table. 'Then we probably only need to know whether she was raped or not,' she said softly, as if to herself. She walked down the table and placed her hand gently on the young woman's hip. Eberard shuddered involuntarily. He was unsure whether he should join her. Averting his eyes from the beckoning cavity in the body's torso, he moved down towards the foot of the table. His mouth felt dry and sour.

Rademan slid the back end of the scalpel between the labia, pulling to one side to expose pink flesh. 'I can't tell you much at this stage,' he began. 'Yes, she did have intercourse, probably within twelve hours of her death. First examination revealed a quantity of seminal fluid on the walls of the vagina. Given that she had been floating in water for a while, the quantity was quite surprising. And in itself may be significant. Specimens will be sent for testing.' He paused briefly, looking up at them. 'Was the intercourse consensual? There are no immediately apparent signs of trauma, whether internal or external. There are abrasions on the inner thigh and small contusions internally.'

'That could be passion as easily as it could be resistance,' Xoliswa interjected evenly.

'Quite so,' Rademan said, adjusting his glasses on his nose. 'Once I've studied the internal wall and smaller veins of the vagina, I'll be in a position to give you a better indication. It would also help if you could find her clothes. That's all I can give you for now.'

Eberard walked towards the doors, relieved to be away from the body. At the entrance to the morgue, the three discussed possible test results. Rademan could test for blood alcohol, stomach contents and narcotics, as well as blood type and basic testing on the seminal fluid, but the cost of a DNA test would need to be justified by reasonable grounds for comparison with a suspect.

'I'll keep a sample available for testing,' Rademan confirmed, 'but I can't justify the cost of the test unless you bring me a suspect. That's about it.'

Eberard walked out into the sunshine. The smell of ammonia clung to him. The tarmac was hot, and he sat in the car for a while with the door open, reading through the terse notes and poorly written statement from Constable Philander. He handed the documents to Xoliswa one at a time as he finished each page. She studied them carefully, reading and rereading each statement slowly, extracting all possible information from the thin docket.

'I think it would be advisable for me to have a female officer working with me on this case,' he suggested. 'It would also be a good case for you. So long as ... well, anyway, I'll ask the superintendent to assign you as my partner in CID for another few months.'

'That would be good,' she said, without looking up.

Eberard watched her as she read. She was so different from him, in all respects, and yet he saw something in her that he recognised. Something that he had once had but no longer sought:

an interest in her surroundings, in herself, an interest in her life. He wondered what he could possibly offer someone like her. Or his own daughter, for that matter.

SLEEP BABY SLEEP

Sleep, baby, sleep
Your father tends the sheep
Your mother shakes the dreamland tree
And from it fall sweet dreams for thee
Sleep, baby, sleep
Sleep, baby, sleep

Sleep, baby, sleep
Our cottage vale is deep
The little lamb is on the green
With snowy fleece so soft and clean
Sleep, baby, sleep
Sleep, baby, sleep

THREE

MARTIN van der Keesel was a man of acerbic comment and rude disposition. His large, veined face was hidden behind a cropped beard and, more often than not, clouds of acrid tobacco smoke. He wore his greasy black hair long, in the fashion of nobility, and was at pains to confirm his status, habitually wearing black slippers with silver buckles and a black coat with gold buttons. The wide collar of his white shirt, yellowed with sweat and grime, flattened against his chest. He had travelled widely on behalf of the Company and had picked up the indelicate habit of chewing *sirih* while in Indonesia. A mild narcotic when chewed raw, the betel nuts blackened his teeth, and when he spat out the crushed fibres, his saliva was the colour of blood. Van der Keesel's overbearing confidence and self-reliance made him an unlikeable but powerful man. He treated his juniors with ill-disguised contempt, while his peers were the recipients of arrogant challenges that bordered on being publicly offensive.

The oft-repeated story in the colony was that he had even dared to laugh in Governor van der Stel's presence on hearing that the man's brother had taken up a position with the Company in Sumatra. 'That family does appear drawn to lands of mixed opportunity,' he had quipped, referring both to the Governor's mixed racial background (his grandmother was Javanese and his complexion perceptibly dusky) and the mixed fortunes that had befallen his father, Adriaan, in Mauritius. The story was that the Governor had pretended not to hear the comment, striking up a lively conversation with the visiting Company official standing next to him.

Van der Stel was not known for his benevolence or humour, and a slight on his family would have caused obvious offence had it come from anyone else. However, Van der Keesel was an important part of the Governor's plan for the colony; his training as a viticulturist and his specialist knowledge of root stock and the art of the cultivated *wynberg* were critical to the success of the wine production in the Cape. In the year that he had been in the colony, Van der Keesel had already made great progress with the vines at Constantia and on the slopes of the hill below Van Riebeeck's original residence at Bosheuvel. It was a matter of record that Van Riebeeck's first attempts at winemaking had been dismal. In Van der Keesel's view, the man's fumbling efforts rendered him entirely useless to the Company.

'What did that infant know about wine stock?' he would bellow whenever the occasion arose. 'Planting muscat on the northern slope, facing the sun all day, when any fool knows that muscat burns ... and planting rotten hárslevelü on the shaded side. Trying to make Tokaji sweet wine in Africa! The man is an idiot! A snotty-nosed child heading a group of weak, scurvy-ridden vagabonds.'

Van der Keesel's vitriolic criticism of the young Van Riebeeck's failures in the vineyards quickly earned him a reputation among the winegrowers. His first step had been to tear out most of the vines, replanting the muscat and discarding the hárslevelü. He had extended the muscat plantings and introduced a field of semillon cuttings from the south of France.

'Semillon is the grape of the future,' he explained in a patronising tone to the Governor's aides, who were shocked at the decision to pull out the established vineyards. 'We will extract a blend for sauvignon blanc, crisp and acidic like a green pepper; we will distil a pure, unwooded wine that is clear and grassy; we will wood it with French oak and prepare a chardonnay-type wine that will grace the tables of kings in Europe, gold in colour, like honey on fresh bread in the mouth. The muscat is the workhorse grape: "hanekloot" – big, juicy berries like a rooster's testicles.'

The grape had first been grown in the valleys of the Nile in ancient Egypt, and from there it had spread across all of Europe. Muscadel was soon drunk in Portugal, Spain, France, Italy, Greece and even Turkey, and Van der Keesel was keen to be the first to produce muscat from the southern tip of Africa. 'I will show you what that little bastard could never have done in his ignorance. I will show you how to make a wine that will bring tears to your eyes and put honey in your veins. "Hanekloot" – not shrivelled, rotting Hungarian hárslevelü!'

Van der Keesel's criticism of his Governor's predecessor was not limited to his botched attempts at winemaking; he heaped equal amounts of scorn upon all aspects of his administration of the growing colony. 'Cabo da Boa Esperança indeed!' he would remark, his voice thick with sarcasm as he spat out the phrase so loved by Van Riebeeck. 'More likely De Kaapse Vlek. The savages running around in the veld could do better than this,' he raged, tormenting the poorly paid employees of the Company. He surrounded himself with noise and vitriol, dominating any company with bluster and bad odour.

'This outpost is the manure shed of the colony, fit only for bandieten and escaped slaves. I see the new inhabitants of this pestilent place – rebellious animals run away from their masters living on the mountainside – I see their fires like stars on the slopes of the Cape mountain. But they are left, unpursued, plotting, by this useless excuse for a garrison.'

He frequently compared the shortcomings of the infant colony in the Cape with the cultural and material wealth of the Company's Asian headquarters in Batavia. 'It is the centre of our trade in spices and the fine fabrics of the East,' he would muse. 'There we throw out our uncomfortable wools, the starched linens we normally have no choice but to wear. Indian cotton, with its fine weave and brilliant colours; Chinese silks, filled with a soft shine; chintz, muslin – these are the fabrics of the future.' He raved on about the exotic spices from Sumatra – mace, nutmeg, cinnamon, cloves – and the rich coffees from Java. The timber – dark and red ebony, rosewood and teak – was also vastly superior. 'And what does this vulgar little outpost offer by way of competition?' he roared. 'Its timber is mean, already we have to look further afield for usable wood; its terrain is ungiving, without opportunity for anything better than ordinary grain; and its people, naked and ignorant, are hostile and resistant to our authority. Even the slaves are better behaved in Batavia.'

He was quick to point to the Company's folly in being tempted by talk of gold and copper, rumoured to equal the wealth of

Monomotapa, and he scoffed at the expeditions that returned only with tales of poisonous snakes, deadly scorpions and vast tracts of scorched, impassable sand and stone. 'It is, sirs, a foul and sadly chosen plot,' Van der Keesel asserted, shaking his head.

But his bluster dissipated when he was in the fields, on his hands and knees, easing a vine into place, rubbing his fingers over the flaking bark or crushing a young grape in the palm of his hand. The sun burnt his wide-brimmed black hat, his neck dampened with sweat and his stockings filled with burrs, but he was silent at these times. He had no respect for the people around him, but the environment at the Cape held his interest – the strong sun, incessant sea winds and long days of penetrating rain. The soil was rich and loamy on the slopes and the stock took well to the conditions. The Cape offered something, in its meanness, that Batavia could never provide.

Van der Keesel had already pressed some wines from the vines planted by Van der Stel at Constantia, and, although he would never have conceded it, the Governor had more than a passing knowledge of viticulture, having procured some good French root stock from a group of Huguenots passing through on their way to the interior. The stock flourished in the more sheltered dales of Constantia, sprouting a proliferation of strong green buds. The Governor had noticed a genuine excitement in Van der Keesel's manner on his first visit to the estate when he showed him the lines of carefully staked plants. The Governor's own view – that this developing territory could be far more than just a granary station and supply point for the Company – was confirmed by the viticulturist's ill-concealed delight at the strength of the growing vines.

Governor van der Stel was an ambitious man. Short in stature and with a temperament in many ways similar to Van der Keesel's, he saw an opportunity to develop the new colony into a flourishing territory that would serve the tables of all of Europe. His will to succeed was tenacious, and his expectations of those around him were as exacting as his demands of himself. His manner was gruff and he displayed great energy and impatience. However, a fiery temper and high regard for his own position often marred his judgement. He had, for example, nearly derailed the commissioning of the building of the Drostdij in the new town of Stellenbosch. The building was to be erected on the very island upon which he had first camped in the valley. The Governor regarded the progress made by his master carpenter, Van Brakel, as being tardy. In spite of the assistance of a team of German builders and a handful of slaves, the man was nowhere near completing the project. Having worked himself up into a rage upon seeing the slow progress, Van der Stel summarily placed the hapless Van Brakel under house arrest. Ironically, it was the equally impatient Van der Keesel who had to intervene, seeking the poor man's part release not because he felt any compassion for the carpenter, but because, without him, the Drostdij would never have been completed at all – a simple fact that the Governor in his anger had overlooked. The Drostdij was completed within the year and stood as a monument to the Governor's will to bring order to the new and untamed land.

The Company was experiencing unprecedented successes in its business ventures around the world, and it was Van der Stel's vision that the Cape Colony – originally intended only as a temporary settlement for passing Company ships – should establish itself as a reliable grain and wine producer. The large schuur, near the thorn grove Rondedoornbosjen, bore testimony to the potential for high yields from the lands in the flood plain of the Riebeeck River.

But of all the newly tilled lands, it was the recently founded area in the valley beyond the settlement at Stellenbosch – named the Jonkershoek – that held a particular interest for the Governor. It was here that he sought Van der Keesel's assistance. Van der Keesel regularly journeyed from the Cape, past the hills of Tijgers Vallei and across the Heiveldt, to Stellenbosch, and he soon made the developing village his permanent home. Van der Stel had come across the valley a year previously when he and a group of twenty pioneers had travelled on horseback from the settlement at Stellenbosch over a range of low mountains. The valley lay at the foot of the range, and Van der Stel was immediately struck by its immense beauty and serenity. The soil was rich and fertile, although it drained easily, and the ferocity of the south-easterly wind was dampened by the peaks above the plains of the river. The dense riparian vegetation in the centre gave way to swaying fields of fynbos, which stretched up to the highest slopes of the mountains. Strong protea bushes, dominated by the pink and white heads of flowers, dotted the landscape, while finer ericas, grasses and lilies covered the ground. Bright red flowers bristled on the ends of slender stalks, offset against the yellows and greens of the bushes.

A male baboon had sounded the alarm as they entered the valley, coughing loudly to its followers and crashing through the undergrowth. The party had only managed to shoot two of the troop, a female and a young male, before the animals had slipped away into the bush. One of the young men had fired a shot at a burnt stump, shouting that he had spotted a lion; they had all laughed, but kept a vigilant eye on the bushes all the same. Iridescent sunbirds, with shimmering green wings, and long-tailed sugarbirds weaved between the flowering bushes. The valley was alive with the chorus of wild animals. Rock lizards and adders scattered before them, and eagles circled overhead. During the course of those first exploratory days, they had filled two sacks with easy trophies: densely feathered eagle owls; sleek yellow cobras; a magnificent black eagle, which the Governor wanted stuffed and mounted in his study; a sharp-toothed honey badger; several klipspringer; a mongoose and the two baboons. After a while, the captain had ordered the men to save their powder and shot in case they came across any 'natives'. But the valley was uninhabited and their exploration was otherwise uneventful.

The route into the valley was now well established by a small party of Huguenots. The group had been persecuted in France and had come to the colony seeking refuge. They had already inspected the area and declared the soil and the surrounding conditions ideal for vineyards. With vine cuttings from their homeland, they cleared small tracts of land for planting – muscat de frontignan, crouchen blanc and semillon for the whites, and grenache, a powerful tannin-producing wine, for the reds.

Van der Stel's difficulty, however, lay in keeping the burgeoning population of free burghers under control. The burghers were attracted by the agricultural promise of the new area, as well as by its distance from the authority of the colony. The land distribution office had experienced a decline in requests for farms along the Liesbeeck River, where the first 'free' slaves or burghers had established their smallholdings and which was still the favoured grain-producing area. Instead, applications for land along the now-named Eerste River flooded in. The Governor had granted title to the religious refugee Jean le Long on the farm Bossendal in the new valley, having tried, unsuccessfully, to persuade him to take land closer to the Cape. He had also received reports of farms being built without any title at all – virgin bush was being cleared alongside the river, and the trade in root stock was apparently swift. The Company laid down strict rules as to which crops could be planted on free-burgher land, but, in spite of this, the Governor had received news of unapproved crops growing surreptitiously alongside the prescribed corn and barley. The Governor had no doubt that these illegal crops were not tobacco (which the Company regulated strictly) but rather variants of the new stock brought in by the Huguenots.

Van der Keesel shared the Governor's vision of a wine-producing empire in their new world. It was his desire to find, or create, a variety of grape that was ideally suited to the conditions of the colony: a vine that could grow in the strength of the African sun without burning, a grape berry that could turn the rich texture of the soil into acids and juice, a variety that soaked up the coolness of the sea breezes without rotting, a wine that had the clarity and depth of the sky under which it was pressed. He was looking for a varietal that could stand on its own, not to be used for blending or for simple sweet wines, but to produce pure, characteristic wines, distinctive wines that would become known across Europe.

But Van der Keesel also understood the inherent risks in the proliferation of freehold-title farmers in the new valley. While the Governor regarded the free burghers as an unruly but useful part of the greater development of the colony, Van der Keesel saw them as a dangerous scourge. His view was that freehold title would undermine the economic control that both Holland and the Company enjoyed over its subjects, and that farms should be established and worked under the Company's name. The free burghers were mostly peasant slaves or artisans who had worked for the Company at the colony. They were released from their employ at the instance of the Governor and allowed to establish small farms. Land and equipment were sold on credit, but they could only plant crops as directed by the Company and had to accept whatever payment the Company offered for their produce. Control lay in ensuring that the profits never exceeded the payment due on debt, thereby locking the new farmers into perpetual servitude.

Van der Keesel was aware that this method of control was more illusory than real, since there was already a thriving black market in crops, equipment, seed and labour. Some burghers had moved further into the hinterland, ignoring the proclaimed boundaries of the colony. Here, they farmed in peace beyond the grasp of the Company administration. Van der Keesel's first step towards restraining the growing burgher population was to reduce the prices the Company paid for grapes. He slashed them nearly by half, intent on starving out the illicit farming of vines. A deputation of burghers arrived at the Landdrost's home in Stellenbosch to complain, threatening to leave the colony altogether. 'Let them leave!' had been Van der Keesel's impatient response to the Landdrost when the man had nervously reported the visit to him. 'There is a list of people waiting for land. They can go!'

However, a few weeks later, at Van der Stel's personal request, he agreed to meet with a group of burghers to consider their grievances. He travelled on horseback with a small commando, heading out from the Company offices early in the morning. The mist lay like a veil across the Liesbeeck Valley, and the horses' hooves clanged on the cold ground. Van der Keesel led the group, pushing his horse mercilessly on the uneven track. The men followed him in silence.

By the time they reached the slopes of the Stellenbosch mountains, the sun was hot and dry. Van der Keesel's horse was sweating and his own face burned with an unhealthy red colour. He pulled his horse up short on the banks of the Eerste River, holding the reins in tight to prevent it from lowering its head to drink. He held that position, surveying the scene in front of him and jerking the animal's head back. White foam dripped from its mouth. The men held back, waiting for the word. When he was sure that no word of dissent would be spoken, he dismounted and draped the reins over the saddle in one swift movement. The horse plunged into the shallow river, slurping at the water.

The air was still. Only snakes and lizards braved the midday heat. Something moved among the rocks on the slope – a flick of an ear or a shudder of muscle that betrayed the presence of some creature. One of the men pointed to a shaded patch beneath a small overhang. A leopard lay with its paws stretched out in front of it, staring at the group of men with large yellow eyes. There was another movement, in the shadow alongside the animal, and a cub emerged, sniffing the air uncertainly. Van der Keesel beckoned his men to stay still as he prepared his musket. Once the gun was ready he picked his way between the rocks, hunched over with the rifle pointed in front of him. The adult leopard sat up at his advance, watching him intently. Once it was in range, he halted, resting the gun on the top of a flat rock. He could see the dappled markings of the beast quite clearly. Its pink tongue was exposed, panting slightly in the heat. The cub had disappeared behind its mother. He aimed at the chest, so as not to damage the head or neck or stain the fur with blood. The musket hissed and banged, releasing a cloud of pungent smoke. The lead ball thudded into the animal's chest, breaking open the skin and muscle and penetrating deep into its flesh. The cat hurled itself into the air, screaming and clawing. She landed on her back and slumped over the rocks, succumbing to shock. He filled his weapon again and approached the shaded overhang. The cub cowered against the face of the rock, hissing pathetically. Its mother was still alive, breathing weakly and growling. Van der Keesel kicked her with his foot and, when she did not respond, turned his attention to the cub.

The cub turned towards him as he fired the shot, and the ball hit its small head just above the left eye, splitting open its skull and destroying the symmetry of its face. Van der Keesel cursed and grabbed the dead cub by its foot. He walked back to the horses where the men were waiting. 'Take her head just above the shoulders,' he ordered, gesturing towards the unmoving body of the mother. He dropped the cub into a sack, threw it over the back of his saddle and rode on.

As the party arrived at the small home of the burghers' spokesman, two farm dogs smelt the blood and ran, yapping, towards them. Van der Keesel pointed his rifle at them menacingly and a young boy ran up to pull the hounds away. A group of six men stood in the dust at the entrance to the house, one waving uncertainly towards the Company's representative. Their skin was scorched by the sun and their clothes were streaked with dried mud. A young man stepped forward to speak, but Van der Keesel did not intend to exchange any pleasantries. He swung the sack out in front of him and opened the mouth of the bag; the bloodied leopard cub dropped out onto the ground in front of the man, who stepped back in surprise.

'Don't try to hunt before you can survive without your mother's milk,' Van der Keesel said in a voice that brooked no argument. The man stared wordlessly at the corpse at his feet and then back at the man on the horse. Van der Keesel crushed the sack into a ball and dropped it alongside the body, before turning his horse around and heading back down the stony track.

GOLDEN SLUMBERS

Golden slumbers kiss your eyes,
Smiles await you when you rise.
Sleep, pretty baby,
Do not cry,
And I'll sing you a lullaby.

Care you know not, therefore sleep,
While I o'er you watch do keep.
Sleep, pretty darling,
Do not cry,
And I will sing a lullaby.

FOUR

THE face from the morgue stared back at Eberard, looking at him without blinking, her features drawn with suspicion and loathing. This girl was younger-looking – the skin along her jawline and just beneath her nose showed traces of unevenness from pimples. Her hair was lighter, cut short, making her look almost boyish. There was a smudge of brownish lipstick on her lips, and she wore a fleece-lined sweater and tight, faded jeans. Her eyes were puffy and red from crying. The girl blinked at Eberard and looked away.

'This is Melanie's sister, my younger daughter Elsabe.' The words were spoken softly, belying the speaker's large frame. Eberard nodded towards the child in a way he hoped seemed both sympathetic and respectful. 'Have a seat, please,' his host continued. Xoliswa's face was stony, taut with concern. She sat closest to the young girl, keeping her hands folded on her lap. The detective chose a high-backed leather chair that creaked as he lowered his weight onto the seat. The room was still and cool.

Professor Dawid du Preez was an impressive man. He exuded a sense of confidence and intellectual intensity. The aura of learning was evident in the room he had chosen for the interview; it was filled with dark shelving that strained under the weight of row upon row of books. Works of fiction, both old and new, were wedged alongside scholarly works on law, art, history and science. Books on botany and ornithology shared shelves with Dostoyevsky and the plays of Bernard Shaw. The collection stretched to the ceiling and loomed over those seated below.

An entire shelf, meticulously labelled, had been dedicated to the history of Stellenbosch and Franschhoek. Books on the history of wine and the art of viticulture and bound magazines on the wine industry were stacked on the shelves, bordered on one side by a tall, dark-veneered cupboard with crisscrossed dowels. The necks of red wine bottles stuck out like the snouts of cannons, a light powdering of dust on their coloured foil.

The shelf closest to Eberard contained the biographies and auto-biographies of various people; he noted Mandela's *Long Walk to Freedom*, a biography on Deneys Reitz and a book on the career of Charlie Chaplin. Although the professor did not smoke, the study suggested the aroma of cherry tobacco and the slight haze left by a pipe smoker. It seemed to Eberard to be the only criterion missing from the otherwise perfect study.

Du Preez himself was a large man. He reminded the detective of a male lion, shaggy and potentially powerful. His frame dominated the room. He was clean-shaven, although his thick, greying hair seemed to grapple unsuccessfully for some order on his head, as if an over-elaborate wig had been carelessly stuck to his scalp.

A respected lecturer in the Law Faculty of the University, the professor was regarded as the successor-in-title to the incumbent dean of the faculty. He was also a part-time lecturer in the history department and was known for his political acumen. In his days as a student at Stellenbosch, he had been a legend of the traditional male residence, Wilgenhof. As a rugby player, he had been blessed with the speed to play in the back line and the physical strength to substitute as a lock or as eighth man. He had captained the university team during some of its golden years, and many of the players under his captaincy had gone on to play at provincial and even national level. Although he had never made it to the national team, his reputation as a swift and powerful athlete was renowned in the university town. He had assisted in coaching the university team for several years before devoting himself to the academic side of his career. He was still a keen follower of sports and was the driving force behind the inter-faculty touch-rugby matches, which took place every year on the first weekend of April.

To the detective, however, Professor du Preez was best known for his strong and outspoken views on the need to protect Afrikaans culture on the campus. His desire to maintain high standards with Afrikaans as the medium of tuition had brought him into conflict with the Student Representative Council. The university was increasingly attracting black students, a move seen by entrenched academics as a threat to the historical culture of the institution. Nearly a decade earlier, Du Preez had started an organisation aimed at pursuing Afrikaans issues on campus – Die Komitee vir die Studie van Afrikaanse Kultuur (KSAK). The existence of the organisation caused some discomfort at the university. Although the professor, as its spokesman, eloquently explained its laudable motivation, the feeling remained in certain parts of the campus that it was an exclusive club aimed at furthering the interests of white Afrikaners at the university. It boasted a number of powerful honorary members, from the academic world to the highest echelons of government, the judiciary, the private business sector and sports administration. For some, this was an indication of the organisation's integrity; to the less benevolent, it suggested nepotism and conspiracy.

Du Preez had exacting standards, but he was equally well known for his generosity when it came to students who battled to keep up with their workloads; he ran extra tutorials on a regular basis to help those who were experiencing difficulties. As a result, his classes generated some of the best pass rates in the faculty.

The professor's manner was polite and dignified, but the strain of the news of his daughter's death was reflected in his face. It seemed grossly unfair to Eberard that a man who had contributed so much to his university community should have to endure such suffering.

'I'm sorry that I have to speak to you so soon, Professor,' Eberard opened awkwardly. 'But, as you can imagine, we need to start our investigations without any delay. The scene hasn't turned up much and we're hoping that you may be able to assist us further … as you can imagine.' The policeman felt the young girl's eyes on him once again, and he started to express his condolences once more but, thankfully, was interrupted.

'I understand, Inspector. You have a job to do and no one wants you to complete your task successfully more than I.' The words were spoken with grim determination, as if speech itself was an effort. 'You must understand: someone has … defiled my daughter. They've taken her away from me. I want nothing more than for you to find this man, Inspector, and may God help him when you do.' A flash of anger passed across the professor's face. He paused, pushing his fingers against his temples. Eberard shifted in his seat.

'God help him when you do,' Du Preez repeated. 'I don't teach criminal law any more, Inspector, although I used to take tutorials many years ago. "Rather free ten murderers than convict a single innocent man." That was the underlying principle in all our debates. We taught it with great conviction and gusto.' He shook his head.

Years of bright, receptive students had theorised about the rights of the accused under Du Preez's guidance, intensely debating the rule of law. The general consensus was that by protecting the rights of the murderer, society upholds the system and makes the rule of law safe for the innocent man.

'It seems very far away now, Inspector,' the professor went on. 'It's always strange to me how academic teachings fail to hold up to the true light of day. Strange and … rather disappointing.' He paused thoughtfully. 'You can't bring my daughter back to me, but you can bring the man who killed her to justice.'

Eberard watched him cautiously, unsure of what to say.

'Justice has been a tenuous concept in this part of the world, Inspector,' the professor proceeded. 'Did you know that one of the first buildings to be erected by the founder of this town was a courthouse?'

The question was rhetorical, and without waiting for an answer the professor told how, within a few years of founding the town, Governor van der Stel had commissioned the construction of a Drostdij, from which justice could be dispensed to the inhabitants of the new frontier. Van der Stel had been so impatient to have the court in place before the town put down its roots that he had the builder arrested and detained for delaying its completion. 'It was built where the seminary now stands,' Du Preez explained. 'The seminary is in fact built on its foundations.

'One of the first magistrates, De Meurs, had been a pipe smoker and he had summoned a house slave to bring him an ember for his pipe one day.' The professor became animated as he told how the slave had carried the ember in an uncovered brass holder, passing by the open doorway. The wind had caught the ember and blown sparks into the thatch. That night the court and its adjoining buildings had burnt to the ground.

The narrative transported Du Preez as he told it, taking him to a different space, a timeless place of historical fascination where death and destruction were matters of cerebral interest rather than emotion. 'The Drostdij was rebuilt after that fire,' he concluded. 'Fifty years later, the building was destroyed by fire once again, despite the efforts of the new magistrate to douse the spreading flames.'

The professor rose to his feet suddenly, as if embarrassed by his account. He moved with surprising agility for a man of his size. He picked up a silver picture frame from the side table. For a moment he was captivated by the image. A shadow passed across his face, and Eberard averted his gaze. Then his host turned the frame around and pulled the backing off. He handed the photograph to the policeman.

'That's Melanie,' he said, almost whispering. 'The picture was taken only a few months ago at her matric dance party. She is … was … eighteen years old. I'll find a copy of her birth certificate for you.' Eberard clutched his pen, writing notes in his pocket-book. Although the information did not need to be recorded, it made him feel more at ease to have his head down, his eyes following the scrawl in the small book.

'As you'll have gathered, she had matriculated. She was planning to come to the university and study English … she was going to start a Bachelor of Arts …' The man's voice choked and he stopped talking.

Eberard turned his attention to the photograph. The girl wore a simple dress, a muted red colour that fell in folds from her shoulders. Her hair was longer, a bright blonde in the flash of the camera, falling easily around her ears and curling up under her chin. Her face was free of make-up and her mouth smiled naturally. She stared into the camera with warm eyes, both happy and shy. It was an endearing picture of a young girl on the threshold of adult life. He rubbed a fingerprint off the corner of the photograph and placed it in the docket.

'Melanie lived at home with me and Elsabe,' Du Preez continued. Eberard looked up at him queryingly. 'My wife – their mother – was killed in a car accident some years ago,' he explained. 'Melanie was eight years old when it happened. Elsabe was only four at the time. I raised my daughters with the help of a nanny.' His voice trailed off once again.

Eberard looked down at his scuffed boots, which looked out of place on the plush carpet. He felt that he had somehow defiled their home. With his scruffy notepad and stained government-issue pen, he represented the dirty reality of the world, the society that had killed the man's child. Professor du Preez folded his arms across his stomach – almost in self-embrace, his body shaking slightly from the effort of control. Eberard wanted to look away, feeling embarrassed by the spectacle of a great man battling with the horror that life had offered up to him. He thought of his own battle. Figuratively, he too had lost a wife and daughter. The possibility of separation had lurked beneath the surface of his marriage for years, but the reality of being alone had struck him hard. Loneliness had bitten down on him relentlessly. The lack of support, so long taken for granted, and the stress of his work in the Organised Narcotics Unit had inexorably worn away his will. When his breakdown hit, he was already physically and emotionally destroyed. Looking at the broken professor reminded him of his own loss, and the memory made him long for a drink.

Unable to sit still any longer, Eberard got to his feet. 'Could I see her room?' he blurted out.

If the professor was taken aback, he managed not to show it. He nodded politely and escorted the detective up a flight of carpeted stairs and into a bright yellow room. Neat and un-cluttered, the room was dwarfed by the two men entering it. A single bed, a desk, a bookcase and built-in cupboards took up most of the space. It could have been anyone's room; it gave no clues as to the personality of its inhabitant. There were no post-ers on the walls, no magazines lying sprawled across the bed. No clutter and no mess. The books on the shelf were nondescript and did not seem to follow any particular theme. A picture of a woman with long blonde hair, tied up in a scarf, stood next to the bed, alongside a book of children's poems and songs.

'That's my wife, Beatrice,' the professor said without elucidation.

Eberard felt a surge of despair. The room held no clues because the girl's murder had been random and indiscriminate. He should not have expected anything else. She was not picked because of the books she read, or because of the friends she did or did not have. Nothing she did determined that she would be the one. Her plans and her dreams made no difference to the choice that someone had made. In an instant, in the flick of an eye, she had been chosen. Because of the way she walked. Because of the colours she happened to be wearing that day. Because she was there. Someone had emerged from the darkness of his own character, taken her life because she had it, and then disappeared back into the gloom. How could he tell a father that there was no real prospect of finding his daughter's killer?

Eberard turned and saw the child standing in the passage, hesitating. 'Professor,' he said, looking towards Xoliswa, 'can my partner ask Elsabe a few questions? And could we carry on downstairs? As you may imagine, there are some questions I must ask you … on your own.' He saw the frown on the professor's face. 'I assure you, I won't keep you much longer.'

'No, it's not about me, Inspector. I'm not sure that Elsabe is up to answering questions at this stage. *Sy's net 'n kind.* Perhaps just one or two,' he said, looking at his younger daughter. The girl nodded and sat down on the bed. Xoliswa sat down next to her and took out her notebook.

'Just one or two,' the professor reiterated warily.

When they were finished, Du Preez showed them to the door. 'Februarie,' he said, smiling briefly. 'That's a slave name: your great-grandfather or perhaps his father must have been a slave in the Cape Colony.' It was customary, he explained, for slaves to take a new surname when they were released – often the name of the month of their release. 'Februarie,' he repeated. 'I can also trace my heritage back to those days; I come from a pure Hollandse line. My forefathers were responsible for the development of the wine industry in the Cape.' The distinctive cultivars of the Cape had been developed by the Du Preez family several hundred years before, and the professor's ancestors had been part of the administration of the new colony since the time of Van der Stel. 'In those days,' he continued, 'there was always a fear of slave revolt, a fear that the slaves would form a unified front – if they had, the small garrison would have been easily overpowered. But the VOC always made sure that the slaves were from mixed nationalities; they used older slaves to keep them in line, often quite brutally, and gave favours to some nationalities while repressing others. Sounds familiar, doesn't it, Inspector? They say that the more things change, the more they stay the same.' He looked at Xoliswa directly for the first time. 'So you see, Inspector, my ancestors may have been responsible for the release of yours.' Du Preez paused and looked Eberard in the eye. 'Ironic, isn't it, that things should be as they are now?' The professor did not wait for a reply and closed the door on them. He had not said a word to Xoliswa during their visit to his home – perhaps simply because she was the junior on the scene, Eberard thought, unconvinced.

The two talked for a while as they sat in the car in the street. Eberard took out his pocketbook and scanned through his notes, but he didn't need them. The facts were already burnt into his mind: a pretty young woman; still a girl really; just finished school; about to start university; ready to start her adult life; sensitive and caring towards her father; brought up without a mother; well balanced despite the loss of her mother; a good daughter; went out with friends for supper; probably walking home; intercepted by some gangster alongside the canal. And the next time her father sees her she is in the morgue.

'Our only avenue of investigation is the friends,' he said to Xoliswa, 'and I can already tell you what they're going to tell us.' His partner stared back at him with intensity, her eyes almost black. 'Xoli, now that we know who the ... who Melanie is; that her father is a lecturer where you are a student, and also, well, who he is – the Komitee and all that – I'll understand if you don't want to be involved. I mean, it may be difficult for you, given your position.'

The young constable did not avert her gaze, but smiled briefly. 'Thank you for caring, Inspector, but I'd like to stay on. I don't think it'll be a problem; he doesn't take me for any courses and, as you could see from today' – she looked back at the house – 'he doesn't recognise me at all.' Eberard tried to interrupt, but she continued. 'I know what you mean when you say "who he is", but I have no difficulty with people protecting their cultural identities. It doesn't make him racist. I've never seen that. If I change my mind, I'll tell you. For now, it's fine.'

Eberard looked back at her admiringly, feeling his ever-present despair lifting for a moment, like a swarm of black flies, briefly disturbed and taking to the wing.

Xoliswa sat looking through her notes for a long while before telling him what she had found out from Elsabe. Melanie seemed to have been close to her and the perfect daughter to her difficult and very precise father. Although he had been loving towards his children, their father had had high expectations. The absence of their mother had obviously complicated things for them. 'They got on all right most of the time,' Xoliswa explained. 'She – the sister, Elsabe – wasn't very communicative, understandably. She seemed very protective of her father.

'Elsabe described her sister as sensitive, to the point of being sentimental. She had no real hobbies, though. No special boy-friend. I couldn't really get a picture of what kept her busy, anything that she took a real interest in.'

Elsabe had shown Xoliswa Melanie's books and photographs and a scrapbook of poems and lullabies that her sister had col-lected from the time of her mother's death. Xoliswa explained that the mother used to sing them lullabies at night to help them sleep. 'The sister says that it was such a part of their life that even she can remember the songs. She would have been four years old at the time. I'm not sure that she could remember that early on, but anyway, she says she can.'

'Lullabies?' Eberard said distractedly.

'It's one of those big old scrapbooks with thick pages,' Xoliswa went on. 'She'd cut some out, written some in, copied some with a photocopier. It must've been a way of remembering her mother ...' Xoliswa's voice trailed off, and Eberard realised how little he knew about his partner. Had she perhaps lost a mother, he wondered.

'Some of the later ones looked like they were printed off the Internet. It was a bit messy towards the end; some of the pages were torn out. She probably lost interest as she got older.' Xoliswa paused, uncharacteristically hesitant. 'The sister says she's going to read from the collection at the funeral.'

'That'll take care of any dry eyes in the audience,' Eberard replied, immersed in his own thoughts – thoughts of the loss of his own child, the life he had let slip through his fingers, like fine sand. That men must face such a turning away, he mused, as he turned the ignition key.

TOORA, LOORA, LOORA

Toora, loora, loora
Toora, loora, li
Toora, loora, loora
Hush, now, don't you cry
Ah,
Toora, loora, loora
Toora, loora, li
Toora, loora, loora
It's an Irish lullaby

Over in Killarney, many years ago
My mother sang this song to me
  in tones so sweet and low
Just a simple little ditty
  in her good old Irish way
And I'd give the world if she could sing
  that song to me this day

Toora, loora, loora
Toora, loora, li
Toora, loora, loora
Hush, now, don't you cry
Ah,
Toora, loora, loora
Toora, loora, li
Toora, loora, loora
It's an Irish lullaby

FIVE

V AN der Keesel first met Jakoba Boorman on the occasion of the Governor's birthday. The weather that October was warm and mild, and the traditional birthday gathering was held on the flat, open common in Stellenbosch. Burghers, residents and Company employees stood in groups, talking and sampling the foods that had been prepared by neatly dressed maids, standing behind their tables. Baskets of fresh bread, sourdough rolls, potjie-brood and roosterbrood sat alongside jars of green fig jam, citrus marmalade and veld honey. Blocks of white cheese had been cut into fist-sized chunks, to be eaten with cubes of watermelon rind soaked in thick syrup. Seared mielie cobs and roasted baby onions were piled onto platters, with trickles of butter running down their sides. Fires roared behind the tables, sending sparks and smoke into the clear sky; male slaves knocked embers from the thick burning logs with iron bars, bringing them to the open braais in hissing metal buckets. The smells of stewing potjiekos and braaied lamb on skewers mingled with pipe smoke and horse manure to form a rich layer of aromas. The Governor's troupe of flautists and pipers were seated on benches and their quiet melodies filled the air. Freshly brewed beer was poured from large wooden barrels alongside uncorked bottles of pungent brandewyn and red and white muscat.

Van der Stel was in high spirits, surrounded by his children and under the watchful eye of Cornelia, his elderly sister-in-law from his first marriage in the Netherlands. He had left the country with his children and sister-in-law under a cloud of accusation; his tempestuous marriage to his wife Johanna had finally collapsed under the strain of her interfering mother and rumour-mongering. His mother-in-law had accepted the word of a chambermaid above his own, accusing him (and not too privately at that) of beating his wife. His move from the Netherlands to the colony, and the vague status of his marriage, remained the topic of hushed speculation within the Company. But whatever the unfortunate events in his past, the Governor was now relaxed and entirely at home among his respectful minions. He had recently taken a second wife, Constance, and her doting attentions only improved his mood. He bustled about the common, his voice raised, lifting the cast-iron lids of cooking pots and admiring the display of muskets and weaponry.

The Governor found Van der Keesel inspecting an assortment of bulbous plants with rough brown exteriors and deep-pink linings to the interior cavities. Next to the strange plants were two separate dishes, reduced to a paste, and some dried cuttings from the plant. The viticulturist was gingerly inserting a small tasting of one of the pastes into his mouth when the Governor loudly proclaimed, 'Now this is something you would not have seen in Europe!' Van der Keesel winced at the intrusion and slowly lowered the spoon without tasting the dish. 'I thought we should show off a little local flavour,' the Governor said proudly, 'so I asked the maids to prepare an example of this local ... plant.' He hesitated as Van der Keesel turned his penetrating stare upon him.

'It looks more like a *kont* than a plant, and not as palatable,' Van der Keesel said crudely, maintaining eye contact with the Governor, whose face reddened. 'But as it happens,' he went on, 'I am aware of this plant, although I admit that I have not as yet had an opportunity to inspect it as closely as this. It is parasitic, probably of the fungus family, known locally as *kannie*.' Van der Keesel warmed to his task as the Governor's face showed his disappointment at not being able to upstage him. He paused dramatically, opening the small silver betel box and inspecting its contents before placing some *sirih* between his teeth.

'It has an extensive underground root structure,' he continued with his lecture, 'and in these parts the locals eat the fruit of the plant raw, baked on a fire or prepared as a paste with cinnamon and sugar. The fruit is filled with small, hard seeds, which are removed in the cooking process. You can add butter or even a little muscadel to take the edge off the bitterness of the dish. The plant itself is very high in tannins, which lend a bitter aftertaste.' Van der Keesel paused again for effect, letting the suggestion that he had reached the end of his knowledge float in the air for a moment. 'I am also told,' he proceeded, just as the Governor was about to intercede, 'that the plant has medicinal qualities; the hard outer shell is ground down into a powder and is used to treat diarrhoea and skin conditions.'

Van der Keesel picked up a large piece of the plant and held it up to the Governor. 'Unfortunately, the stem of the plant can produce its own smaller flowers, which have a distinctive smell' – he beckoned to his host to smell the plant – 'of rotting carrion, so as to attract certain pollinating insects.' The Governor jerked back in distaste. Showing no emotion, Van der Keesel turned to the table, placing the plant carefully beside the plates of food. 'A most fascinating plant – rather a portrait of the new colony itself, wouldn't you say, Governor? The allure of cunnilingus undermined by the foul smell of dead flesh? A stinking *vleesroos*.'

Van der Stel scowled at the man. 'Your humour is not appreciated, sir. Nor is it understood, I might add. I trust you will refrain from making such comments in the presence of my sister-in-law or other members of my family.'

Other than a faint smile, Van der Keesel did not respond to the rebuke. The Governor paused and then, considering the matter closed, took his employee by the arm and directed him to the adjoining table. The sight of a man pouring brandewyn for the guests raised his spirits after the viticulturist's indiscretion.

'This is Frederick Boorman,' Van der Stel announced, gesturing towards the man. 'He makes those wooden vats that we were looking at in the cellar.' Boorman was a leathery-skinned man with a thin layer of curled black hair and a dark-brown complexion. His eyes were circled with wrinkles and shifted nervously from the Governor to Van der Keesel. He stepped from behind the table and murmured a greeting. Van der Keesel nodded imperceptibly.

Ignoring the servant's discomfort, the Governor continued in a loud voice: 'Frederick has applied for his release onto land in the new valley. He has his eye on a nice piece along the banks, just as you come over the ridge. He thinks he can make a living for himself and his family there. What do you think?' The Governor's eyes glinted with mischievous pleasure, but Van der Keesel did not take the bait. 'You see, if I were to say yes,' he went on, 'I would be losing my valued cask-maker. But if I say no – well, I fear that I may be presented with inferior vats for my wine.'

The unfortunate man tried to say something, mouthing some unspoken protest before falling silent.

'Should I accede to his request to my own detriment?'

At this point in the one-sided conversation Jakoba appeared at Frederick's side, taking her husband's hand firmly in her own. Van der Keesel noticed an immediate soothing of the man's disquiet; he seemed both more confident and comfortable. It was this remarkable transformation that drew his attention. Jakoba was a solid-looking woman, with strong bones bordering on the masculine in their definition. The smoothness of her skin and her wide eyes gave the impression of lasting beauty. Hers was not the petite prettiness of the wealthy ladies of Amsterdam tottering along the canals with their laced umbrellas held aloft. Van der Keesel's interest in the conversation rose.

'I would think that some mutually beneficial arrangement could be met,' he said guardedly, his eyes meeting those of the interesting slave woman in front of him. She returned his gaze without wavering.

Jakoba was an intelligent woman. She had no illusions about what was at stake. She swiftly took account of the shifting powers that danced between her and the Governor's acquaintance; the patent imbalance of slave and master was, in a moment, usurped by a barter. Her family's freedom was a matter of great importance, but she was aware, too, of the weight of the challenge that had sprung up in the viticulturist's eyes.

Van der Keesel's gruff, dismissive manner did not alter in the presence of women, and yet he had remarkable success bedding a growing number of widows, mothers, wives and single women. His domineering attitude overpowered those beneath his social standing and was somehow intriguing to the women associated with his peers. While boorishness and crudeness were disdained in polite society, his irreverent energy and confidence emitted an apparently attractive sexual undertone. He had, on a number

of occasions, both within his short time at the colony and before
that in the Netherlands, been confronted by angry husbands and
suitors, threatening him with physical violence and damnation.
He took neither threat seriously and rejected their complaints
with arrogant declarations: 'If you cannot keep her at home, then
you do not deserve to have her at home.' Rumour had it that,
as a younger man, he had been challenged to a pistol duel after
sending a lover back home with a note saying, 'I am finished
with her now. You may have her back.' Van der Keesel did not
admit to or deny the story, but it seemed to hold an element
of truth. Certainly, his reputation was already well established in
the colony.

Jakoba squeezed her husband's calloused hand and forced a
smile. 'We are in your hands, sir,' she said softly, but pointedly.

With that weighted line, the wheels of freedom and of misery
were set in motion. Van der Stel released Frederick from some
of his duties on the estate the following month. His status
remained that of a slave, pending the Company's confirmation of
his reprieve, but he was granted leasehold title to a small piece
of land next to the river. The smallholding was bordered by the
Eerste River on three sides, cupped in the crook of the river like
a small lump of dough. The plot was on the northern side of the
river as it snaked westwards towards the town. The expanding
vineyards of the Company lay immediately to the north. Stretching up the slope away from the smallholding was an established
field of vines, crouchen blanc, already a metre tall, with gnarled
stems as thick as a child's arm. The western boundary of the
field, almost in line with the smallholding, was a rough dirt track
leading to an earth-and-clay dam, fed by a canal that ran up the
length of the slope towards the mountains. On the other side
of the track, the fields continued, newly cleared and destined to
be planted with young semillon cuttings. Fresh plough troughs
lined the slope, the earth cut open in anticipation. Boorman's
ground ran the risk of being flooded if the winter rainfall was
too heavy, and the ground was too wet for vines, but the soil was
dark and rich and had much to offer the family.

'We can plant mielies away from the river where the water has drained out of the soil,' Jakoba pointed out enthusiastically. 'We can build there as well, where the water won't pool when it rains. Then, closer to the river, we can clear a patch for green vegetables. The ground is too wet for potatoes or onions, but soft-fruit trees like plums will do fine. Maybe we can plant some tubers and beets in the summer, when the soil is drier.'

Frederick grinned, his tobacco-stained teeth pushing out behind his lips. The piece of land was small enough to be worked by his family in the evening when they returned from the Company fields, and would provide them with a quick and sustainable source of food. When the confirmation of their free-burgher status came, they could devote more time to the land and perhaps expand. Until then, Frederick, Jakoba and their daughter Sanna would work in the newly prepared semillon field with other slaves. The work was arduous, overseen by a caffer, an ex-slave used by the Company to control the slaves. Fearful of returning to slavery, the caffers were eager to please their masters and often brutal as a result. The caffer in charge of the new fields was a jet-black Madagascan called Bakka. No one knew his real name, or dared to ask; his face seemed perpetually screwed up in fury, or pain, and his back was lined with scarred welts. He was a vicious man, given to bouts of uncontrollable rage and abuse. He threatened the slaves under his control with the Slave Lodge, an overcrowded and frightening place, no better than a prison, where *bandieten* and lunatics mixed with terrified slaves in windowless barracks. The misery of their conditions in the field was bearable only in comparison to the plight of the poor souls trapped in the barbaric lodge.

But Bakka's abuse was tempered when it came to Frederick's family. He was aware of their undefined, but somehow improved, status; he knew that Frederick worked directly for the Governor. He was contemptuous of the prospect of their release, but was nevertheless more cautious in his approach towards them. For his part, Frederick made sure that he was respectful and retiring in Bakka's presence. The arrangement with the Governor was not ideal, but there was the hope of a better future for his small family. Van der Stel required that even once Frederick's release had been formalised, he would have to ride into town on two days of every week to attend to the manufacture of his vats. This was the sacrifice Frederick had to make in order to secure his release.

It was seven months after Van der Keesel's intervention at the Governor's birthday party that Frederick discovered the true nature of the sacrifice. He found Jakoba huddled, crying, in their half-built kitchen, her knees scuffed and her feet stained with the dust of the clay bricks. She waved him away, refusing to explain her condition, sobbing and sucking in the air with heaving gulps. But the moment Frederick saw her there, he understood. The barter had not been his to make, and what had been bartered was beyond value. How can you place a price on freedom? Its value can only be measured against things equally as precious, things that cannot be owned or bought, like trust, like love, like fidelity. Jakoba had no possessions to trade but herself. He stood and watched her groaning on the floor of their new home, a home bought with her soul, bartered for lust and power. The cruelty of the transaction was brutal and it tore at his heart. Yet, to a man who had spent his life subservient, cowering from raised hands and striking whips, there was no anger, no bitterness or rage. Frederick had been born into a system that took from him and gave little back; he knew that his masters could take his wife from him, that he could lose his daughter, that he could be sent to any part of the world on the Company's whim. These decisions evoked no anger in him, only a resigned sadness at the indelible harshness of the world.

Jakoba made regular weekly visits to Stellenbosch after that. She would return stony-faced and tired. Frederick would wait for her, a pot of vegetables simmering on the open hearth, but she would invariably go to bed without eating. It became an unspoken rule that her visits to the viticulturist would not be mentioned or discussed. She would announce in the morning that she had to go into town, and he would nod without expression. On her return, he would wait for her to climb into bed before slipping into the room and tenderly tucking the covers in around her.

But the knowledge that he had bought the land with his wife's body bore down on him; in his mind, it poisoned the ground and soured the water. His vision of being master of his own family had been destroyed. He had simply exchanged one master for another, and his new master had taken something that he would never have offered. Not a man to take revenge or seek to even the score, Frederick felt a growing misery with each passing day, comforted only by the presence of Sanna, bright and energetic, happily oblivious to the price of her family's freedom.

LAVENDER'S BLUE
(DILLY DILLY)

Lavender's blue, dilly dilly,
Lavender's green
When you are King, dilly dilly,
I shall be Queen

Who told you so, dilly dilly,
Who told you so?
'Twas my own heart, dilly dilly,
That told me so

Call up your friends, dilly dilly
Set them to work
Some to the plough, dilly dilly,
Some to the fork

Some to the hay, dilly dilly,
Some to thresh corn
Whilst you and I, dilly dilly,
Keep ourselves warm

Lavender's blue, dilly dilly,
Lavender's green
When you are King, dilly dilly,
I shall be Queen

Who told you so, dilly dilly,
Who told you so?
'Twas my own heart, dilly dilly,
That told me so.

SIX

DETECTIVE Inspector Februarie walked along the shaded pavement on Dorp Street from the Drostdy towards Market Street. Bistros, art galleries and wine shops sat between historical buildings with solid whitewashed façades and curved gables. Two elderly women chatted on a first-floor balcony, framed by dark-green broekielace, oblivious to the noise of traffic up and down the narrow street below. Their conversation reached him briefly – the attractive sounds of well-spoken Afrikaans filtering down before being drowned out by the roar of a diesel engine. The tall trees and the pretty surrounds made the street one of the highlights for visitors, but he had never felt at ease with the conflicting diversity of the town, and Market Street, in particular, was a testimony to that dichotomy. The town seemed to be in the grip of a schizophrenic seizure, proudly projecting its colonial heritage while trying to assimilate the impossible challenges of its contemporary existence. The rich history of its minority squatted on the cultural genocide of its majority; the wealthy enjoyed luxuries built on the backs of the poor; and histories of saviours and slaves twisted in a parasitic knot.

The VOC kruithuis – the historic powder magazine – served as a prime example. It was one of the favoured and proudly preserved structures of Stellenbosch, with its distinctive white-domed roof and nearly windowless walls. But its history was fraught, having been used to store arms and ammunition for the suppression of natives and other belligerents. There were indications that its perimeter had been used for the sale of slaves. It faced onto the Braak – a jealously protected village square in the centre of town, where the militia had been inspected before embarking on sorties into the hinterland. Later, the organised armies of the British had gathered there before moving off to do battle with the Xhosas. The disquiet of Stellenbosch, however, could not simply be ascribed to the racial distinctions that dominate all South African towns and cities; it was a more complex association of rich and poor, wine farms and squalid locations, old traditions and new politics.

When first moving to Stellenbosch, Eberard had visited the oldest shop in town, at the insistence of the female office staff, who were keen to prove their town's worth to the newcomer. The small general trader in Dorp Street was started in 1904 by Samuel Johannes Volsteedt. The owner had reportedly suffered from a weak back (more likely a hunchback) and found farming too strenuous an activity. '*Oom Samie se Winkel*', as his shop became known, had traded ever since. The white limewashed shop tried to continue Volsteedt's tradition of selling anything and everything, and in so doing displayed a diversity that was both rich and flawed.

Eberard had walked through the small, haphazard array of rooms with a sceptical smile on his face. The shop reminded him in some ways of the old general dealer stores in the small Namaqualand towns of his childhood, but it was more densely packed, thick with memory and the immediately forgettable. The noses of visitors were assaulted by the aromas of rooibos, lavender pillows, sun-dried bokkems, masala, smoked snoek, old hemp sacks and biltong. Oblivious to the smells, Eberard had wandered past shelves that supported opaque marble-stopped bottles, old glass milk bottles from the Union and the Royal Dairy, and whisky tumblers etched with gaudy depictions of buffalo and lion. 'Blob top' soda bottles, some still with soil encrusted around their rims, perched next to blown-glass hippos with gaping pewter heads, and traditional enamel mugs peeked out from between fake-fur waistcoats and gold-painted ostrich eggs. Old-fashioned mampoer, red and white muscadel – '*Ouma se Wyn*' – and koeksisters were offered for sale next to bottles of old and undrinkable red wine, each selling for hundreds of rands, the labels rotted and peeling away. A faded picture of Volsteedt's mother gazed down at unnaturally bright drawings of game animals stacked beneath her, and the sawn-off head of a springbok surveyed the scene forlornly.

Eberard sifted through the piles and drawers of cultural

artefacts and kitsch souvenirs, the attractive and the tasteless, the timeless and the superficial.

An American tourist stood at the counter, camera straps crisscrossing his shoulders and chest like a combatant. He forced an array of coloured notes out of his thick fake-leather wallet with his fat thumbs. Next to him, a wizened woman from the township, a shawl wrapped tightly around her head, spoke Afrikaans to the assistant, clutching her small parcel of dried apricots and bokkems, her eyes averted from the red and brown notes at her fingertips.

How things change and somehow stay the same, or move backwards, Eberard had thought to himself.

He stopped outside a whitewashed building a few streets away from the store. He climbed the cool concrete steps to the first floor, where the apartments perched on top of grocery stores and shoe shops. The dark-green door was open and he did not bother to knock as he stepped inside. The small reception area was minimalist in its furnishings. A few simple steel chairs lined the cool, white wall, and a receptionist sat behind a low counter. The grey-haired woman, dressed in a neat jacket and matching trousers, put a mark against his name in the large diary opened in front of her. Eberard noted with relief that the reception area was empty.

'Mr Februarie, Dr Primesh will be with you in a moment. Please have a seat.'

The latest *Femina* magazine lay on a small table between the chairs, its glossy cover turned towards him. A young woman with swollen red lips and mischievous eyes looked up at him. Her mouth was slightly open, the hint of her wet tongue lurking. Her low-cut silky dress pulled tight against the swell of her breasts, pushing out to him, inviting. He picked the magazine up. Underneath, another glossy cover, another invitation: a tall, lean model in a slit dress, her pale, smooth thigh bent and turned, just slightly, outwards, opening. Her lips, also thickly smeared with red, pouted. He turned the *Femina* magazine over and put it down on top of the pouting model. Now you can fuck each other, he thought heatedly. Whores!

The door to the consulting room opened and a middle-aged

woman emerged. She avoided eye contact with Eberard and walked briskly to the receptionist. They started discussing appointment dates in hushed tones.

'Mr Februarie. Eberard.' Dr Susan Primesh beckoned him into the consulting room. 'Sorry there was an overlap, but I was running a little late.' The woman seemed ill at ease and bustled him into her consulting room.

Eberard picked up on her disquiet and immediately started with an apology. 'I'm sorry I missed the last appointment. I realise that we haven't been together for that long and that every session counts. My work just wouldn't allow me to make the time. I had to ... I had a ...'

'Eberard, I understand the pressures you're under,' the woman interrupted, almost sternly. 'It doesn't matter. I'm sure it won't become a pattern.'

He found her manner unnerving. There was something authoritarian about it. She was a mixture of compassion and concern, and severity. It was as if she was fighting her natural urge to be friendly, aware of the need to maintain careful boundaries. He felt that just as he was starting to trust and even like her, she would suddenly impose an artificial space between them. Maybe it was because he had not chosen to come and see her; it was a condition of his transfer to the station that he attend evaluation sessions with a state-appointed psychiatrist. But he still felt the need to develop a sense of trust, and he felt hurt when she enforced her professional role.

Their interaction was complicated for him by the fact that she was an attractive woman. She had a beautiful grace to her; her arms were thin but not scraggly; her face defined but not gaunt. Her skin seemed to shine from within. She would sit opposite him with her back up straight, her hands resting on the folder on her lap. When she smiled, her teeth showed in a line of clear white enamel. He had sensed maternal warmth in her interest in his vulnerabilities. However, the moment he responded to it, looking into her eyes, trying to question her on her own attitude, she would pull back, leaving him feeling isolated. Maternalism was mixed, necessarily but uncomfortably, with sexuality.

Today, as they moved to their seats, Eberard could not fail to notice how the sunlight from the window caught her white blouse, offering the subtle hint of underwear. She sat down and the glimpse was gone. He thought of the two women in the magazines, lying on top of each other. He sat down opposite her and looked at her expectantly. Even without the sunlight shining through the fabric, her top was full of suggestion. The white – colour of innocence and oppression – contrasted starkly with her smooth brown skin and black hair, and made him feel impotent and titillated. Anger welled up in him again. Doesn't she understand, he thought, looking at her as she paged through his file, that a man cannot interact with a woman outside the realm of sexuality? In Muslim countries, men cover their wives and daughters from head to toe when they go out because they understand this fact. They are not only protecting the women in the family, they are removing sexuality from public interaction. If she wants me to relate to her outside of that realm, he thought, then she must present herself without suggestion. His inability to consider her asexually left him depressed, confused by his own male frailty and the ease with which his base instincts could dominate. But at the same time, he felt angry. He was angry with her, for not understanding and for dressing the way she did. He was angry at all the stimuli that were thrown at him every minute of every day; his sexuality was exploited mercilessly, in every advertisement, in every film, in every magazine. Women were presented to him like whores, droves of half-dressed prostitutes imploring him to buy their product, to follow their lead. The excitement was momentary – a fleeting breath of orgasm – and abusive.

'You seem distracted, Eberard,' Primesh noted simply.

'Oh,' he responded with a forced smile, 'it's everything and it's nothing.' He could not bring himself to explain to her, and sat for a while without speaking. His eyes wandered about the room. Next to her, a large wooden chest served as a table; the crack between the lid and the side was just wide enough for the flat blade of a screwdriver. When you turn it sideways, he thought, it would lift enough to get a finger hold. He imagined filling the gap and pulling the lid open. The mechanical logic calmed his thoughts. She watched him, quizzically, before taking control.

'Last time we met,' she began, 'we talked about your dependency on narcotics.' It was a brutal start to the session and Eberard felt chastened. He was, after all, here for a particular reason. 'You were telling me how you had started experimenting with crack cocaine, after a big arrest' – she ran her finger across her notes – 'in the Eastern Cape. And you spoke about the dependency and the drinking. What we didn't get to last time was the extent to which the drugs resulted in your breakdown, or whether you feel it was a symptom of another crisis.'

Eberard was taken aback. It seemed an impossibly complicated question. He was not even sure that he understood what she was asking. He stared at her blankly.

'I don't know,' was all he managed to say in answer.

She frowned at him, and then let her face soften. 'What's on your mind, Eberard?' She placed the notes on her lap and leant forward. 'There's plenty of time to talk about the past. If there's something bothering you now, we can look at that first. Are you struggling with dependency now?'

'Only with regard to women,' he blurted out, laughing to make light of the comment, although the truth of the statement was immediately apparent to him. 'I've been assigned the case of a young student who was found floating in the river. It was on the front page of yesterday's newspaper.'

'Yes, I saw the article. What a terrible thing to happen.'

'Well, I've been given the case to investigate and ... well, seeing her in the morgue was ... I know that I'm supposed to be a hardened policeman, and I've seen lots of bodies, but a bullet wound or a knife wound, they don't destroy the sense that you're dealing with a human being. But that girl laid out on the table, cut open like that. It made me very uncomfortable.'

Eberard thought back to the lump of meat in the morgue – the walking, talking person with hopes and dreams who had turned, in the blink of an eye, into a carcass on a table. 'I mean, is that all we are at the end of the day? It just seems grossly unreasonable that we end up like that ... and ridiculous.' He looked down at his hands.

'And how do you feel about taking on the case?' Primesh articulated the question that had been nagging him ever since he had taken the docket from Captain Fourie.

'What do you mean?'

'Well, it's going to be a high-profile case. There'll be a lot of pressure.' She spoke slowly and deliberately. 'You were referred to me on a brief, as you know, both to assist you personally and to assist you in maintaining your current position at the station. The idea – as I understand it – was that you were transferred to Stellenbosch to rest and find your feet again. Is this case going to help you, or even allow you, to do that?'

'I don't know. I don't know if it's a good idea,' Eberard replied. 'But at the end of the day, I'm a detective inspector in the force. That's my job. I'm experienced and hopefully I can do a good job. If I can't, then I shouldn't carry on in the force at all. Then I should just give up now.'

'That's a rather uncompromising attitude towards a complex issue. There must be other suitable detectives to take the case on? At least for now?'

'There may be. You're right. I'm sure there must be. But senior management have decided to assign it to me. Perhaps they'd like to see me fail. Maybe they think I can do the job. I just don't know. But I do know that if I can't do the job, I must leave the force. I mean, I can't sit in some back office pretending to do my work and still call myself a police officer.' Eberard took a deep breath, trying to assess how vulnerable he was making himself.

She let the topic go and asked after his general health – his drinking, his eating, his sleeping. He wanted to tell her how his own body had become foul to him. He knew he could never articulate it to her, but his body's own smell, the very feel of it, had become unbearable. The heaviness of his hand, the odour of his own breath, were nauseating. He wanted to explain to her. He needed her to understand. How he loathed his every reaction. How bile stung the inside of his throat.

'And how are you sleeping, Eberard?' she broke his train of thought. 'Is that any better?'

'No, it isn't.' Eberard slept intermittently and with little routine. 'When I lie in bed at night and I can't sleep, if I'm restless or overtired, do you know what I think about to soothe my mind?' he asked rhetorically. 'I create scenes in my mind, scenes where I've stumbled onto a crime in progress.' Primesh listened attentively, her hands still and her fingertips touching. 'I'm the only officer there. There's no backup. I'm on my own. I draw my gun – sometimes my pistol, but often the R5 rifle. With pinpoint accuracy, I shoot each one of the criminals.' Eberard became more animated as he described the scene. 'There's the commotion of people running for cover around me, but I'm calm and focused. Each one appears in turn in my gun sights; each one is struck down by my shot. Some shoot back or try to hide behind a car, but I turn my attention from one to the next, gunning them down one by one with single shots. In some of the scenes I'm injured in the leg or the shoulder, but there's no pain, and no distraction.' Eberard sat forward and placed his hand on his shoulder. 'I can ignore the injury and track each one of them down. They're like rats running around an empty room, clawing to get out. Once I have the scene in my mind, with all the small details in place, I can play it in my head over and over until I fall asleep.'

'I see.' Primesh did not appear unnerved. 'And what do you think its meaning is for you?' It was the therapist's standard question.

'I don't know,' Eberard said half-heartedly. 'It puts me to sleep. I suppose in my mind I'm competent and strong ... invincible, really.'

'But it still bothers you?' she pressed.

'Well, it isn't soothing unless I shoot them,' he confessed. 'It doesn't work if I run after a suspect and catch him without hurting him. Even if I just wound them, or arrest them after firing a warning shot. The soothing part is the shooting and the killing. I have to imagine killing other people to feel calm.'

He was watching her to see her reaction; instead of being

horrified, she seemed captivated by his confession. 'I'm someone,' he concluded, 'who falls asleep dreaming of killing people.'
Eberard looked out of the window as she scribbled down notes.
He wondered what warped things she was writing down. It was
a strange form of medicine, this, he thought: talking, writing,
analysing. What could it really do to help him? Could it really
change his dreams?

'I'm not sure it's as "warped" as you think,' she said, as if she
had just read his thoughts. 'Some people dream of adultery, others of rape, some of sexual encounters with under-aged children,
but that doesn't make them adulterers, or rapists or paedophiles.'

'Ja, but if I dreamt about having sex with a child, I would be
very worried about my mental health, or at least my emotional
health.'

'That's true,' Primesh agreed, 'but there can be no justification
for a sexual encounter with a child, whereas in your case, your
conscious mind is taking an acceptable subconscious thought
and articulating it in a particular manner. What about your *bad*
dreams? Your nightmares?' she asked.

'When I was going through a difficult time, before my breakdown' – Eberard let the word hang in the air for a moment,
intrusive and unpleasant – 'my mind was filled with terrible
images, even hallucinations. But, apart from that period, I don't
have bad dreams. Not often, at least. When I do, they're usually
the same. I'm on duty, a crime has taken place, and the suspects
are running towards me. They can see me, and I can see them.
I reach for my gun, but it won't come out of the holster. It's
caught on some small thread of nylon that's holding it down.
I feel weak and don't have the strength to break the thread.
They're grinning and shooting and I'm pulling at my gun, but I
can't break it free. Sometimes I get it out, but I'm too weak to pull
the hammer back, or something has caught behind the trigger,
holding it forward. They shoot me in the leg, the stomach, and
I'm lying on the ground, crying. They keep shooting and I can't
get my gun out. I'm helpless, because of something ridiculous,
some thread that has come loose. They stand over me. They laugh
and shoot me again and again. I want them to stop. I put my

hand up and plead with them. But my voice is gone. My mouth opens and closes like a fish. I wake up sweating, sometimes screaming or crying, and then I can't go back to sleep. I'll be up for the rest of the night.' Eberard smiled as he remembered how his partner in the Organised Narcotics Unit used to laugh at him; the man could always tell when he'd had one of his dreams, because for the next day or two Eberard would wear a bulletproof vest. 'And the next day at work I'll be all skittish.'

'Your good dream is about being in control, strong and powerful,' Primesh concluded. 'Your bad dream is about being weak and vulnerable, out of control and unable to defend yourself. Now if we look again at this new case that you've taken on, how is it going to make you feel if you can't make any headway in catching the girl's killer?' Eberard shifted uncomfortably in his seat. 'What if this case is one where you can't be in control, where you can't be the protector, where you can't win, because there's no evidence, because the killer is never to be found? Forget your job for a moment. Think about yourself. Is this going to be a good process for you?'

'Ag, maybe it's meant to happen,' Eberard shrugged. 'There are some people who believe that everything happens for a reason. Maybe this is a process that has been brought to challenge me. I'm not going to run away from it. Not yet.' He looked at Primesh for some sort of approval, but she just blinked at him. 'We do have leads in the case,' he went on. 'It's confidential of course, at this stage anyway.' She nodded seriously and he felt encouraged. 'We found her clothes in a dustbin along the road from the canal. Semen stains on her dress suggest sexual activity a few hours before her death. We know where she was last seen, at a club nearby. My partner is interviewing the friends and people from the club at the moment. So I think we'll end up with something to go on.'

'And if you don't work it out? If you don't catch anyone?' She sat with her pen poised. 'What are your feelings about that possibility?'

'Well, I feel sorry for the girl. Of course, one has to feel terrible for her. But it isn't her ... I mean, I don't want to catch the culprit because of her. It'll make no difference to her now. But her father deserves it. Life has dealt him one blow after another. To lose your wife and be left to bring up your children on your own, then to lose your daughter, just when she was ready to leave home on her own.' Eberard shook his head. 'He's trying to be strong, but you can see him buckling under all the suffering. I see something of myself in him, my own loss. I don't think I could go back to him and tell him we've closed the file without an arrest. So, ja, there's pressure on me, my own pressure.'

He felt stronger now. Somehow, talking about his motivations had given him resolve. He did not mention that he had started drinking again, just a glass of whisky to help him sleep at night. He felt embarrassed by his earlier confessions. He had been indulgent, he thought, as he watched her making some notes in his folder. His life was simple and clear compared to the trauma of the professor's position. His own daughter was alive and being looked after by his wife in Cape Town. He glanced at the clock; he still had fifteen minutes, but he didn't want to get started on the next problem without reaching any conclusions. He always felt deflated when she interrupted him to make way for her next client; it reminded him of the artificiality of their discussion and made him uncomfortable.

'I'm sorry, Doctor.' He stood up purposefully. 'I need to get back to the investigation. Do you mind if we finish early today?'

Primesh looked up at him, surprised. His expression was resolved and she did not argue. 'If you need to go, then you must go, Eberard.' She stood up. 'For what it's worth, I hope that you catch him, whoever he is.'

Momentarily, he felt proud. It was the feeling he searched for in the scenes he created lying in bed. He smiled and opened the door. He was halfway across the reception room when she spoke again.

'Eberard' – he stopped and turned back towards her – 'don't forget the prescription for your medication.' She closed the door to her room. Once again, she had left him stranded and deflated. The receptionist pushed an envelope towards him on the desk without looking at him. He snatched at it and left.

Out in the sunlight, a drumming sound droned in his head. The bright light irritated his eyes and he stopped, looked down onto the concrete and wiped the moisture from the corners of his lids. The noise grew in strength, pounding on his temples. The ground seemed to vibrate around him. As he squinted apprehensively into the glare up Bird Street, a figure ran past him, trailing a thin silk scarf that brushed against his face. Eberard jumped in fright and had to stifle a shout. The street was packed with people, energetically jumping up and down, shaking their arms in the air. The tar seemed to pound with their stamping feet. Their presence was surreal; he could not make out whether they were excited or angered or frightened. Suddenly, a strange shadow loomed over him. Turning slowly from Merriman Street, behind the crowd, a colossal animal was lumbering towards him. It stood at least five times the height of a person, towering over the figures at its feet. It had the appearance of a huge leopard, its canary-yellow coat gleaming in the sunlight, and massive black spots scattered like paw prints across its flanks. Its expansive jaws were open, revealing an unnaturally scarlet tongue and intensely white teeth. He expected a guttural roar to rush out at him, but the only noise emanated from the students leaping across its path. Eberard started involuntarily and stepped back into the doorway. The creature moved forward smoothly, relentlessly, completing the turn into the street.

The crowd parted to allow the animal to proceed up the road; it was led by a contingent of men and women dressed in traditional colonial clothes and appeared to be some sort of harvest festival. The women wore layered dresses of simple colours, tied in at the waist and wrists; the men tight-fitting trousers and over-layed jackets. The leader was ringing a bell and intoning some message from a scroll held out in front of him.

A long-haired figure pushed between two young women; they seemed not to notice him and carried on laughing and shouting indiscernible slogans. The figure loped towards Eberard, his back hunched, and his hair, grey and matted together into dreadlocks, swung in front of his face. But through the curtain of hair, his eyes glared. The man pushed up closely against him. Despite the heat, he was dressed in a long woollen overcoat, musty smelling and littered with grass and dust. Suddenly, unexpectedly, the stench of old urine invaded Eberard's nose, sour and pervasive. He tried to step back, but the figure gripped his hand, squeezing his wrist tightly with his bony fingers. The man's hands were coarse and scarred. Eberard recoiled instinctively, but the man held on, pulling the policeman towards him.

'You think I'm just your fucking bergie, *né*?' the figure hissed, stale liquor swirling up into Eberard's face. He looked away, but the man tugged at him aggressively to keep his attention. 'I'm a white man. Don't forget that. A white man in Africa. I'm your street bergie, hey? I'm your animal – I live under the bridge, where the water's cold. I see you. I know what you do. I'm your bergie.'

Eberard felt strangely intimidated by the man. Normally, he would have held out his police badge, confidently flashing his status before bundling him into a side street. But he stood on the pavement, young students swirling around him in a carnival of colour and movement, trapped by the noise, motionless in the stream, his arm tugged and pushed by a wild man. He felt unable to move; there was no reaction in him. He remembered standing in the surf at Macassar as a child, watching a set of waves rushing towards him, gathering power. They sprayed their foam droplets at him like spittle from a bellowing mouth. He had stood, buffeted from side to side, pulled by the backwash and thumped by the foaming waves, powerless to challenge their force. His uncle had dragged him onto the beach, with his eyes stinging from the salt water. He had lain on the sand and let the sun warm his body, telling his uncle that it was the shock of the cold that had paralysed him.

But he knew then, as now, that he had been overwhelmed – by the noise and the undeniable power of the threat. Now he stood, immobile, his will not only to move, but even to live, deeply threatened. This time, the danger had no physical form; it did not move or sway or thunder towards him. It was a greater terror. The threat lay somewhere inside him, not in his mind (he had not constructed it) and not in his heart (he could not feel it, in the way that you could feel anger or sorrow). It lay within his own definition of himself, at the core of his being.

His character in life was flawed, a Shakespearean figure whose function is to develop the tragedy. He could not help but destroy his marriage; its failure was ordained in his frailty. He was led, like a pack animal, to the collapse of his career, unable to steer away from the abuses that waited confidently for him. When, then, is it the end, he wondered. When do you finally know? Surely when you see yourself standing absolutely still, as now, not moving in any direction, while everyone else carries on moving; no one feels the need to stand with you, and you can do nothing else.

Eberard felt a single cool tear run down his cheek, running dry at the corner of his mouth. He wiped his eye tentatively, looking at his hand in surprise, as if he expected to see blood on his fingers. His thoughts had closed him off from the noise of the street for a short while, but now the sounds of screaming and laughter crashed about him again, even stronger, grating in his head like gravel.

'Yey, you *blerrie hotnot*, you don't even listen to me, *jou fokking* ... I'm telling you, here, I'm telling you ...' The man was still gripping Eberard's hand, now sticky with sweat, and swaying in front of him.

'Leave me alone,' Eberard said weakly.

The man's face transmuted from a scowl into an insane grin. He beamed as if he had just been complimented, throwing his head back and flicking his hair up. His mouth opened, revealing the stumps of yellow teeth and a tongue caked with white residue, slithering from side to side like an injured snake. 'Wah hah hah hah hah hah!' A roar of uncut laughter pushed up from his throat. He laughed as if he was running into battle, emitting screams of derision, which died as swiftly as they had arrived.

'*Fok jou, hottentot!*' His voice was filled with malice. '*Jy's die een!* The one who stole my land. The kaffir who threw me out of my house and told me to live under the bridge. *Jy is die een!* You sleep with jintoes and shit in my house. An animal's better than you. Not even an animal ... not even an animal.'

Eberard started to walk, pushing at the man's hand in an attempt to brush him off. The man hobbled alongside him, pulling at his arm. 'So, where's my money? You owe me money!' he persisted. 'I want to buy *brannewyn* for tonight, then we can drink by the river. You and me, your bergie.' Eberard tried to walk faster, but people jostled against him, shouting in his ear and rubbing against his shoulders. He broke free of the man's hold and wiped his hand against his trousers. The man's hand searched for his arm again, but Eberard turned his back on him.

They were soon separated, although Eberard could hear him still swearing at him, demanding money and shouting incoherent abuse. No one seemed to pay him any attention. Only Eberard remained aware of his presence, a few paces behind. Then, to his relief, the man latched onto someone else.

'Hey, my larney. How are you? I'm your bergie ...' His voice drifted away as Eberard moved down the road and turned into a side street to get away from the crowd.

Everyone has their story, he thought, exhausted, but not everyone has someone to tell.

BRAHMS LULLABY
(LULLABY AND GOOD NIGHT)

Lullaby and good night, with roses bedight
With lilies o'er spread is baby's wee bed
Lay thee down now and rest, may thy slumber be blessed
Lay thee down now and rest, may thy slumber be blessed

Lullaby and good night, thy mother's delight
Bright angels beside my darling abide
They will guard thee at rest, thou shalt wake on my breast
They will guard thee at rest, thou shalt wake on my breast

Guten Abend, gute Nacht, Mit Rosen bedacht,
Mit Naeglein besteckt, schlupf unter die Deck
Morgen frueh, wenn Gott will, wirst du wieder geweckt
Morgen frueh, wenn Gott will, wirst du wieder geweckt

Guten Abend, gute Nacht, Von Englein bewacht
Die zeigen im Traum, dir Christkindleins Baum
Schlaf nun selig und suess, Schau im Traum's Paradies
Schlaf nun selig und suess, Schau im Traum's Paradies

SEVEN

THE address was in a developing industrial area of the town, across the railway line and away from the business district. The road crossed the line on a high bridge leading through the Kayamandi settlement before turning back on itself and running next to the electric fencing alongside the line and the depot. A large sign advertising Coca-Cola stood over the entrance to the township, which appeared as a quilt of rusted roofs stretching from the road and sweeping up the slope of the hill towards the pine trees at the top. Lone trees pushed through the roofs in places, their scraggly limbs hanging precariously over the small dwellings below. The shacks in Kayamandi used more wood than in the city townships: long, roughly cut planks were nailed together, merging with the browns of the soil. Narrow corridors of earth, wet and eroded with mud, squeezed between the walls. Makeshift signs advertised cash stores, games houses and shebeens, and a large bright-green Boxer tobacco board stood incongruously among the homes. The doors of the shacks all looked out across the valley, over the town below and towards the manicured vineyards on the other side, interspersed with Arctic White roses and blushed with red bougainvillea. The township ended abruptly where the pitch of the slope made the building of houses too difficult, and only the road proceeded further towards the industrial zone.

The building faced onto a large open space used by the municipality to house its trucks. People had dumped their garden waste in part of the open lot; piles of broken concrete paving, branches, torn tree trunks and clumps of dried grass marked the edge of the property, spilling over the pavement onto the road. Heaps of dead leaves swirled up and down the length of the street, blown by the wind. The drains were blocked solid with soil and twigs, and watermarks showed where the road flooded in winter.

The two-storey building was flanked on one side by a warehouse. Its large receiving-bay door was secured with a rusted padlock, ferrous marks streaking down the door and staining the cement pavement. The windows of the warehouse were boarded up with chipboard. The building itself looked unused, and there was no sign of any business operation. The single door, painted in a stressed green, was the only break in the façade.

Eberard had been heading back to the station when Xoliswa had called him on his cellphone, sounding uncharacteristically tense. 'I think we have something,' she had said tersely.

She was waiting outside the single door to the building when he arrived. He was again struck by her stature. His ex-wife, in her critical and sour way, would have called her big-boned. But to him, she seemed athletic and strong. She carried herself upright, with dignity and a certain natural poise. Her braids were buffeted by the wind, flying out behind her neck as if alive.

Xoliswa did not wait for him to ask questions. 'I spoke to Melanie's friends,' she started as soon as he was within earshot. 'She had supper with them at the Keg & Barrel in town. She had a bit to drink, just beer. Maybe two cans. A young tutor from the university was with them. Apparently, he had an interest in Melanie. They all stayed at the pub until about ten, half past maybe. Then she asked this tutor guy to give her a lift. I spoke to him on the phone.' The constable briefly looked at her small notepad. 'Jeremy Wilder. His name's Jeremy Wilder. He wasn't very helpful. Anyway, he told me that he gave her a lift at about ten o'clock to this club ... that operates from this building.' Eberard looked up dubiously at the battered façade.

'He left her here in the street. Apparently she told him that she was meeting someone here, but wouldn't say who. She didn't want him to come in – said it wasn't his sort of thing. He sounded a bit straight. Not the clubber sort. Academic. Quite rude and condescending. And quite a bit older than her.'

'I didn't realise Melanie was the clubber sort herself,' Eberard said under his breath. 'Carry on.'

'Well, he left her here. Waited long enough to see her go in. Then he went back to the pub. They didn't see her again that night.' Eberard was nodding impatiently. 'There's more, don't worry,' Xoliswa reassured him. 'Her friends told me that recently she'd been occupied with something … or someone else. She stopped spending time with them and wasn't at home a lot. They think she had a serious boyfriend that she didn't want anyone to know about. They said her behaviour was a bit strange as well – as if she was distracted. She was irritable with them. Started to keep to herself more.'

'Good. That's good. What else?'

'Then I spoke to a female bartender inside the club,' Xoliswa continued. 'She's in early to check the stock. No one else seems to be around. Anyway, she's new at the club, and she doesn't seem to know much about it or the people who come here. The night of the killing was her second night on the job.'

Xoliswa summarised the witness's story. In a dark alleyway behind the club, she had seen a black man arguing with a young white girl who fitted Melanie's description. The man had grabbed the victim's arm and pulled her into the gloom, out of sight.

'That's when I called you,' Xoliswa explained. 'I didn't want to be the only person hearing this. She's very nervous and I think she's holding something back. When she saw my excitement, she stopped. If she gives me anything more, I think you should be here to hear it yourself.'

'Well done.' He felt genuinely grateful to the young reservist for having had the sense to call him. 'You did the right thing, Xoli.' His heart beat strongly as he patted her on the shoulder. A faint smell of perfume reached him. 'Take me to her, and take careful notes for a statement. We've got to nail this down right now.'

Xoliswa led the way, pushing the unlatched door open and stepping into the dark interior. Eberard stumbled on the step as he followed and had to pause while his eyes adjusted to the poor light. Three concrete steps, painted with bright-yellow road paint, led down into the large club area. A long bar counter ran along the length of the wall to his right. The lighting was dim, but Eberard could make out clusters of coloured lights and mirror balls hanging above him. The floor was also concrete, painted in wavy patterns that swayed towards the bar. Across the dance floor, on the far left side of the expansive room, was a second, smaller bar, with high tables and chairs scattered in the space in front of it. The walls were drably painted, in similar patterns to the floor. Indecisive strips of yellow and dirty pink ran down the walls. Little effort seemed to have been made to establish a theme for the venue. Eberard wondered how long the club expected to last.

The smell of stale cigarettes and spilt alcohol made Xoliswa wrinkle her nose, but Eberard was oblivious to the assault, although he briefly eyed the bottles of spirits lining the back of the bar. The club was quiet, except for the occasional clink of bottles from the smaller bar area. He followed his partner across the dance floor, their shoes echoing noisily on the hard surface. A young woman stood up from behind the bar counter.

'This is Detective Inspector Februarie, Maria.' Xoliswa put her elbows on the bar counter. 'He would like to speak to you.' As he got closer, Eberard saw how frightened she was. And how young. Perhaps nineteen or twenty, with bright-blue eyes and bleached hair. An obtrusive nose ring circled into one nostril; her fingers moved up to touch it. It looked uncomfortable, and her skin was red and inflamed around the top edge of the metal. A new addition, he thought.

'I don't really have time.' A flash of silver appeared on her tongue as she spoke. 'Like I have to finish checking the stock, you know.'

'Maria? That is your name?' Eberard asked. She nodded briefly, flinching defensively. He moderated his tone. 'I understand that you're busy. This probably won't take long. But it's a very serious matter. A young girl ... woman, your age, has been killed. We need to find out exactly what you saw. Please, will you tell me again?'

He tried to look as patient and caring as possible. The nose ring and the stud in her tongue irritated him. He felt like shaking her, taking her outside into the light of the real world. The girl vacillated for a few seconds, drumming her fingers on the counter. Eberard leant forward expectantly.

'Okay, like I'm new here, see. I only started a few days ago.'

The girl's eyes darted around the room as she spoke. 'I can't cause any trouble, and like, well, I just need to get my work done and that's it,' she whined. He stood waiting silently. She looked at him imploringly, and then at Xoliswa, who had the same set expression on her face. 'Okay, look, like two nights ago, Saturday night, I was working behind the bar. At about two o'clock, maybe a little before two, I went out back to have a smoke, out the back over …'

'Can you take us there now?' Eberard interrupted her. 'Before you carry on?'

'Ja,' she replied uncertainly. 'It's unlocked at the moment, for deliveries, you know.' They followed her across the dance floor to the main bar. At the one end, a wooden door had been painted to blend into the vague paintwork of the walls. She pushed the door open and almost flinched as the bright light flooded in. The sunlight picked out her blotchy skin, smeared with brown base along her chin to cover her acne. The alleyway ran between the club and another building. A few windows, screened by dirty chicken wire and plastic bags, faced onto it. The sides of the alley were lined with rusting drums and black rubbish bins. The drainpipes from the roof led down the buildings and opened directly onto the alley. Patches of green slime and black oil marked the uneven surface, and the smell of garbage and stagnant water filled the air. The alley ended against the brick wall of the adjoining building a few metres away from the door. The other end opened up some distance away onto a small back road.

'I was standing here having a smoke, you check. I was sitting on that drum, resting my feet. I'd been standing all night, you know,' she offered in explanation. Eberard nodded, exasperated, willing her to continue. The girl pulled a scrunched-up packet of Camels from her back pocket and lit one, squinting into the sun. 'As I came out and sat down, I heard like someone arguing. I couldn't hear what they were saying, you know, but it was a woman and a darkie … a black man, ja … with a deep voice.' She sucked on the cigarette. 'The girl was very upset about something. She was shouting at him, and he was angry as well. They were at the top of the alley.'

'Could you see them at all? Are there any lights in the alley?' Eberard asked.

'Well, there was some light, I reckon. From the road, you know … and a little light coming down from the first-floor windows. I could just see it was a white girl, like a girl maybe my age, and … and the black man. They were fighting. Like shouting. Then he grabbed her arm and sommer pulled her around the corner. Fucked if I know what it was about. I didn't see them again.' She looked back at the door to the club. 'Okay, so can I go now?'

'Maria, you can go when you've told me everything you know.' Eberard felt his temper rising. 'The moment you've told me everything, you can go and carry on with your work. Did you recognise either one of the two people you saw at the top of the alley?'

Maria looked at Xoliswa in distress, but the constable was unmoved. The girl fidgeted with the cigarette, dropping it on the ground and stooping to pick it up. As she straightened, Eberard noted a tear running down the side of her cheek. He knew she was holding something back.

'You didn't know the girl, but you do know who the man is, don't you? Maria?' She nodded almost imperceptibly in agreement and then shook her head. Tears started rolling down her cheeks in streaks.

'I don't know for sure.' She wiped her nose with the back of her arm, her skin dragging against the nose ring. Eberard winced involuntarily. 'It looked like a man who works here. A man from Burundi, I think,' she added in a soft voice, like a child apologising.

'What's his name, Maria?' Xoliswa asked, handing her a crushed tissue from her pocket. The subtle combination of the compassion of the gesture, together with the firmness in her voice, impressed Eberard. The barmaid's face crumpled into tears.

'He's a bouncer who works here on … on the main door. I only know him by his nickname. They call him Bullet.'

'A Burundian bouncer called Bullet. You saw him arguing with a young white girl in the alley. Then he grabbed her arm and pulled her around the corner.' Eberard was speaking more to himself than to the girl, but she nodded nonetheless. 'Tell me more about the woman. What colour was her hair? What was she wearing?'

'I don't know. I didn't really see. It looked like a short dress. Like a black dress.' He glanced at Xoliswa. She nodded once in return. 'I didn't see her properly. Please, I don't know anything else.'

'Maria,' Xoliswa said calmly, 'the girl who was killed, we found her dress this morning. She was wearing a short black dress when she was killed.'

'We think that you saw the man who may have killed her, Maria,' Eberard added.

The girl started to sob uncontrollably. Xoliswa touched her shoulder gently and escorted her inside the club. They sat down with her around one of the high tables, and the constable brought her a glass of water and a serviette. She gulped the water noisily and blew her nose. Eberard turned away while she negotiated her jewellery. They sat in silence for a while.

'She had light hair,' the girl went on, before Eberard could start asking questions again. She had lost all her adult pretences and spoke quietly and simply, like a child. 'The lady showed me a picture of her. I don't know if it was her. The girl I saw had short light hair. She was wearing a short black dress. The man was Bullet. I don't know any more. Please.'

'Where can we find this man, Bullet?' Eberard asked.

'There's a bunch of Nigerians living around the corner, at the back of the warehouse alongside this building. If you go around the corner, you'll come to a door. They live in there. I think he lives there. Or he sometimes stays there. You can ask them.'

'Thank you, Maria. You've helped us a lot. If you can remember anything else, then just call us at the Stellenbosch station.' Eberard wrote his name and telephone number on a torn piece of paper and gave it to her.

She looked at them carefully, as if assessing their sincerity. Eberard was about to get up to leave, when she spoke again. 'I won't sign my name to this. If you ask me if I said it, I'll say that I didn't ...' – they waited expectantly – 'but as the guy pulled her around the corner, I think I heard her scream at him that her father would kill him. Like she shouted, "My father will kill you!" It sounded like that. I don't know for sure.' Her eyes filled with tears again and she started sniffing. 'I should've said something to someone. I know I should have. But I was scared. And I wasn't sure what had happened. He's the bouncer here. The boss is also an African. I didn't know what to do. So I just left it. I tried to forget about it. Then I saw the newspaper. I knew it was her! I knew it!' She was almost shouting at them through her sobs. Small bubbles of spittle landed on the table top.

'Maria. You can't stay here,' Eberard said firmly. 'We're taking you away from here. I'm sorry, but we're going to take this man in for questioning. You can't stay here.' To his surprise, Maria did not resist his suggestion.

'Constable Nduku will take you home. I don't want you to come back here until this has finished. Do you understand?' The girl nodded, her hands cupped over her face. 'Xoliswa, Constable, take her home to her parents, wherever they are. Explain what has happened, but ask them to keep it quiet for now. Prepare a full statement, and get her to sign it. Before you leave, will you call the station and ask for a patrol van to come here right away? I want some uniformed members with me when I look for this suspect.' Xoliswa put an arm around the young girl and walked her towards the entrance.

The police van arrived shortly after Xoliswa had left with the waitress, still whimpering. Eberard gave the two uniformed men a quick briefing before leading them around the side of the warehouse. The policemen unclipped the leather bands that held their pistols. The narrow road was empty, except for two men sitting on drums on the pavement and smoking. They were bare-chested and their dark skin gleamed with sweat. Eberard smelt their odour as he passed, thick and pungent. One man had a lesion on his head, a scar from the deep cut of a blade. The other man grunted and spat onto the road; a blob of mucus sprayed across the tar. Eberard looked at them with distaste.

He stopped at the doorway and turned to them. 'We're looking for a man called Bullet. *Ons soek 'n man by die naam van Bullet.* Is he inside here?'

The men looked at him scornfully. The one with the scar shrugged his shoulders and turned back to his friend. '*J'arrive du Congo. Je ne suis pas là pour vous aider.*' His friend snorted in agreement.

The policemen glared at the men, but Eberard gestured to them to follow him. He pushed the door open. A narrow passage led away to the left before turning out of sight towards the warehouse. Three doors with makeshift handles opened onto the passage. The first stood open, revealing a small room with dry walls and a low ceiling. The room had space for a single bed, a low chest of drawers and a table with a kettle, toaster and two-plate stove. Clothes were hung against the wall on nails. The second door opened into a similar room.

The third door was locked. A radio, tuned to a music station, was playing. Eberard knocked loudly on the door and stood back, letting the uniformed officers take up their positions on either side of the door. One officer had drawn his firearm. A male voice sounded from inside the room. Then someone turned off the music. The lock grated on the other side of the thin door. As it started to open, the uniformed officer with the firearm kicked at it hard, forcing it open and pushing the person on the other side backwards. The three of them stormed in. The occupant was alone. He shouted in surprise and fell back onto a single bed against the wall. The room was slightly bigger than the others. In addition to the bed, it had a cupboard, a bookshelf with two shelves of books and papers, a stand-alone basin and a small kitchen area. The air was thick with smoke. Eberard vaguely detected the sweet, cloying smell of dagga and could see that the man's eyes were deeply bloodshot.

'*Pourquoi ne me laissez-vous pas tranquille?*' The man's voice was bass and resonant, and his tongue showed bright pink against his dark skin. He was shorter than the policemen but strongly built, with thick biceps and muscular forearms. His chest was broad and well defined, and a thin roll of skin marked the divide between his head and the start of his neck. His scalp was smooth and polished like a metal ball. Eberard was in no doubt that this was the man he was looking for.

'Your name is Bullet? Where are your papers? I want to see your papers. Now!' He was shouting at the man, who shouted back at him in French. 'You're working at the club, isn't that right?' Eberard pressed. 'You can speak some English. So speak to me. Where are your papers?' The uniformed policemen moved around him aggressively.

'*Mes papiers sont en règle!*' the man spat. '*Que voulez-vous de moi? Vous m'harcelez parce que je suis noir! Et parce que j'arrive d'un autre pays!*'

'Handcuff him!' Eberard instructed, noting the man glance towards the open door. 'And watch him; he's been smoking. He looks bloody strong. Cuff his ankles as well if you have to.'

The policemen closed in on him, turning him over on the bed with force. He was still shouting abuse at them. As he tried to break free, his fist slammed into one officer's jaw. The officer's partner brought the back of his firearm down into the small of the Burundian's back. He groaned in pain and tried to turn over. Eberard heard the handcuffs click over the man's wrists before the policeman hit him again with all his force, his fist cracking against the side of the man's face. The Burundian lay still on the bed, heaving. Eberard moved forward and forced the handcuffs even tighter against his wrists, the metal ridge pressing hard into the man's skin.

'Fucking Nigerians!' one officer said loudly, pulling the man to his feet. The blows had winded the suspect and he was unable to stand up straight. The officer searched him roughly, his forearm thudding up into the man's groin. The man stood uncertainly, gasping for breath.

'All right,' Eberard intervened. 'Take him back to the station in the van. I'll meet you there. One of you stay and start a search. Once you've dropped him off, come back here and help. Looking at this place, we probably won't find anything to help us. But look carefully. Women's clothes, blood, semen. Possible weapon.'

He paused. 'Apparently he's from Burundi. Check for hard drugs as well,' he said cynically. The men nodded.

'Oh, yes. Read him his rights. Tell him he's a suspect in a murder. Fill out that constitutional rights form and make him sign,' he added.

'Fucking aliens got more rights than our own women, isn't that right?' one policeman hissed, smacking the handcuffed man on the back of the head. 'You can read your fucking rights off the back of my hand, you bugger.' They dragged the suspect out of the room. The road outside was empty; the two men were nowhere to be seen. The suspect was thrown unceremoniously into the back of the police van.

Eberard returned to the station. He had an urge to phone Professor du Preez to tell him that he already had a suspect in custody and that he felt confident about an arrest. But he knew that he needed something more to link the Burundian to the dead girl, and he held back his impulse.

The suspect sat in the dark cells for a few hours before being hauled up to the interview room. The man sat hunched up on the wooden chair, pushing his thumbs into his thigh. He glowered at Eberard at every question. When he was pushed, he shouted back at him in French. He had refused to sign the property register and had left the constitutional rights form lying on the floor, unread.

After a while, Eberard gave up, and had the man returned to the holding cell. He walked back up the stairs to his office. He was halfway through his own statement when the telephone rang.

'We didn't find much, Inspector. No blood. No drugs either. But we did find a woman's earring next to the bed. Small silver half-moon. I'll bring it to you once we've finished off here.'

'Okay. Bag it and seal the room off. I'll ask Constable Nduku to come past and pick the earring up. We'll need the father or sister to ID it for us.'

Eberard continued with his statement. He was restless with anticipation but forced himself to complete it. When he was finished, he went down into the charge office again. The Burundian was lying on his back on the bench in the holding cell, with his shirt pulled over his face. Eberard was about to knock against the bars when the charge-office commander called him to the telephone. He took the call in the charge office.

'Good news, Inspector.' It was Xoliswa, sounding excited. 'I'm at the house. I've spoken to the sister. The father wasn't here, but the sister's positive: that earring belonged to Melanie. I think you've got him.'

Eberard put the telephone down. An uncharacteristic surge of hope filled him. The satisfaction that he used to get from the job, could he still find that, could it still be there? Could he dispel the doubts, he wondered, regain some of what he had lost? Maybe his name would be printed in the newspaper. Maybe his wife would see. Perhaps she would read the article to Christine. Maybe she would feel proud.

He dialled the pathology laboratory and waited impatiently as he was put through. 'Dr Rademan, I have a suspect.' It felt good to tell someone. 'I need you to do a DNA match for me. I'll arrange for a sample to be sent to you tomorrow.'

'Certainly, Inspector. As you know, however, to call for the test, I'll have to have copies of all the statements implicating the suspect. Just for record purposes, you know.' The doctor laughed nervously. 'Just so that I can't be accused of wasting precious state funds. On wild goose chases, you know.'

'That's no problem, Doctor. I know the difficulties with these things. Can you also do me one other favour? We've found a single earring that belonged to the deceased, and we were wondering ...'

'Well, she had no earrings on her when she came in here,' the pathologist interrupted keenly. 'But she does have pierced ears. But no earrings. Must have come off in the water. Or in the struggle when she was hit on the head. Sorry. Can't help you there.'

Eberard felt mildly disappointed at this news. It would have been far cleaner if the other earring had still been in her ear when she was found. But it was a small matter; the important thing was that Melanie could be placed in the Burundian's room, and he had been identified pulling her out of the alley. Eberard had no doubt that the DNA test would be a match.

ALL THROUGH
THE NIGHT

Sleep my child and peace attend thee,
All through the night
Guardian angels God will send thee,
All through the night
Soft the drowsy hours are creeping,
Hill and dale in slumber sleeping
I my loved ones' watch am keeping,
All through the night

Angels watching, e'er around thee,
All through the night
Midnight slumber close surround thee,
All through the night
Soft the drowsy hours are creeping,
Hill and dale in slumber sleeping
I my loved ones' watch am keeping,
All through the night.

EIGHT

JAKOBA kept to her side of the agreement with Van der Keesel. She gave what she had agreed to give. Frederick had not received notice from the Company of the lifting of their status as slaves, but nevertheless they had cleared the smallholding alongside the river and had started to construct a rough home from sun-baked clay bricks and rocks. The family's situation as informal free burghers was tenuous. Jakoba was not in a position to assert her independence, and years of slavery had taught her acquiescence. She was now Van der Keesel's *nyai*, a Batavian word for a housekeeper, which, in Company parlance, was used to describe female slaves taken as sexual companions by their masters, isolated from their families and lonely for a woman's touch. But while some women were afforded a position of respect in the social structure of the colony, Jakoba remained nothing more than a slave to serve her master's passing desires.

For Van der Keesel, as for all men whose egos steer their lives, the satisfaction lay in the initial conquest of carnal property rather than the ongoing tedium of governance. His interest in her sensuality soon started to wane as other challenges arose. He developed an attachment to the young fiancée of a Dutch draughtsman, and was also pursuing a captain's wife, who was left alone at the colony while her husband conveyed supplies from Holland. Jakoba filled the occasional gap between these activities, and her presence became almost a chore. The short-lived and immediate thrill of sexual dominance gave way to a bored and dismissive acceptance of her visits. Van der Keesel treated her like a servant, a personal employee, occasionally demanding sexual gratification to confirm his power, but increasingly using her to perform chores around his unkempt residence. He showed no interest in his home or the clutter of ill-matched furniture that filled it, and rarely spent much time between its walls. Jakoba would arrive on the designated day, not knowing whether to expect to be dismissed with a torrent of abuse, ordered to his unmade bed, or find herself on her knees scrubbing week-old ash from the hearth. The absence of any pattern in his behaviour made the anticipation of her visits all the more intolerable and demeaning.

Van der Keesel had the use of a room on the Company's estate at Constantia, but he rarely visited the Cape for any length of time. His permanent residence was in the new settlement of Stellenbosch, where he could keep an eye on his vines. The Company-owned house was situated off Schreuder Street in the centre of the growing village. It looked out onto a site that Van der Stel had designated for a new row of Company houses. The work was slow and the site had deteriorated into a series of small interlinked pools of muddy water, breeding mosquitoes and filled with dragonfly larvae. Glossy-winged hadedas and elegant grey-headed herons stalked about the shallow fringes, stirring the soft mud with their feet and darting their sharp bills into the water. Van der Keesel had chosen the house partly in order to keep an eye on the progress of the site, but he had lost interest in the continual shortages of building materials and the need to source suitable wood and clay locally. He occasionally shouted abuse at the foreman, but otherwise ignored the slaves deployed there.

The uneven roadway was filled with mud from the building site, and, when the wind blew, fine grit swept through the open windows of the house. Jakoba could feel the prickle of the dirt on the bed linen as Van der Keesel pressed her down, his rough hands on her shoulders and breasts. The mud caked her soft leather shoes, and the folds of her skirt collected thick layers of dust and grime. When she returned home, the state of her clothes mirrored her internal defilement.

The harsh sun reflected off the whitewashed terrace of the house, and the steep thatched roof and white gables kept the interior cool, although the new thatch still deposited flakes from the lining of the reeds, spreading a thin carpet of dirt across the floors and furniture. Light filtered into the rooms through the mullioned windows. Glass was still hard to come by in the new colony, and gauze, sealed with beeswax, was stretched over the window frames to keep insects and dust out. A large open hearth, its stones blackened by fires, dominated the kitchen, together with a roughly hewn table in the centre of the room. Two half-length benches sat at either end of the table, the one solid and the other made with young oak slats strung with strips of buck skin. Cast-iron and earthenware pots were stacked in the corner of the kitchen, and hooks for hanging vegetables hung empty on the rafters. It was usual to hang strings of onions, beetroot, herbs and salted fish from the beams, out of reach of meerkats and other scavengers. The previous tenants of the house had done so, but after Van der Keesel had moved in, the strings of vegetables had been left unattended and had dried to husks, and the fish had been pulled off when they started attracting flies. Despite his energy and stocky size, the house bore no evidence that he ever used the kitchen for cooking, and Jakoba assumed that he obtained his sustenance elsewhere in the town. The young male slave assigned to the Company house had orders to light the fire at night-time, but was never called upon to prepare food in any form for the tenant.

As was the custom among the gentry of the Company, the front room was used to display the inhabitant's status. While the remaining spaces in the house were largely bare, the expansive front room was cluttered with furniture, carpets, cloths and trophies from Van der Keesel's travels. Richly piled carpets were draped over huge sea chests, five feet wide, while the floor was left bare. A large stinkwood and amboyna cabinet dominated one wall, with blue and white china plates, some displaying the VOC emblem in the middle, lined up along the open shelves. Ornaments from China vied with spice boxes from Indonesia for pride of place on the table tops. Figures carved from dark ebony, a globe of the world made from cloth stained with henna, tea chests, silver snuff and *sirih* boxes piled up around the room in a disorderly fashion. Some of the side tables were made from cheaper wood, lacquered with red varnish to look like the expensive red ebony from the Indonesian islands.

The living area led directly into the bedroom through a large opening, without curtaining or door. The room was as bare as the wooden floor, save for a wide four-poster bed in the middle, positioned so that it could be seen quite easily from the living room. A thick quilt lay across the sheets, infested with fleas and lice. The four posts were elegantly carved in the form of plaits, snaking upwards towards the square canopy, like the roots of a gnarled old tree. A traditional Asian-designed muslin cloth was draped over the canopy; the Tree of Life was depicted in its centre, with large red flowers drooping from its boughs. The headboard was also carved from dark ebony, a floral design running like waves along its length, separated into strips by thin dowels. Jakoba would lie on the bed, her fingers hooked around the pillars, the sturdy and cold bars of her prison.

The hardships of slavery had taught her to make use of any scraps of material or leather to keep her family clothed. She was an accomplished seamstress, able to patch holes and mend tears with great skill. Van der Keesel took to handing her clothes that required mending: sour-smelling shoes that had split the stitching, coarse socks with holes pushed through at the dirty toes, frayed breeches and sweat-stained shirts. She never brought the clothes home and always finished her darning before leaving. She had no wish to remind her husband of the price of their land, or to give the viticulturist cause to intrude further into her family's lives.

Van der Keesel sensed her fear of his intrusion – or perhaps it was simply his boorish disregard for his subjects – and he insisted on visiting the Boorman smallholding from time to time. He would arrive on horseback, unannounced and usually inconveniently close to mealtimes. He would dismount impatiently, dropping the reins without waiting to be received. He would expect one of the younger children to catch his horse, before it entered the vegetable fields, and tie it up for him. (On one such occasion, he exploded when, on departing, he found that his horse had not been watered and fed.) He entered their home as if it were his own, throwing his coat onto the table and sitting down without acknowledging the family.

'Jakoba!' His use of her first name in front of her husband carried with it the deliberate suggestion of ownership and intimacy. It was all Frederick could do to remain in the house during these visits. 'Jakoba! I need you to come tomorrow. There is work for you to do. My trousers need fixing.'

'I thought I had mended your trousers, Master van der Keesel,' she replied carefully.

'These are other trousers, girl,' he glowered at her, his look warning her not to challenge his orders. She demurred and nodded quietly.

'Of course, Master van der Keesel. I will be there tomorrow morning.'

There was an awkward pause as the visitor cast his eyes around the bare kitchen, turning up his nose in distaste. He would invariably insinuate their return to the work of slaves during these visits. 'I think you'd be better off back at the colony. I'll tell the Governor that his idea to release your husband from his duties was a foolish one. People like you cannot be left to look after yourselves. Look how you live here.' He cast his arms in front of him in an arc. 'You live like the animals that you are. You can't look after yourselves. I have told the Governor this time and time again, but he will not listen,' he blustered, shaking his head. 'He's too soft, Jakoba. He thinks that he is doing you a favour by letting you live like this. But your freedom, Jakoba … your freedom is a curse on you.'

Jakoba was close to tears. She sat down opposite him, her hands wringing on the rough table top between them. 'Please, Master van der Keesel, please. We are happy here … we have worked hard for the Company, and Frederick is still working for Master van der Stel every week. Please, Master van der Keesel, I beg you. We are just starting here. You'll see, we'll make it nice …'

'Don't snivel and beg.' He dismissed her with a wave of his hand as if she was a dog begging for scraps. 'It is pathetic.'

Frederick placed a plate of food in front of the man, carrots and potatoes mixed with thickly cut onions, hot from the hearth fire. The visitor snorted.

'Look at the food you eat,' he said with scorn, picking up the vegetables with his grubby fingers. 'You might as well forage in the fields with your snouts. Grovelling animals feed better than this.' He continued speaking as he shovelled the food into his mouth, dropping bits of half-chewed potato onto the table and floor. 'You half-breeds are a real problem. Van der Stel thinks you can be trusted with your freedom, but I've told him it's nonsense. Only yesterday I had a new burgher flogged within an inch of his life; he has forfeited his release and he'll be doing hard labour for the rest of his days. Caught him planting illegal vines along the river bank. Can you trust a half-breed? Never. But then Van der Stel's one himself, so what can you expect?' Jakoba averted her eyes at the mention of the Governor, trying not to associate herself with Van der Keesel's treasonous comments. The visitor wiped the plate with his fingers and pushed it across the table. 'Dogs must be put back in the kennels, Jakoba. We cannot have dogs roaming around the land.'

Jakoba could not withstand the taunting any longer and tears spilled from her eyes. 'Please, Master van … please …'

Frederick stood up from his seat in the corner where he had been sitting out of sight. The viticulturist leapt to his feet as if someone had threatened him.

'Sit down, slave!' he ordered. 'How dare you get to your feet while I am still seated! I am talking here and you dare to interrupt me before I have finished. Do you want a flogging, boy? Do you? I'll let the caffers have you!'

Frederick stood on his feet for a second, more out of shock than any determination to hold his ground, before sinking back onto the stool. Jakoba was sobbing with her head on the table.

The room was still for a moment, save for Jakoba's heaving breaths. Then Frederick spoke, his voice strong and clear. 'We are grateful for everything that you have done for us, Master van der Keesel, but my wife is very upset and I think that you should leave us now.'

Jakoba looked up in alarm, waiting for the visitor's reaction. To her surprise, Van der Keesel rose calmly to his feet. 'I have other business to attend to,' he said, 'and you have your wife to comfort, Boorman.' He turned on his heel and walked through the doorway into the fading light.

Jakoba waited for the sound of the horse's hooves on the

stony ground to recede into the distance before calling out to her daughter. 'Sanna,' her voice quivered, 'come to me, my little one.' Her husband remained seated in the shadows of the room, a prisoner of his sadness and impotence.

Sanna fell into her mother's arms, her smooth hands stroking Jakoba's head, murmuring in her ear. She crooned the lyrics of an old lullaby, calming her mother with her soft words and gentle touch.

The girl was now fourteen years old and tall for her age. She had developed a strength of character and resoluteness that had long been beaten out of her parents; where her mother was stoic, she was defiant; where her father was broken, she was resilient. She had a young prettiness that would soon swell into the understated beauty sometimes seen in her mother's tired face. Hers was uncontaminated ground upon which a man like Van der Keesel would be wont to place his boots.

Sanna knew instinctively that she should remain out of sight when the viticulturist visited. Her parents did not acknowledge this directly, as the direction of such thoughts was too painful. But, in her heart, Jakoba knew that it was just a matter of time before her taunter would register the unspoiled beauty of her daughter.

SUO GAN

Sleep, my baby, on my bosom,
Warm and cosy, it will prove,
Round thee mother's arms are folding,
In her heart a mother's love.
There shall no one come to harm thee,
Naught shall ever break thy rest;
Sleep, my darling babe, in quiet,
Sleep on mother's gentle breast.

Sleep serenely, baby, slumber,
Lovely baby, gently sleep;
Tell me wherefore art thou smiling,
Smiling sweetly in thy sleep?
Do the angels smile in heaven
When thy happy smile they see?
Dost thou on them smile while slum'bring
On my bosom peacefully.

Huna blentyn yn fy mynwes
Clyd a chynnes ydyw hon
Breichiau mam sy'n dyn am danat,
Cariad mam sy dan fy mron
Ni cha dim amharu'th gyntun
Ni wna undyn â thi gam
Huna'n dawel, anwyl blentyn
Huna'n fwyn ar fron dy fam.

Huna'n dawel, heno, huna,
Huna'n fwyn, y tlws ei lun
Pam yr wyt yn awr yn gwenu,
Gwenu'n dirion yn dy hun?
Ai angylion fry sy'n gwenu
Arnat ti yn gwenu'n llon
Tithau'n gwenu'n ol dan huno
Huno'n dawel ar fy mron?

Paid ag ofni, dim ond deilen
Gura, gura ar y ddor
Paid ag ofni, ton fach unig
Sua, sua ar lan y mor
Huna blentyn, nid oes yma
Ddim i roddi iti fraw
Gwena'n dawel yn fy mynwes
Ar yr engyl gwynion draw.

NINE

MISTING rain sparkled in the spotlights, drifting like a gossamer sheet across the length of the courtyard. The orange lights reflected off the puddles collecting on the tarmac, and traffic hummed in the background. The serenity of the scene belied the stories of misery that clung to the walls, seeping from the cracks in the high windows of the surrounding cells. A deep, soulful voice started singing; a prisoner had climbed up and pushed his head against the thin strip-window panels. Songs of sadness resonated from deep inside his chest – songs from the mines, far and long away. Songs of sorrow and longing for home. The melancholy of the minor keys made Eberard uncomfortable. Am I your persecutor, he pondered, am I your oppressor because I locked you in the cells? For stealing? For taking what was never yours?

He suddenly felt irritated with the man, singing his pathetic songs of hardship and freedom. He slouched down on his seat and closed his eyes. Small white dots played in front of his eyes, and his head felt swollen. He quickly slipped into a state between sleep and wakefulness, his head lolling back against the headrest. His thoughts – half-conscious dreams – were warmly familiar. Standing in front of the bank on the main road, waiting for the suspects to come out. The sun is warm on his back. There is no other sound, just the stillness of anticipation. Shadows move behind the plate-glass windows. A woman calls to her child, briefly breaking the silence, pulling the young boy into the doorway of a nearby shop. The air holds its breath. The glass door is pushed open and, in slow motion, replayed, then played again, a figure emerges. Dressed in black, balaclava pulled over his head; no ambiguity about good and evil. Dressed for the part. Clean and convenient. The figure is carrying a case in one hand and an automatic rifle in the other. Light-coloured wooden butt. AK-47.

A second figure emerges. The details replay over and over,

savouring the tension and warmth of the moment. Still Eberard waits. Watching. The third figure comes out, and the door closes behind them. A click of glass on glass, like a safety catch. Like a shotgun shell loading onto the base plate. Eberard stands up, emerging from behind the vehicle. He is towering over the car. His shoulders flex as he shouts a command to them, his chest swelling soundlessly with authority. They hear him and look up, squinting into the sun and lifting their guns slowly. A gloved hand points in Eberard's direction.

They appear in his sights as black targets against the brilliant background of the sun on the bank's windows. He focuses on the closest figure. The target fills his sights. Bigger than the sights. Large, unmoving. Eberard feels the metal ring against his thumb. He touches it with the extremity of his finger. If you curl your finger on the trigger, you will pull to the side. Squeeze slowly, he tells himself, with the pad of your finger. A popping sound as the weapon jerks in his hands. He feels a rush of air as the cartridge tumbles out the side, spinning in a slow arc in the air. He sees it in his mind's eye: a smoking empty cartridge tumbling slowly through space; everything blurring around it. It lands on the tar at his feet with a thin, brassy clatter. The figure in his sights lurches backwards. The sights move onto the second figure. Like a machine. A single movement from one to the next. He locks onto the new target. The figure already has his gun raised. Squeeze again. A rush of air, the clatter of the cartridge. No other sound. The figure jerks away.

The last suspect is hiding behind a car. The target steps out into the light, firing blindly with a handgun at his pursuer. Eberard is perfectly calm. His breath comes in a slow, easy routine. He focuses on the last figure. Unhurried. His sights are filled. He squeezes the trigger. Slowly.

The sound is loud and frightening; a harsh bang cracks against his head, leaving his ears ringing. The scene explodes in light.

Eberard jolted awake in his chair, blinking into the fluorescent lighting of his office. His ears buzzed with a low grating sound, but the room was quiet. It was dark outside and the evening shift would have taken over. Had he dreamed the gunshot so realistically, he wondered. He listened for noises in the corridor. A light breeze pushed through the open window, and summer crickets whirred outside. A Christmas beetle bounced against the pane, pushing against the glass and sliding towards the opening. Someone shouted something outside in the courtyard. A car sped past the station. A siren started on the main road of the town. The radio crackled downstairs.

Eberard rubbed his gritty eyes and picked up the report on his desk. Rademan had scribbled on the top of the file: 'DNA test requested. Request confirmed. Results next week.' The pathologist had summarised his findings in a typed addendum. Despite the man's eccentric manner, the report was succinct and clearly written.

> Semen was found to be present in the vagina of the deceased. The ejaculate contained both viable spermatozoa and a disproportionately large quantity of seminal fluid. This may be indicative of multiple intercourse with a person of low sperm count. It also suggests that she may not have been submerged in water for very long. The condition of the ejaculate suggests intercourse occurred within a period of a few hours prior to her death: intercourse could have taken place immediately prior to her death. Abrasions were found to be present on the upper thigh and labia. The presence of petechial haemorrhages on the inner wall of the vagina indicates that intercourse occurred prior and not subsequent to death. It is also suggestive of non-consensual intercourse, although not conclusive in this regard.

The clatter of thick cell keys jangling outside Eberard's office distracted him. He took a sip of cold tea. Again someone shouted from the station yard below.

> The cause of death was drowning in fresh water. The deceased would have been deeply unconscious when she entered the water. She sustained a severe injury to the left

side of her temple and forehead. The cranium was crushed over the temporal and frontal lobe, causing massive damage to the brain, prior to immersion. Death or extensive permanent disablement would almost certainly have resulted from this injury had she not been placed in the water. The wound to the skull is jagged and resulted from a crushing, rather than a penetrating, blow. The presence of grains of sand and natural detritus deep in the wound suggests that the object used may have been a rock or a brick. This would suggest a lack of premeditation.

I am informed that the deceased was found floating face down in a freshwater canal. I am also informed that a patch of blood was located on the side of the riverbank, upstream from where she was found. The blood-type from the sample taken from this patch matches the blood-type of the deceased. The blood-type on the dress found nearby also matches the blood-type of the deceased. Further test results will be forthcoming in this regard. However, at this preliminary stage, the inference that the deceased was struck while lying on the grass next to the river and that her body was then placed in the river would be consistent with the pathological findings to date.

The commotion in the yard grew. Someone shouted up to Eberard. Another voice swore loudly. He dropped the report back onto the table. He stood up and put his jacket on. He was halfway down the stairs to the charge office when a young constable intercepted him, bounding breathlessly up towards him.

'You'd better come quickly, Inspector!' he shouted. 'We've got a problem in the cells. I mean, a real problem.'

The young man turned and charged down the stairs energetically. Eberard followed more sedately. The sky was clearing and the half-moon shone brightly. Eberard thought of Melanie's earrings with some irony as he walked across the tarmac towards the cells. The young constable was shouting into the radio, pressing the call button down without waiting for control to give him air time. Eberard felt a surge of impatience and kicked an empty chip packet into the gutter. The pale yellow paint of the cell building glowed weakly in the floodlights. The first gate stood open, its black paint chipped and scratched to show the bare metal underneath. Several shift officers were standing in the small quadrangle leading to the individual cells. The smell of disinfectant.

'What's going on?' Eberard asked dismissively. No one answered him, but they parted to allow him through. 'Just don't tell me we've had another fucking escape!' he shouted in exasperation. A juvenile housebreaking suspect had escaped the week before; because of his youth, the duty officer had decided not to handcuff him while leading him to the cells. The suspect had tripped his escort and bolted from his grasp. But the men shook their heads at Eberard, and one officer gestured towards the orange glow of the first cell.

Inside, a coarse grey blanket and thin mattress lay unused on the cement floor. The steel push-button tap over the basin was running, jammed by the fingers of frustrated prisoners. Otherwise, the space was empty, except for a figure lying slumped against the wall next to the toilet. Eberard moved closer and crouched down beside him. The Burundian was lying with his legs astride, as if he had been standing and bracing himself for a blow that had knocked him out. His strong arms hung uselessly at his side, and his neck was twisted awkwardly. The wall had pushed his head forward, and Eberard could not see his eyes. He reached forward and turned his head to the side. Blood leaked out of a neat round mark on his forehead, running in a dark rivulet between his eyes and down the side of his nose. His eyes were wide open, filled with surprise, but quite still.

'How the hell did this happen?' Eberard felt dizzy and stood up slowly. He turned towards the door in fury. 'For God's sake, how did he get a gun into the cell? Who was on duty when this happened? Christ, didn't you search him?' Then he remembered the search in the room, on the bed. His heart clenched. Had he missed it? Was it his fault? In the heat of the moment, the fight to subdue the suspect, had he missed something as obvious as a firearm? He felt faint and clammy.

The men were frowning, but no one spoke. The same officer who had gestured for him to enter the cell now pointed to the adjoining cell. His shuffling, uncommunicative attitude only infuriated Eberard more.

'Jesus Christ, now what?' he shouted. 'What?' He strode out of the cell and into the adjoining one. This space was similar in all respects, except for the presence of a man sitting on the concrete bench, his head in his hands. He was shaking with emotion. Eberard felt a shift in his reality, as if he had walked into a hallucination.

'Professor du Preez,' he managed to say, not as a question, but simply a statement of fact. He stared at the professor, trying to gain a hold on the situation. 'Professor du Preez,' he heard himself say again. He could not think how to react. He stood in the cell, watching the professor sobbing into his hands. He caught himself before saying the man's name again. Then he turned and walked out.

He pushed angrily past the officers standing outside. One of them asked him what they should do with Du Preez. 'You let this happen,' Eberard snapped. 'You work it out. What a goddamn mess!'

Once outside in the courtyard, he vented his frustration at the night sky, letting out a roar of anger. He stormed into the charge office and took a cigarette out of the pack on the table. He lit it and retreated back up to his office, where he slumped into his chair, knocking it against the wall behind him. A small chip of paint and plaster landed on his trousers. He felt overwhelmed with fatigue. He wanted to sleep, to be unconscious. When he woke up, everything would be back to normal. He would have his suspect. He would prove his case. He would show the professor that the system worked. He would avenge the girl's death. He would be in control. He would be the protector. He would act. He would participate. But the sand beneath his feet was shifting; the foundations were being washed away. He had no idea what had just taken place at the station; all he knew was that nothing would be the same again.

'Superintendent, it's Inspector Februarie,' he announced,

speaking into the slim black handset. 'Yes, I'm still at the station, sir. There's been a shooting. In the cells.' He paused while this extraordinary information sank in. His superior was silent. 'I think you'd better come down here,' he added unnecessarily, dropping the telephone receiver into the cradle. It bounced out and clattered on the desktop. He picked it up wearily and placed it back more carefully. He rummaged in his wallet for a five-rand coin and went downstairs to the soft-drink vending machine. The can was cold and solid, and the cool bubbles eased his stomach.

The on-duty officers had placed the professor in the holding cell inside the charge office. The same holding cell that had housed the Burundian earlier that day, Eberard noted. The man was still sobbing, although less violently now. Eberard leant against the bars of the cell door without talking. He sipped his Coke as he watched the large man trying to deal with his pain. Neither of them spoke.

The superintendent arrived in his off-duty clothes, jeans and a shirt, and Eberard left the professor to join the discussion.

'We came on duty, Superintendent. I was here from about 6:45.' The on-duty charge-office commander was explaining the events in a nervous, high-pitched voice, shifting from one foot to the other. 'I was told we had one prisoner. That was the Burundian man in Inspector Februarie's case. He was in cell number one. The book shows that he'd already had his telephone call. So I just left him. Then, at about 7:30, that man arrived.' He gestured towards the holding cell. 'He was dressed in a suit. He showed me an advocate's card and said he'd come to see his client, the Burundian. He said that we were holding his client and that he had come to consult with him. He said he needed to see him before he spoke to any of us. I mean, he said he wanted to see his client, the Burundian, before he spoke to the detectives or anyone. So I told him that he was the only prisoner and he could speak to him in the cells. He said that was fine. So we took him there and left him with his client. It was all standard procedure, Superintendent,' he squeaked.

'Okay, okay, what happened next?' the superintendent snapped impatiently.

'About five minutes later, there was a shot. We ran back to the cells and we found the prisoner had been shot. The advocate … the man … was standing in the cell, crying. There was a gun on the floor. A 7.65 pistol and one empty cartridge on the floor. The prisoner was already dead. He'd been shot in the head. I don't really know what happened. We didn't think … I don't understand, Superintendent, what's going on?' The young constable was close to tears.

'What's going on?' Eberard interjected, infuriated. 'What's going on is that you let the father of the child – the child who the suspect had raped and killed – into his cell with a loaded fucking firearm. You let the father of the dead girl kill the suspect in our own cells! How the hell do you plan to explain that one to internal complaints? For fuck's sake!'

The muscle above the superintendent's left eye jumped. 'But where did he get an advocate's card from?'

'He's an associate member of the Bar. He's a law lecturer and a professor. They're allowed to be members of the Bar. He's admitted as an advocate,' Eberard said icily. 'Didn't you notice the name?' He glowered at the constable.

The uniformed officer looked morose. 'I don't know anything about your case. Do you think I'd have let the father anywhere near this guy if I'd known what was going on? I thought he was his lawyer. Superintendent, we don't ever search legal representatives before they consult. I mean, he's an advocate. Must I do a body search on him?'

'Can you imagine the shit from the Law Society if we started frisking their members?' the superintendent responded. 'This is one big fuck-up. I'll call the area commissioner; he'll be happy with this, I'm sure. Februarie, you'd better open a murder docket. It's your case – it's ended your one murder case, so you might as well take the next one. They sort of belong together,' he said, without humour. 'And get the body guys over here. I don't want that body in my cells any longer than it has to be.' He looked at the distraught man in the holding cells and shook his head in disbelief.

Eberard nodded compliantly. He had hoped that the second

killing would be assigned to another officer. He sighed and took another cigarette out of the pack on the table. The padlock on the holding-cell gate clicked loosely as he opened it. He pulled the dirty bolt across and swung the heavy grate inwards. The metal hinges shuddered, and the professor looked up momentarily as it clanged against the inside wall. Eberard caught the bars as the door swung back to him, pushing it closed behind him. He did not bother to replace the padlock.

He leant back against the grate, his shoulder blades pushing between the round bars. He remained in that position for a while. The professor reminded him even more strongly of himself now. Eberard, too, had been swept along in events over which he felt he had no control. Although he had committed the very acts that had caused his downfall, he had behaved as if he'd had no choice. He had taken the drugs. He had skimmed narcotics off the top. He had struck deals with merchants. He knew that now. But at the time it had seemed as if another person was at work, destroying his life, wrecking his every attempt to regain his balance. He had not thought about keeping the stash of crack cocaine; it was inevitable, indeed it had been a necessary and obvious link in the chain. Losing his wife, watching Christine go; it had all been scripted for him and he could no more walk off the stage than the professor could now walk out of the open cell door. How do you break the circle, Eberard thought, still watching the man in front of him. How do you lift yourself out of the hole and not dig it even deeper?

'What happened, Professor du Preez?' he asked, trying to keep his voice even.

Du Preez did not answer. His cries were dry now, desperate gulps of air. He ran his hands back and forward through his hair, pulling at his scalp. Eberard repeated the question.

Du Preez looked up. His eyes were red, and the lids looked tender and puffy. He appeared to have shrunk, and when he tried to speak, his lips trembled. He looked down, away from his questioner.

'After you phoned, I thought ... I came ... I came to confront him,' he murmured. He waited and then spoke more clearly.

'I came to confront him about what he did to my … to Melanie. I can't sleep at night. Can you understand that, Detective? Not to sleep at night. Not at all. I hear Elsabe crying in her bed; I don't have the strength to go to her any more. He has robbed me of the last humanity that I had. He's taken away my daughter. And I wanted to know why.' He looked up at Eberard. His voice was filled with emotion, but his eyes were lifeless.

'I wanted to know why he had done this to me. To Melanie. To Elsabe. *Wie anders kan ek vra?*' he pleaded. 'When my children's mother was taken from them, I tried to ask God why. I never received any answer. This time there was someone I *could* ask. So I came to ask him. Why did he do this thing?'

'Did you get an answer from him?'

Du Preez looked down again. 'I confronted him in the cells. When I told him I was a lawyer, he dismissed me. He said he had his own lawyer, and he didn't need a white man to help him. He was very abusive. Then I told him who I really was. He didn't believe me at first. But I kept telling him, over and over again: "I am her father." It suddenly dawned on him that I was telling the truth. He looked at me carefully, looked me up and down. And then, do you know what he did?' Spittle had collected in the corners of the professor's mouth. Eberard felt a sudden need to take a cloth and wipe it away. The lack of dignity disturbed him. He felt that he should be talking to the learned man in a study, surrounded by books, the aroma of imported coffee permeating the air. Instead, the smell of urine drifted up from a damp patch in the corner of the cell. The walls were smeared with unidentifiable streaks, fingerprint ink or dried faeces. Someone had scribbled obscenities along the wall above the concrete bench. The graffiti mixed racist slurs with lewd diagrams and meaningless scribbles.

'He laughed,' the professor's voice rasped. 'He burst out laughing. He looked right at me, into my eyes, knowing that I was her father, and he started to laugh.'

'Is that when you shot him, Professor?'

'No, I was too shocked to do anything. I hadn't come to shoot him. You must understand that, I hadn't come to shoot him.' He turned all his attention to Eberard. 'I brought the gun with me – it was a stupid thing to do – but I brought it with me in case he turned nasty. I couldn't ask you guys for protection – if you knew who I was, you would never have allowed me to speak to him. I planned to speak to him, but I brought the gun for my own protection. When he started to laugh, I was too shocked to do anything. I realised that I'd made a mistake in coming to confront him. He's an animal, he's not going to give me an explanation for his actions. He did it because she walked past him, because she was there, and afterwards he didn't think anything of it.' He put his head in his hands and started to sob again. He breathed deeply for a few moments, trying to control himself.

'You have no idea how much more difficult that makes it, Inspector.' He looked up again. 'I realised then that he couldn't give me a reason. Not because he didn't want to. He didn't *have* a reason! *He didn't have one!*' He was shouting now, and Eberard raised his hands to placate him.

'What happened then?'

'I turned to go. I was about to knock on the bars to call the policeman who had let me in. I heard him – the Burundian – get up and move towards me. My back was to him and I took my gun out. I thought he might be about to attack me. When I turned around he was close to me. But he was smiling. He looked right at me, with his thick lips and his stupid face. Then he said, with that French accent, "Your daughter, she tasted so nice."

'I felt like I'd been burned from head to toe. Like hot oil had been poured over me. I pointed the gun at him. I think I was screaming at him. I can't remember. I can't … I heard the gate keys jangling behind me. He had stepped back from me, but he was still smiling. He opened his mouth to say something else. Something disgusting. I could see it forming in his eyes. It was something disgusting and horrible about Melanie. Something about the way she died. I could see it. It was about to slide out of his mouth. I saw it coming and I pulled the trigger. His mouth closed and that disgusting thing stayed inside. He fell back next to the toilet. I dropped the gun. The policeman grabbed me from behind. The rest I think you know.'

Eberard was still for a moment, shocked by Du Preez's account. 'Professor' – he forced himself to carry on – 'you do realise that I have to arrest you and charge you with murder?'

The man nodded in silent compliance. He dropped his head and groaned into his hands. 'Do you think I'll be granted bail? Not for myself. For Elsabe. She can't be left on her own. Not now. Not after all of this.'

Eberard made a decision on the spur of the moment. 'I won't oppose your application for bail, Professor,' he reassured him. 'You can bring the application first thing tomorrow morning when you appear in court. You aren't a flight risk and you aren't a danger to society generally.' He felt embarrassed even as the words left his mouth. 'I'm sorry to speak like that, Professor. But that's the test.' He felt the blood rise in his cheeks. 'Now I'm making a fool of myself, pretending to teach the law professor about law.'

Du Preez looked up at him and smiled for the first time. 'I appreciate your attitude, Inspector. Please don't be embarrassed. Right now, I need as much help as I can get. I think I've shown quite dramatically that I can't take care of myself.'

The professor – usually so self-contained and stern – suddenly reminded Eberard of his father, who had been a proud and strong man. Fiercely independent and irascible, his age and growing illness had weathered him. He had fought against it, trying to hold back the storm. And then, one day towards the end, he lay on his bed with his hair greying and his eyes straining behind his spectacles, and he let go a little. He had been struggling to read a book all morning and, in one swift movement, he turned to Eberard, closed the book and handed it over to his son.

'Here. Take this. I can't read any longer. You read to me now.' His father had let him help him. By doing so, he had shown him his vulnerability without losing his dignity. Eberard had looked at his father and felt equal to him for the first time in his life. The older man was letting go and passing something on, no matter how small, for his son to continue. His father had died a few weeks later, quietly and with determination, like everything else he had done in his life.

Eberard thought he saw some of that letting go now: an acknowledgement of vulnerability. But it seemed ironic that the professor had chosen to reveal his weakness to someone who was himself so fragile.

LULLABY

I shall find for you shells and stars.
I shall swim for you river and sea.
Sleep, my love, sleep for me.
My sleep is old. I shall feed for you lamb and dove.
I shall buy for you sugar and bread.
Sleep, my love, sleep for me.

My sleep is dead. Rain will fall but Baby
   won't know,
He laughs alone in orchards of gold.
Tears will fall but Baby won't know.
His laughter is blind.
Sleep my love, for sleep is kind.
Sleep is kind when sleep is young.
Sleep for me, sleep for me.

I shall build for you planes and boats.
I shall catch for you cricket and bee.
Let the old ones watch your sleep.
Only death will watch the old.
Sleep, sleep, sleep, sleep, sleep, sleep.
Sleep, sleep.

TEN

THE road outside the warehouse was unrecognisable. Empty and windswept by day, by night it was filled with cars, parked at angles on the pavement, and motorcycles, leaning one into the other in a line from the corner. Several bicycles were bound in an ugly mass to a light pole. A Volkswagen Beetle, with stripped paint and pictures of sunflowers splattered across its bonnet, was parked between a five-series BMW and a fire-engine-red V6 Nissan Sani. On the pavement, to the left of the entrance, an emerald-green Ducati speedster dwarfed a maroon Vespa. A loud bass thudded from inside the building. The ground itself seemed to vibrate, the dust lifting off the asphalt with each beat. The door opened briefly and a blast of fast-paced high-tech music burst onto the street. The sound was exhilarating. The door closed again, and the muffled bass returned. Outside, a few couples sat on the bonnets of cars or crouched on the pavement with their feet in the gutter. The red tips of their cigarettes glowed brightly, and the sweet smell of dagga, like overripe fruit, drifted down the street on the wind, overpowered suddenly by the sharp smell of crack being burned. The smells and sounds gave the faceless building an atmosphere of anticipation – the characteristics of the young, on the move, superficial, intangible, but always somewhere. The wind would clear the air; the sounds would fade; the building would be left. But the next night, again, rising from the ashes of the day, here, somewhere else, a new venue. The same sounds, the same smells.

A massive man blocked the entrance in front of the closed door. His deep black skin melted into his T-shirt and trousers. Only a thick gold chain glinted in the street light. He looked the visitor up and down before shaking his head.

'Not today, sir. Sorry there.'

Eberard raised his eyebrows in surprise at this statement. The man's accent was a confusing combination of African depth and American twang.

'Isn't the club open to everyone?' he asked, uncertainly at first. He was already feeling for his identity card in the back pocket of his jeans. 'Is it because I'm not black?' he asked more assertively.

The man guffawed at the suggestion. 'Da black mon always happy to take money from da white man or da mixed mon like-a you, mon.' The statement amused the speaker, and he laughed again, his strong white teeth showing. 'You offering to pay den?' he asked, grinning. Eberard shrugged and nodded. The accent was perhaps more European than American. 'One hundred an' fifty bucks,' the man said. 'That's seven-five for da door to open, and seven-five for me to open it.' He laughed again and shook his head, enjoying his own joke.

Eberard took out his wallet, careful to hide the police identity card. He counted out one hundred and sixty rand. The man took the notes and pushed open the door in a manner which suggested that no change would be forthcoming. 'Where are you from?' Eberard asked, before stepping inside.

'Middl' of Afrika,' the man replied through the blast of noise. 'Welcom' to Club Pécheurs.'

Eberard found it hard to believe that this was the same space he had been in the day before. The auditory assault was over-whelming. Powerful bass beats filled every inch of the room, drumming against his stomach, while brilliant top notes stabbed at him like ice picks. The space was packed with bodies, all moving and gyrating in different directions; yet all following the same rhythm – half-naked figures painted with fluorescent paint, streaks of luminous pink, purple, lime, shimmering under the ultraviolet lights. At a glance, the individual bodies were indis-cernible – a flaming back, a glowing pink cheek, the outline of an eye, a painted nipple. Bare torsos bounced off the skin of backs; arms met and intertwined; hands flashed in the white light of strobes; tight tops brushed across forearms. With every beat the positions changed, and the pace was fast and furious. Eberard stood at the top of the steps in awe, watching the beast in front of him bounce and weave at a speed he could never have imagined. New figures joined while others left the fringes, but the creature kept its form, a massive dancing python, a writhing collage of black and white and brown shapes, streaked with un-natural colour, each independent and connected to the other. The mass moved in time to the high-pitched but even notes that penetrated the dance floor. The hairs on Eberard's neck stood up in reaction, and he felt a shiver of anticipation flood down his spine.

'If you don't go in,' a guttural voice growled in his ear, 'I can't close da door.'

He flustered an apology and moved onto the second step. The door closed with a thud behind him. The sound only served to heighten the effects of the music, as the rhythm surrounded him and swept past him like a hurricane; he was in the eye, stand-ing still and watching the space swirl around him, picking up people and images. The tempo of the music grew; the air around him roared. A sweet tension rose with the music, pushing, draw-ing, higher and higher. His ears screamed. The dancers waved and jumped and stomped in anticipation, making the beast move even faster, with jerking, frenetic movements. The lights swirled and Eberard's muscles tensed, his heart pounding. The pace, the energy, was unbearable. His eyes were dry, but refused to blink in the face of the onslaught.

And then ... a moment of absolute stillness. A break in noise so pure, so sudden, that it took his breath away. The walls hummed quietly, suspending the energy of the dance. A purity of stillness, like cold water in the morning. Eberard felt like laughing out loud. For a second or perhaps two, the beast on the dance floor held itself, panting without noise. Waiting, unmov-ing. The sublime second of passion before release. And then it came: an explosion of dramatic beats. The sound rushed over the mass, through them, like a great wind, and the dance floor erupted into motion again, faster than before. Eberard stood on the steps, motionless, his mouth half-open and his palms pressed against his thighs. He had never witnessed anything like it.

'Music based on the human orgasm. Makes perfect sense, *non*?' Eberard started at the voice next to him. It was warm and languid, spoken with confidence and conspiracy. The accent was

African-French, and the delivery was commanding. He turned to the man standing next to him. He was looking onto the dance floor, smiling. The man was probably in his late thirties, and he sported the same smooth head as the dead Burundian suspect. He was suavely dressed in a cream suit. A black shirt pulled tightly against his strong chest under the loose jacket, and the neat triangular fold of a red handkerchief in the top pocket gave him an amusing dapper air. He turned to Eberard with a playful look.

'Why do you think it took so long to come up with this idea? Shall I tell you why?' Eberard shook his head and then nodded in response. 'Because the music needs drugs to really make sense. This is the first music since reggae to be composed specifically for a particular drug – music tailored to the effects of a drug. *La musique de l'imaginaire*. Isn't that fantastic? Well, it's either an indication of how developed we've become, or how far we've gone back.' He laughed freely, his clean white teeth shining in the ultraviolet light.

Eberard looked at his acquaintance with some suspicion, but the man's manner was easy and disarming. He put out his hand, and, without thinking, Eberard engaged in a firm handshake.

'My name is Laurent Kitsire,' he announced firmly, above the noise from the dance floor. 'I am from French-speaking Zaire, now called the Democratic Republic of Congo. *Le coeur sombre de l'Afrique*. Where the dark heart of Africa resides, where the blood is at its thickest. I come from Rutshuru in the province of Kivu, a wonderful and terrible place … near the Ugandan border. Well, I lived there once. I was a teacher in literature.' His eyes twinkled with mischief. 'And now I have a permit to be in your beautiful country. And I am also the owner of this club. Welcome.'

The man took Eberard's hand in an almost childlike way, and led him down the remaining stairs. A pink neon sign waved across the wall behind the main bar; Eberard wondered why he had not noticed it on his first visit. It traced the name 'Sinners' in a series of connected whorls. The drably painted walls were gone; in their place, under the ultraviolet, bodies weaved towards him erotically, shining and three-dimensional. Lithe shapes with pointed nipples and smooth muscles lured him closer. The murals seemed to move in and out, towards him and away, in time to the beat of the music. He wondered whether that was at all possible. We are so easily absorbed in the surreal, he thought dryly.

The enigmatic Laurent ushered him to the bar counter and offered him a shot glass filled with clear liquid. Eberard hesitated: his drinking was taking hold of him once more. He had started drinking straight after work, at home, on his own, until he collapsed in exhaustion on the couch. He watched as his host tipped the glass into his opened mouth, his head tilted backwards and his pink tongue extended to catch the last drops. Impulsively, Eberard followed suit. The alcohol hit his tongue and palate in a single assault of taste and sensation. His tongue burned with a clean pain, like the deep cut of a blade, saliva weeping from the walls of his mouth. His nostrils filled with the smell of naartjies and cough syrup. And a darker aftertaste. Was he tasting his own blood, he wondered. He gulped and felt his belly warm. His torso shivered as he touched the corners of his eyes to stop tears from running down his cheek. He blinked slowly at the man, who was grinning at him.

'I mixed some things together,' his host said casually. 'A drink I call *un péché* – a sin. It's a drink to toast my club. And you won't get it anywhere else, my friend. Where I come from, we're not shy to try and mix new things together. Where I come from, all things are to be eaten or drunk. I come from a country where we turn our dangers into our food.' He smiled warmly. 'For example, the kihuta adder is both a dangerous killer and a delicacy in my town. We roast simbriki – the cane rat, our enemy in the field. We eat the insects that bother you at night: crickets, grasshoppers and termites. We sear them in burning pans with salt and hot peppers. Our children take the young of birds and monkeys from their fighting mothers for food. We make luku bread from roots. We snack on boudin made from peanut flour and Kikanda root. We are not a people who are afraid, my friend. *Nous dévorons nos ennemis.*'

The barman, a muscular man dressed in a red leather vest, had already refilled the glasses. Eberard threw the liquid into his mouth again. He expected the effect to be reduced on the second occasion, but the bite was as strong, like an insect gripping onto his tongue. This time he thought he detected an aftertaste of cloves. He felt his body starting to glow. A young woman, a teenager in a tight black bikini top, pushed between them. She winked at Eberard, a slow luscious closing of her eyelid, before turning to the barman. She did not look at Eberard again, but her attention had made him feel reckless and happy.

Eberard turned to his Congolese companion, but the man pre-empted him. 'I know why you are here, Mister Inspector Detective Eberard Februarie.' He waited for the effect of his words to be felt.

Eberard looked at him in surprise. Gratified, the man continued. 'Your presence here is obvious, Mr Februarie. You have arrested and killed my friend and worker. Now you are here to see whether you should feel guilty about that or not. *Tu veux mon absolution.*'

Eberard started to protest, but the man raised his hand good-naturedly. 'You don't need to explain yourself to me, Inspector Detective. I'm sure you didn't know you were sentencing Bullet to death when you took him in. I'd like to think that, had you known, you would have prevented it from happening.' The man took his hand again, friendly but firm. 'Please, come and sit with me at the smaller bar, where we can talk more easily. *Mets-toi à l'aise.*'

Still the beast weaved, bodies circling and folding, as they edged past. The two men moved along the fringe of the dance floor. Up close, Eberard could see how the dancers were glistening with sweat, slick and oiled, sliding over one another. He imagined himself standing in the middle of the floor, erect and still, a sliding mass of soft bodies rubbing against him. The figures were arousing, both in their individual detail and in their collective form. He felt as if he could wade through them, parting them like warm seaweed. He wanted to feel drunk, to let go and swim through the shining dancers.

'Is it not the most exciting act?' Laurent read his thoughts. '*C'est la véritable essence de la sexualité*. It is sexuality distilled and concentrated into a pure drink. Do you not think you could drink what you see? Just tip the floor up and drink it in like the juice of oysters? But it is a drink that can never take your thirst away. It is like the palm wine from my own country; it will leave you needing more and more.' His host did not wait for a response. He pulled out a tall stool for the policeman before turning to the bar counter. Eberard was relieved to notice that the witness, Maria, was not there.

The barman placed new shot glasses, already filled, on the table – two glasses each. Laurent nodded to Eberard. 'So, you will call me Laurent, and I will call you Eberard. You will tell me what you know, and I'll tell you what I know. And then we will have a party. *C'est bien.*' He threw back the alcohol and clapped the glass onto the table top.

Eberard felt relaxed and confident. 'Laurent. Laurent, that sounds fine to me.' He looked down at the empty shot glass. 'I'm not officially on duty. So this is actually fine,' he said. 'What I mean is, the party side sounds like fun. Thank you.' The room swirled around him, making him feel recklessly at ease.

'All right, my friend,' Laurent smiled, 'then let me tell you what you think you know, and what I know.' Eberard did not react to his presumption. 'The daughter of an important man is found dead in a canal. She has been murdered. She was in the company of a Burundian man. A man who was in this beautiful country of yours illegally. He is arrested. By a hard-working policeman, our Mister Detective Inspector Eberard Februarie. Our friend, *non*?' Eberard nodded, his head loose on his shoulders.

'All right. And there is evidence.' The word was spoken with a marked French accent – *evidéns*. 'This evidence, *preuve*, is found to bring him to the murdered girl. Once in custody, at our friend the policeman's jail … he refuses to speak, *n'est pas*? This is certain, of course. He's an illegal and he knows not to say anything. But then the angry father finds him and kills him. *Et le tueur est tué*. So the killer is killed. Justice is done. We're all happy, *non*?'

'No, thas not quite correct.' Eberard knew that he was slurring his words, whereas his host still seemed fresh and alert. 'The father's been charged with murder, and we now ...' His voice trailed off unconvincingly.

'Ha!' Laurent snorted, his voice rising in pitch. 'Ha! The father's already out on bail. He was granted bail this morning of a few thousand rand. Now he's back home, as if nothing ever happened. He has friends who can help him, *non*? And Bullet ... he's lying in the morgue. In a refrigerator. With no one to bury him. Convicted and sentenced in a few hours. Justice is fast and certain in this country of yours, my friend. Very quick, this justice of yours.'

They both downed their second glasses. Eberard coughed violently as the alcohol caught in his throat. His host waited patiently while he regained his breath.

'There *has* been a crime, my friend,' Laurent continued. 'There has been a crime which is easy to identify, although no one will be prosecuted or sentenced for it.' He paused. Despite the seriousness of his words, his eyes were still half-laughing. Eberard found his mischievous manner unnerving. It was as if he did not take himself, or his statements, seriously. 'Your conclusions are too obvious. And simple conclusions have no place when it comes to human behaviour,' Laurent went on. 'The answer to the murder of this girl is not so easy. Your case was given to you, prepared on a plate of fear, and you've taken it with both hands. *Merde!*'

'I haven't accepted that Bullet was responsible,' Eberard protested loudly. 'The plate is still on the table.'

'I don't see you sending it back to the kitchen,' Laurent responded derisively. 'But anyway, the fact is that this little town sees the matter as closed. Life moves on, my friend. Prejudices run deep. We need to categorise; it makes us feel safe. I saw it in my students when they spoke about characters in literature; I see it in you and your work. But the truth is that this crime was not committed by a black man.'

Eberard looked at the man warily. There was of course a chance that the DNA results would be negative, but the witness's account, the earring ... Eberard doubted it.

'I see the way you look at me,' Laurent continued. 'But I'm

telling you, this crime was not committed by a particular *type* of man.' He paused again, cocking his head towards Eberard. 'It was committed by a man. Just a man, my friend. This crime is about men and their needs and their wants and their sex. Not sex, *sexualité*, yes, *sexualité*. A Burundian didn't rape her; a man raped her. And that man was driven by his being a man, not by his nationhood. She wasn't raped by a man with a passport! She was raped by a man with a penis. Am I not right, Detective? You cannot say no.'

Eberard tried to consider his host's statements seriously, but he could not stop a glimmer of a smile forcing its way onto his lips. He found the man's argument, and turn of phrase, fascinating. He let himself be entertained.

'You will find, Eberard, that I have a lot to say about manhood. And about men and their needs. Their lusts. But we can talk about that later. Let me tell you what I need to say. You know that a young woman was murdered. She was a teenager, starting years of hard study at the *université* ... happy to follow in her father's proud footsteps, yes? Probably a virgin, *non?* Well, maybe she was and maybe she wasn't. But do not believe that any teenage girl, no matter how proper she seems, is pure. Your hormones, Eberard, my friend, are at their most aggressive as a teenager. Your upbringing may tell you how to behave, but you'll always be answerable to your body, not to your parents. You can escape your parents, your teachers, even the police,' he chuckled, 'but you can never escape your body.'

'Look at these young girls here.' Laurent waved his hand towards the dance floor. Eberard gazed at the young bodies bouncing off one another like echoes from the music, their individual features all combining into an orgiastic mass. He looked away. 'Do you think that they are oblivious to the sexuality of this music?' Laurent asked. 'This music was created for them – they come here *because* the music is as sexual as it is. They aren't here to drink or smoke cigarettes. Most of them don't even smoke your weak marijuana. The only drug they take is the drug that increases the sexual ecstasy. Clean-burning sexuality. Serotonin. That is what they are after.

'You are wrong about the dead girl, Inspector. She wasn't

dragged here unwillingly. In the last two months, I noticed her here often. She was on the dance floor, tight dresses and perky tits, just like the rest of them. She rubbed her arse against her dance partners just the same as all the others. She performed for them. She *put out*. You know what it means to put out, Inspector? She played with her hair and touched her body, just so, just here and there.' Laurent touched his chest and crotch in imitation. 'She was ready to explore. She was out there and she was looking. She didn't find what she was looking for, in the end anyway. But she was out there. Looking. Who knows what she found. Who knows what was attracted by her scent.'

Laurent stood up suddenly. 'Bullet was a good man.' He leaned forward and looked at the policeman keenly. 'But he was just a man. He had his needs and he was not someone to hold back. Neither am I, Inspector. Does that make me an evil person? I like stimulation, Inspector. I like to be stimulated and excited and surprised. Surprise me, Eberard,' he challenged. 'Surprise me! I am Laurent Kitsire. *Etonne-moi!*'

The ease with which the man acknowledged his need for stimulation, for satisfaction, was exhilarating. Unexpected and long-buried feelings of arousal and a lightness of being momentarily welled up in Eberard. He felt almost as if he had been given a gift, a present that would lighten his life for ever, and he grinned drunkenly at Laurent, his eyes half-closed.

'Bullet liked to be satisfied and intrigued, Detective Inspector. But, and very importantly, he had his own particular – and perhaps strange – interests. Ms du Preez was not one of them. If you understand nothing else of what I have told you, understand this' – he waved his finger at the policeman – 'Bullet followed challenges. His life was a hard one, harder than you can ever imagine. It was filled with impossible tasks, with survival against great odds. And he survived. He liked things that were different. Things that were difficult to possess. And he did not like to wait. His taste for woman was insatiable; yes, this is true. But it prowled on the edges of your world, my friend.

'Bullet was hunting something in particular before you killed him. Something bright that glows under the right light, but disappears in the morning sun. Elusive. Unforgiving. A very special lady. She is as different from your Melanie du Preez as night is from day. You may have the pleasure – or the discomfort – of meeting her one day. Maybe I'll introduce you. If you're patient and adventurous enough. Once you've been with a woman like that, Inspector, your taste for children will wane.' Eberard frowned at the man's choice of words, and his head dropped briefly from the effects of the drink. The lightness had gone and the liquor had dulled his mind again, closing in darkly.

'As different as night is from day. As lightness leads into darkness. You are looking in all the wrong places, Inspector,' the Congolese man hissed, aggressive for the first time. Eberard flinched as his host clapped him on the arm, before watching him walk, untouchable, into the midst of the seething mass on the dance floor.

A LOVER'S LULLABY

Sing lullaby, as women do,
Wherewith they bring their babes to rest;
And lullaby can I sing too,
As womanly as can the best.
With lullaby they still the child;
And if I be not much beguiled
Full many a wanton babe have I,
Which must be still'd with lullaby.

First lullaby my youthful years,
It is now time to go to bed:
For crookèd age and hoary hairs
Have won the haven within my head.
With lullaby, then, youth be still;
With lullaby content thy will;
Since courage quails and comes behind,
Go sleep, and so beguile thy mind!

Next lullaby my gazing eyes,
Which wonted were to glance apace;
For every glass may now suffice
To show the furrows in thy face.
With lullaby then wink awhile;
With lullaby your looks beguile;
Let no fair face, nor beauty bright,
Entice you eft with vain delight.

And lullaby my wanton will;
Let reason's rule now reign thy thought;
Since all too late I find by skill
How dear I have thy fancies bought;
With lullaby now take thine ease,
With lullaby thy doubts appease;
For trust to this; if thou be still,
My body shall obey thy will.

Thus lullaby my youth, mine eyes,
My will, my ware, and all that was:
I can no more delays devise;
But welcome pain, let pleasure pass.
With lullaby now take your leave;
With lullaby your dreams deceive;
And when you rise with waking eye,
Remember then this lullaby.

ELEVEN

Van der Keesel's discovery of Sanna took place some months later in the fields on the mountain slopes on the northern side of the canal running down to the large dam. The bulk of the stock planted on these slopes was Spanish grenache, a heavy vine producing big, round berries in large straggly bunches. The grapes yielded a tannic red wine and grew well in the drier parts of the Mediterranean; but the vines battled with the Cape's lengthy wet winters and cool sea breezes. Initially, they had flourished, showing promise in the warmer months. But Van der Keesel, who was a regular visitor to the fields, noted their slow decline with growing displeasure. The new leaves had developed a greyish fungal growth on the underside, and the berries had lost their firmness before ripening, producing slack-skinned and shrivelled grapes. The soft fruit was attacked with determination by flies, ants, red beetles, *witogies* and various rodents.

He had left the stock in place, waiting to see if the next summer season would not be more productive. In the meantime, he had cut tiers into the steeper slopes above the fields of grenache and crouchen blanc. On these tiers he had started his experimentation with new vine stock – one that would not only cope with the conditions of the new colony, but which would also be unique, a pure African wine, a symbol of the Company's conquest of the new worlds. As a younger man, Van der Keesel had spent time in nearly all the established wine-growing regions of western Europe. Relying on this knowledge, he had assembled a range of root stock, in small quantities, from all over Europe. For red wines, he brought souzão from Portugal, a grey-coloured berry that produced deep red wines high in fruit and acid; tempranillo from the north of Spain, a strong-growing vine used to blend complex deep wines; spätburgunder from Rheinpfalz on the Nahe River, producing a low-tannin, fruity wine; and gamay noir from Burgundy, juicy and thick-skinned like cherries. For white wines, he gathered silvaner from vineyards planted along the banks of the Danube, a tough-skinned, sugary grape that dominated German winemaking; muscat de frontignan from France for a white muscadel; weissburgunder from Rheinhessen from the region of the Rhine. He also had a quantity of riesling, obtained from the small surviving estates at Schloss Johannisberg in the Rheingau region, named after the town in the area. He had spent a year in the region and learnt the use of botrytis and the benefits of late harvesting in producing sweet noble wines. He intended to use these first vines to seek out a reliable stock that was tough enough to withstand the battering southerly winds, scorching summer temperatures and drenching winter rains. He sought a wine that was high in fruit, with a balance between tannin and acidity to provide subtlety and complexity on the nose and palate.

The viticulturist's expectations of himself were as demanding as those of the new lands he found at the Cape. It sometimes seemed too ambitious a goal, but he was adamant that he would find the right grape and produce a wine that would grace the tables of the finest homes in Holland and Europe.

But his plans were frustrated at every turn. An unseasonable deluge had eroded deep channels into the tiers, tearing the soil from the newly planted roots and causing some of the steps to collapse entirely. A swarm of locusts had descended on the vine-yard and damaged some of the new shoots, before being chased off with horse-hair brushes. But by far the biggest obstacle was the workforce. The slaves who were assigned to the fields were incapable of appreciating the delicacy with which the new stock needed to be treated; roots were crushed under heavy boots, the side stems were snapped and new shoots were damaged. The caffer Bakka hurled abuse, Van der Keesel strode up and down the fields in fury, but still they forgot to water new stock, leaving it dry and gasping in the midday sun, or they flooded the shallow trenches, causing the side berm to break, wasting the water carried up from the dam. The more their acerbic master shouted at them, the less his servants seemed to care about the fields. He had noticed that the women took greater care and were more delicate in their movements when planting, and so replaced most of the male slaves working along the tiers with women, although a few men were still assigned to take care of the digging of trenches and extending the field.

He spent most of his days surveying the fields on horseback, trotting up and down the rows of growing vines, talking to Bakka and intimidating the slaves. Occasionally, he dismounted to plunge his hand into the soil or to threaten a worker who had applied too much pressure when tying a stem.

The bright-green buds had spurted from the inhospitable bark, and light leaves were opening out to soak up the summer sun, but the work was backbreaking, as the vines were still so low on the ground. Van der Keesel had ordered that the rows closest to the clay dam be watered by bucket once every four days, and he watched over proceedings with a glare, spitting blood-red *sirih* juice in contempt. Those who seemed to tip too much or too little water onto a vine were strongly disciplined, and a worker who wet the vine itself, instead of pouring the water into a trough dug around the roots, was liable to be struck without warning by Van der Keesel's leather whip. The conditions in summer were hot and sweaty, and the labour was even more arduous, but the taskmaster paid little attention to the workers' hardship, concentrating only on the successful outcome of his project.

Both Jakoba and Frederick worked the tiers, as well as the lower fields of semillon, clearing the ground of weeds and tending to the new stock. Their status remained uncertain, and they worked in the fields with slaves during the day and tended to their free-burgher land when they were finished. Sanna worked with them in the fields, pulling weeds out of the ground alongside her mother and collecting piles of stones to be used on the roadway up the hill. She had recently turned fifteen and was tall and slender. Her mother had braided her hair behind her head, coaxing the tight curls into bunches. Her severe hair and height made her look boyish, but her smooth skin and developing breasts suggested a strong and attractive femininity. Though the sweat dripped off the end of her nose, and her back ached from the long hours, she never complained. She would often fetch water for her mother to stop her becoming dehydrated, making her sit down in the shade and watching her drink.

One February afternoon, when Sanna had just returned from

fetching water at the dam, she heard the familiar groan of one of the workers. Van der Keesel could be seen leading his horse along the narrow path around the dam at the bottom of the field. Sanna helped Jakoba to her feet and they walked, her mother bent over, towards their row among the vines. Sanna knelt down, facing the dam to keep an eye on the horseman. He had stopped to chastise a worker who had been resting in the shade of some scrub bush. Frederick was working higher up with a group of men, sinking poles into the ground and tying up the growing vine stems. Her father appeared unaware of the horseman's approach, but Sanna saw that Van der Keesel was eyeing Frederick's group while tapping the base of his whip on the horse's flank. One of the men muttered something, and they turned and caught sight of their master, before quickly turning back to their work. Their fingers worked with care; their faces wrinkled in a frown of concentration.

As he progressed up the hill, Van der Keesel did not seem to notice Jakoba bent over a few rows away from him. He directed his horse straight towards the small group of men working on the stakes.

The horse came to a halt a short distance from them. 'Frederick Boorman!' Van der Keesel bellowed.

The words echoed off the face of the mountain, bouncing back and forth across the valley. Jakoba saw the look on the man's face; the tone of his command left her in no doubt that there was trouble to come. Frederick stood up and gave an uncertain half-wave towards the man on horseback.

'Come here, Boorman!' Van der Keesel shouted.

The workers in the field all rose and watched in silence. A mottled francolin flew up from the undergrowth, squawking in fright and landing gracelessly further up the hill. Sanna turned to her mother. 'Leave now, Mama. He'll only upset you, and there's nothing you can do.'

Jakoba shook her head. 'Maybe he'll listen to me ... you know, we ...' Her voice trailed off weakly.

'Mama, I know about you and that man. I know what happened and I know why it happened. There's nothing you can do. If he sees you here, it will only make it worse. If he thinks you're watching, he'll try to humiliate Papa in front of you. He always does that. Go, Mama, go now and don't turn around until you are home.'

Jakoba nodded fearfully, tears welling up in her eyes.

As she made her way towards the edge of the hill, Frederick approached Van der Keesel. Bakka watched from further up the hill, his thick arms folded across his chest. Frederick trod slowly, careful not to snag his clothes on the vines or damage any of the troughs dug around the roots.

'Come, man, move! I want you here now.' Frederick nodded and tried to move down the hill faster, stepping over the vines in single strides. As he neared the horse, his foot caught on a thin branch of one of the vines; it snapped with a crack.

Mortified, Frederick turned around to survey the damage. The viticulturist erupted with rage. He screamed obscenities at the unfortunate man, accusing him of deliberately damaging the crop. Frederick mumbled apologies as he half-walked and half-crawled to his master. Sanna watched her father cower before the rider, a pathetic figure wringing his hands and pleading. She started to walk towards them, oblivious to the dismayed whispers of the workers around her. Her ears were filled with a ringing, thumping sound. The air seemed thick, like a heated mohair blanket. She pushed forward towards her father. Out of the corner of her eye, she noted Bakka starting to move as well.

'*Boooorman!*' Van der Keesel boomed. 'Now I see what kind of an animal you are. You are the kind that sleeps by the fire and eats my food, but when I am not looking, you turn around and bite me. You're a treacherous lying bastard, Boorman. Do you think that you can cross me and get away with it? Now I see how you break my vines.' He paused and put his hand into a hessian bag slung over the back of the saddle, pulling out a small piece of vine, freshly pulled out of the earth. Soil trickled from between the short roots, leaving a soft smear on the side of the horse's neck.

'Now, Boorman. Can you tell me what this is? And can you tell me where I found this thing?' Frederick looked at the vine without comprehension and shook his head. 'You have no idea where I found this vine … this *illegal* vine, and a whole lot of other illegal vines planted next to it? A whole field of illegal vines planted under my very nose. You have no idea?' He was shouting loudly, deliberately, so that everyone could hear.

'Let me tell you, my bastard slave. I found this vine growing in a clearing in the bush next to your property. You have been growing illegal crops, Boorman. And not just any illegal crops, you have been stealing my vines and growing them for yourself!'

Van der Keesel was red in the face, and his shirt was streaked with sweat. He lifted his whip and brought it down with a violent crack; the knot on the end of the leather thong smacked Frederick's cheek, tearing the skin open from the side of his eye down towards his jawline. The blood ran between his fingers as he clutched his face, falling onto his side on the ground. 'You have been stealing from me! I will not have it! I will have you flogged and hanged by tomorrow!' Van der Keesel's voice suddenly dropped to a sinister hiss, his whip raised again for effect. 'In front of your wife. In the public square. Tomorrow.'

Satisfied, the horseman wrenched the right rein of his steed and turned to go, the horse champing at the bit. Just as he was about to depart, Sanna stepped forward, her arms hanging loosely at her side. 'I know who planted those vines,' she said firmly, 'and it was not our family.' She was aware of the massive shape of Bakka close behind her; she could smell his unwashed body, tensed and waiting. The whip shook in Van der Keesel's hand.

'Are you talking to me, girl? Because if you are, God help you!' The whip still shook in his raised hand, ready to strike a blow. Sanna looked up at it; the knot at the end bore the traces of her father's blood, and many others before him. It swung in the sunlight, crossing the path of the sun, back and forth. She watched it and waited for the horseman to strike. To and fro, backwards and forwards. The moment seemed to last for eternity. The workers watched Van der Keesel; Van der Keesel watched Sanna; and Sanna watched the knot swinging in the sunshine. Bakka waited for the sign. Then Frederick moaned loudly and rolled over onto his back in anguish.

'Good God, girl, you have some nerve,' Van der Keesel said simply, dropping the whip to his side. Sanna did not acknowledge his statement but walked over to her father, placing the edge of her dress against his bleeding face.

'My father did not plant those vines, sir,' she said more politely, her voice soft but firm. Her lips were pressed together in an effort to hold back her fear and anger. Van der Keesel stared at her incredulously.

'Your daughter – for I see that she is your daughter, Frederick, by her upstart and treacherous nature – has crossed me in front of the Company's slaves.' The anger had left him and his words were spoken as if he were commenting on the state of the vines or the weather. 'I cannot say what her punishment will be, but it will be in keeping with her crime. As will yours, Frederick. I shall investigate the origin of those vines, and if I find your complicity in the crime, my retribution will be terrible.'

The viticulturist looked around him and seemed to awaken as if from a dream. 'Get back to work. What are you doing standing around like idiots? Bakka, get them back to work, or I'll have you sent back to the Lodge!' The dark man turned angrily and lumbered towards the group of slaves, sending them scuttling back to their work. Van der Keesel turned back to Sanna. 'What is your name, girl?'

'I am Sanna,' she said formally. 'I am the daughter of Frederick and Jakoba Boorman.'

'Jakoba Boorman's daughter,' Van der Keesel mused. He looked at her once more, slowly and with appreciation, before turning his horse down the slope. The look in the man's eyes was one that Frederick knew too well.

LULLABY

The light is losing all its charms.
The minutes shot; the shadows won
as night adopts you in its arms

and nets the threat of worldly harms
or worldly loves. No longer young,
the light is losing all its charms.

You're dreaming soon, mouthing psalms,
dispelling in a wondrous tongue
as night adopts you in its arms,

unmoors your dreams, and disarms
your wide-eyed thoughts. Your eyelids hum.
The light is losing all its charms.

Sleep steals you now and embalms
your stolen eyes. I cannot come
as night adopts you in its arms.

But in your dreams the darkness calms
our breathing breaths into one.
The light is losing all its charms
as night adopts you in its arms.

TWELVE

EBERARD sat, deep in morbid thought, beside Xoliswa in the pew. His bones felt bruised against the wooden slats, and his mind kept conjuring up the image in the photograph: the image of the professor's loved ones – Beatrice du Preez sitting on the bed, her shoulder-length hair woven into a thick blonde plait. With all the maternal beauty of a woman at ease with her children, she was enjoying her two daughters, obedient and intelligent, keen to please their mother and eager to soak in her warmth and love. She sat on the bed, stroking the hair of her eldest child. She smiled to herself as her daughter's eyes started to close, dreamily mouthing the words of a lullaby.

> *Lay your sleeping head, my love*
> *Human on my faithless arm;*
> *Time and fevers burn away*
> *Individual beauty from*
> *Thoughtful children, and the grave*
> *Proves the child ephemeral:*

Elsabe read the words now, standing upright in front of the pews. She seemed both mature, dressed in a plain but tailored black dress and stockings, and young, her voice straining against her tears and wavering like an injured bird between the walls of the church.

> *But in my arms till break of day*
> *Let the living creature lie,*
> *Mortal, guilty, but to me*
> *The entirely beautiful.*

The words were all the more poignant in her soft and girlish voice, and Eberard envisaged Melanie's wooden casket moving into the blue and yellow flames, roaring as the gas fed their hunger, the fresh pine immediately scorched by the heat. The sides blackened, like a dark stain spreading out rapidly across the surfaces, and the thin boards burnt quickly. Soon the heat and flames broke through and licked inside.

> *Certainty, fidelity*
> *On the stroke of midnight pass*
> *Like vibrations of a bell ...*

Eberard closed his eyes. Melanie lay still, her eyes closed, her hands folded on her chest. The flames danced and crackled around her, flooding inside the box and fanning out across the lid above her. The fire sang and whispered to her. Her skin seared, and her hair singed to the scalp. The fire held her tightly and cut into her deeply. Her mother opened her mouth, and the flames rushed out to devour her child.

Elsabe's voice intoned on rhythmically:

> *... but from this night*
> *Not a whisper, not a thought,*
> *Not a kiss nor look be lost.*

He kept returning to the image, his mind drawn to it like fingers to a fresh wound, brushing the torn edges of the skin and pulling away, smarting. His thoughts strayed, like a distressed animal pulling on a leash, fascinated by the stake that secured it to its own misery.

The floppy book trembled in Elsabe's hands, and she glanced towards her father who sat, bent forward, in the first row. Auden's 'Lullaby' seemed a complicated choice. Surely there were simpler, more moving poems available to the young girl, Eberard thought. She struggled on.

> *Soul and body ... have no bounds ...*

She stopped and looked at her father. Tears were running down her cheeks, but she did not try to wipe them away. She read the line again and proceeded. Soul and body have no bounds. Perhaps that was why she had chosen this poem, Eberard pondered. He was sure that the priest would latch onto the phrase in his sermon, wrapping it in religious meaning, picking at it with pious hands and turning the morbid and tragic into a reason to celebrate: 'Even in this time of mourning, let us celebrate the life of Jesus.' He had heard it before, at countless gravesides, from platforms in countless churches – preying on the gutted and grief-stricken, peddling religion to the desperate.

Eberard felt no connection to the concept of a soul, the idea that every person has something sacred within them. He had seen too much of human behaviour, the banal stupidity of self-interest playing out on the streets, in the homes of ordinary people. Perhaps it provided some meaning to the professor, he thought; perhaps in a time of real loss, it was all that was left to cling to. He thought of the two girls, still only children then, trying to talk to their mother, standing bewildered at her graveside and trying to communicate with her. Would religion have made it any easier for them, he wondered. He doubted that Professor du Preez would try to talk to his daughter now, as if she were in the spirit world around him. He seemed too rational, too sceptical, to take such an easy route.

> ... *the winds of dawn that blow*
> *Softly round your dreaming head*
> *Such a day welcome show*
> *Eye and knocking heart may bless,*
> *Find our mortal world enough;*
> *Noons of dryness find you fed*
> *By the involuntary powers,*
> *Nights of insult let you pass*
> *Watched by every human love.*

Elsabe closed the book and returned to her seat beside her father. The congregation sat in silence.

Eberard felt Xoliswa stir next to him. His blunted nose again picked up an unexpected hint of soap and skin. He felt a warmth bloom in his chest. Was she crying, he wondered, turning towards her in a show of sympathy. But to his surprise, the constable had her small pocketbook on her lap and was scribbling down Elsabe's words. 'Nights of insult let you pass, watched by every human love.'

The open pages neatly recorded her movements for the day. Sometimes Eberard missed the instant gratification that came with being a uniformed member on the shifts. Criminal investigation as a detective was drawn out; success was measured in slow steps taken over months, sometimes even years. And even then the success of an investigation was often out of your hands, jeopardised by the vagaries of the justice system, the unpredictability of witnesses and legal rules that lined the route like hurdles. The uniformed members – crime prevention and complaints – could be faced with twenty problems in a shift: car accidents, disturbances of the peace, family violence, burglaries, assaults, trespassing, drunkenness. But by the end of the shift, when the bulletproofs were stripped off and the firearms locked away in the safe, the work was done, the paperwork completed, and the policeman would never deal with the complaint again, except perhaps to give evidence in court. Success or failure was immediate – an arrest made, evidence found, a suspect lost. When the shift was over, none of it mattered any more.

But it was this immediacy, this constant state of crisis, which had forced Eberard out of the uniformed branch and into the specialised units. At first, he had enjoyed the excitement, the adrenalin that came with working in the heat of the moment – crushed glass underfoot, the screech of sirens, red and blue lights strobing off your face, the gratification of easing someone's fear, of forcing control out of a state of chaos, of reducing trauma to simple lines in a small black book. But with the chaos came human unpredictability, the unrelenting irrationality of people's reactions. Drunk drivers who vomited abuse even as they stumbled from their mangled cars. Suspects who kicked and swore, asserting their rights, spitting at the uniform in contempt. Calm men who became violent in a second of inattention. Women who screamed and tore at their protectors when they tried to subdue battering husbands. Children who sat quietly in the corner, watching, their thumbs in the mouths, their eyes wide. It left him bruised and dirtied, and no amount of streaming hot water could wash it away.

Xoliswa's eyes met his briefly. They were almost black, deep and dark, with small flecks of brown at the edges of the iris. The corners of her full mouth turned up slightly in a wry smile. He was many years her senior, in age and in rank, but he felt strangely calmed by her presence. He felt comfortable sitting next to her, watching her carefully recording details in the pocketbook. He half-closed his eyes and tried to capture her scent once more – an almost imperceptible hint of her body. She looked at him again, this time drawing her eyebrows upward quizzically. He turned away, trying not to show his embarrassment.

Mercifully, the service came to an end without Professor du Preez saying any words for his daughter. The congregation filed out solemnly, shaking their heads and dabbing their eyes gently. Eberard escaped to the car without offering his condolences. He sat in the driver's seat, watching Xoliswa drive away in her own car. It would not be long before she left for good, he was sure. She had a bright future ahead of her. He sat for a while, paging through the scrapbook, retrieved by Xoliswa after the service. It had an old-fashioned cardboard cover, with pictures of pens, pencils, scissors and glue scattered across it. The colours must once have been bright and eye-catching, but had faded to a blue-grey sheen over the years, and it gave off a musty, papery smell. He ran his hand over the front cover. Melanie must have bought it with her mother's death fresh in her mind. He opened the book to the first page. A fishmoth had been squashed, close to the spine; its body was flattened and dried like a small piece of rice paper. He blew into the pages, and the remains fluttered off the edge of the book onto the floor of the car. Someone, Melanie he supposed, had written in black koki pen on the inside cover, in broad childish strokes:

THIS BOOK BELONGS TO MELANIE DU PREEZ
9 YEARS OLD.
STELLENBOSCH

The faded purple pages were thick and, where she had written with ink or koki, the absorbent paper had spread the ink in fine tentacles, blurring the edges of letters. On the first page, written in childish but careful letters, was 'Hush, Little Baby'. A lump formed in Eberard's throat as he started to read: 'You'll still be the sweetest little baby in town.' He murmured the last line to himself and closed his eyes. He could taste the cold bite of whisky on his tongue. He longed for release, for a moment of being so drunk that he no longer had to care. His armpits felt sticky and they prickled as he brought his hands up to his face. A loud knock on the window startled him, and he looked up, stressed and drawn.

Professor du Preez stood next to the car. Eberard rolled the window down. 'Are you all right, Inspector?' the professor asked with genuine concern.

Eberard nodded unconvincingly. 'That is hardly a question you should be asking me, Professor. In the circumstances, I mean. I feel a bit run-down, that's all. How are you holding up? What a terrible day for you, sir.' Du Preez nodded his head, but said nothing. 'I'll return the book to you shortly,' Eberard continued.

'There's no rush. I really don't think I could open it right now. I would like to have it back, of course, but in your own time.' Du Preez looked exhausted. Eberard gestured to him to sit down, and the professor walked slowly around the front of the car, sitting down heavily in the passenger seat.

'Should you be talking to me, Inspector?' Du Preez asked. 'You're the investigating officer on my case ...' Eberard did not really care what others thought of the situation, but the professor did not wait for an answer. 'I wanted to thank you,' he announced. 'Both for coming today – it is good that you were here, for all of us. And for being so decent about my bail. There's no excuse for what I've done, I know. But it helps to know that you understand, that you have some insight into ... the situation.' He ran his finger along the dashboard in front of him. 'My life is over,' he went on. 'We both know that now. My life has no meaning to me. Whether I'm here today, dead tomorrow, that makes no difference to anything any more. But it's not about me. It's about Elsabe.'

Eberard looked up at the girl standing near the church door. She was talking to a young man with styled, mousy hair and glasses. They hugged each other in a stiff, formal way. The two men in the car watched them without speaking.

'Who's that man?' Eberard broke the silence.

'Oh, that's Jeremy Wilder. He's a tutor at the university. He took Melanie out on a date once, a few weeks ago. I didn't really approve. He's quite a bit older. A postgraduate.' Eberard nodded, remembering Xoliswa's account of the boy. 'It is ... was ... an ongoing problem,' the professor said softly, 'how much to interfere. And one's interference is most certainly never appreciated.' He fell silent and the two men contemplated the scene in front of them.

After a long pause, Du Preez spoke again. 'What do you think will happen to me, Detective? What kind of plans should I be making for Elsabe's future?'

Eberard found it difficult to think clearly and could not concentrate on formulating an honest answer. He stammered the beginnings of a reply and then stopped. He paused and started again. 'Professor, there's a lot of mitigation in your favour.' He tried to sound encouraging. 'You already know that. I don't think there's been a similar case before. There was that case a few years ago where the father beat his daughter's attacker. The court gave quite a heavy sentence, but that case was different. It's so difficult to say what a court will do. You aren't a threat to society ... it embarrasses me to talk about you like this ... but I for one won't be asking them to ... to sentence you to imprisonment.'

Eberard wished he had not started the conversation. He took a deep breath and continued reluctantly, avoiding eye contact with the professor. 'Now that I think about it, Professor, we got your records from Pretoria this morning, and that might be a problem.' Du Preez had a prior conviction for assault. It had happened a long time ago, and the records indicated that he had only received a warning, not even a fine. Still, Eberard was sure that the prosecutors would use it against him. 'I'm sure there's a good explanation. But the court may be worried that you lost control on a previous ...'

'That assault,' Du Preez interrupted, 'that assault took place in very particular circumstances.' Eberard was surprised at the grim determination in his voice. 'My wife was killed in a car accident, Inspector,' he said evenly. 'A drunkard drove through a red robot and crashed into the side of our car. I was driving and Beatrice turned towards the car as it rammed into us. The drunk driver had not even touched his brakes. They had to cut her out of the wreckage with some special machine. He wasn't hurt. He was driving a fancy luxury car and he stepped out. He swore at me. He came right up to me, swearing. His breath stank of drink. Beatrice was lying in the car. *Ek het nie geweet hoe* ... I didn't know then that she ... how badly she was injured. I wanted to walk around the car to her side to help her, to get her out. And this man stood in my way, shouting at me. I hit him, Inspector. I hit him with all the force I could muster. I broke his jaw with one punch. Then I left him and I went to my wife. She died in hospital the next day.'

The car felt claustrophobic and Eberard's head pounded. He wound the window further down, but, as he did so, the professor opened his door and climbed out. He closed the door gently but firmly behind him, making sure it clicked into position, and walked away without saying another word. Elsabe was standing on her own now and her father took her in his arms. She put her arms limply around his waist. Then she pulled away and ran into the church. The professor followed her, drained of energy.

Eberard opened the tattered cubbyhole. A twenty-packet of cigarettes lay unopened on top of the car's logbook. The plastic wrap pulled off easily, and he ran his fingertips over the orange filters. The comforting feel of a new pack of cigarettes. He pulled one out from the tight bundle and ran it under his nose; he wished he could savour the scent of fresh tobacco – the undertone of clean chemicals that he remembered. But he smelt nothing. He lit the tip with the car lighter and drew heavily. Pungent and familiar tastes flooded his mouth and throat; his chest tingled and he felt light-headed. He blew the smoke out in funnels from his

nostrils, and it swirled up against the windscreen before streaming out of the open window. It had been a year since he had
stopped smoking. As the nicotine smoothed the raw edges of his
thoughts, his mouth burned for the taste of alcohol.

Eberard paged through the scrapbook as the hazy smoke
clouded the car. The first half of the book was filled with
children's lullabies, written in the same large, neat print. The
writing gradually became smaller and more mature. Occasionally, Melanie had carefully cut out and stuck down a printed
page or a page photocopied from a book. The child's songs slowly
gave way to sophisticated lullabies – more poems than simple
lullabies. The WH Auden one had come from this section of the
book. He could not imagine how some of them could be sung;
they would be spoken, he imagined. But still, the writing was
true to the tradition – light and soothing, intended to comfort a
child, sung by a parent before sleep. Lulling, warm songs about
loving fathers and doting mothers, about not having to worry.
A song that told the unknowing child that all was well. A child's
version of religion.

The songs were more contemporary in the second half of the
book, often typed on computer and printed out. Many seemed to
have been printed off the Internet, displaying a website address
in small print on the bottom. Their mood was lonelier and increasingly desperate. With the onset of adolescence, the writing
became messy and careless. Someone – presumably Melanie –
had scrawled some of them down like notes, slanted sideways up
the page like careless afterthoughts. Some were stuck down only
on one edge, creasing and flapping open. There was a coffee stain
on the one page, a smear of dark brown rubbed away indiffer-
ently by the back of a hand. Towards the end, a page had been
torn out; the jagged edges of purple paper stuck out of the spine.
He ran his finger over the edges. The remaining pages were bare
and would remain so for ever.

Eberard tossed the book onto the passenger seat. He turned
the key in the ignition, and the car spluttered into life. He could
not imagine the pain that Professor du Preez had experienced
in life: his had been a life of extremes – the joy of a family and the

pain of its destruction. Eberard's own life seemed all the more pathetic in contrast; not dull but dulled, lacking in substance and meaning. Du Preez had a reason to keep fighting; the policeman had lost his in a small cloistered room years before.

Eberard spent the rest of his day chasing witnesses in one of the many petty assault cases that burdened his working life. Three people had supposedly witnessed an exchange of blows. Only two had been identified, and Eberard had only managed to locate one of them. It had been a day of false information and failed leads. It was dark when he finally gave up, with only one thin statement to show for his labours. Driving past the township, he noticed blue lights flashing up ahead in the road. The brake lights of the vehicle in front of him lit up. He saw a traffic officer behind his car, taking out red traffic cones from the boot. Setting up a roadblock, Eberard thought, although it was a quiet Sunday evening. The traffic officer, a burly man with a midriff that bulged against the cotton of his shirt, caught sight of Eberard's car and beckoned him to stop. He pulled up alongside the officer, putting the orange hazard lights on. The indicator light clicked rhythmically inside the car.

'What's the matter?' Eberard asked reluctantly. 'Do you need any help?'

'Pedestrian! Cut … him … in … pieces!' The man spoke in an animated, almost hysterical way, blurting the words out individually, each word its own sentence. He gestured up the road. For the first time, Eberard noticed a car on the left-hand side of the road, parked slightly at an angle. Someone was leaning through the back window, talking to the passengers. There was something else, a lump like a large handbag, lying in the middle of the right-hand lane.

'Is anyone hurt?' Eberard asked, and then, feeling foolish, added, 'In the car?'

'Nah! Just … neck …' The traffic officer seemed out of breath, although he had only just arrived on the scene. The adrenalin was clearly pounding through his body. Eberard felt drowsy, but he could see that the traffic officer was out of his depth.

'All right,' he said, turning off his car, 'let me have a look. But you're doing all the paperwork.' The man nodded and stepped back to let him out the car. Eberard took out his black metal torch and a small first-aid pouch from under the seat.

He left the officer to set out the traffic cones and started walking towards the parked car. As he neared the object in the road, it slowly came into focus. It was dark, the colour of roasted coffee, with pink and white ends. He slowed his pace, frowning, trying to identify it before he got too close. It reminded him of a seal pup he had found on the beach, its head savaged by a shark. It had the same consistency and weight, lying thick and meaty on the road surface. Eberard stopped about five metres away. He zipped the first-aid pouch open and took out the surgical gloves. As he pushed his hand into one, it tore, splitting along the cuff and over the thumb. He swore quietly to himself. The other glove slipped onto his hand more easily, but his middle finger pushed through the top. The broken gloves only added to his unease.

'Fucking seal pup in the middle of the road?' he whispered to himself. He stepped closer and carefully lowered himself to one knee on the tar. He reached out his hand, the end of his finger obvious against the white latex glove, and placed his palm down on the mound. It was warm on his hand, and dry and firm. He switched his torch on and pointed it at the object. He could see the round edge of a bone nestled into the pink flesh, drained of all blood. It was the thigh of a man, severed at the knee and the hip, lying like a discarded animal in the road.

Eberard stood up and wiped his forehead with the back of his arm, careful to keep the latex glove away from his face. He shone the torch onto the side of the road. The rest of the body was lying in the grass. Strange not to have noticed it before, Eberard thought. The man's trousers had been torn off with the impact of the collision, but thankfully his boxer underpants still covered the jagged hole at his hip. Eberard went round to the figure's head and felt for a pulse at the neck. The man's eyes were wide open, staring up at him. Eberard recognised an old scar running across his head. It was the Congolese man who had been sitting outside the warehouse, who had shouted at him when he was looking for Bullet.

All people had the same look in death, death by trauma rather than natural causes: the eyes still and superficial, the mouth drawn back and the teeth, top and bottom, exposed in catlike aggression. A dry crust of spittle marked the corners of the man's mouth. Fearful that he might suddenly blink or reach out and grab his arm, Eberard had to resist the urge to look away, to step back. Bile stung the inside of his mouth and throat.

This is pointless, he thought. Even if he felt some faint pulse, the blood loss from his torn leg would make any attempt at resuscitation impossible. He looked down at the small first-aid pouch in his hands. What did he think he was doing? Trying to save lives with a Band-Aid and a thermometer? He stood up, nearly stumbling over the body as dizziness took his balance away. The light from his torch swung across the grass and tar.

Eberard walked past the traffic officer and climbed into his car without a word. He slammed the car door and threw the torch and pouch onto the back seat. The torch clattered onto the floor of the car as he started the engine. He heard the officer shout as he accelerated past him: '*Maar wie gaan my nou help?*'

'Just do your own fucking job,' Eberard muttered under his breath. The severed thigh lay still, accusingly, forcing him to drive around it.

Later that night, Eberard tossed in his bed. Every position was uncomfortable, every thought searing. Some time after midnight he got up and poured himself a tumbler of brandy, gulping it down. The alcohol only made his head throb more, and he lay on his back, sweaty and groaning. In the early hours of the morning, he finally drifted off, only to awake with a start from a dream: he had come across a car accident. A Ford Sierra had collided with another car, but had somehow also managed to hit a person, a man, who lay wedged at the front of the car, his hip and one leg held by the bonnet like prey in the jaws of a crocodile. Only his arm reached the ground, draped listlessly with his palm open. Eberard approached him, his foot knocking against the arm. The man moved his hand out of the way, so that the inspector would not step on his fingers. Eberard walked around to the driver's side; the door was already open. He reached down for the bonnet catch and pulled, hearing the thud of the bonnet releasing and the man tumbling to the ground. When he moved back to the front of the car, a paramedic was already attending to the victim.

'No,' the paramedic said, looking up at Eberard, 'he's dead.' Eberard stared in disbelief. He tried to say something, to explain that the man had moved his arm – that he had not realised that he was dying. He felt that somehow releasing the bonnet had killed him, that he was responsible. Someone was standing next to him, putting his arm around him to comfort him. He could not see who it was, but felt tears running down his face.

Someone else – the paramedic? – was saying something, murmuring the same refrain over and over again: 'It always happens like this ... it always happens like this ...' Then Eberard turned to the man beside him. The nightclub owner smiled back at him compassionately. 'But you were driving the car,' Laurent said quizzically.

MY CHILDHOOD

Momma rocked my sobs away.
Her breasts had long ago gone dry,
so I cried both night and day
till no tears were left with which to cry
…

Through interminable winter nights I heard
momma's cry of wrath.
With thunder in her every word
she chased the Angel of Death.

All the nights of childhood through
upon her breast I shut my eyes,
and she never knew
her curses had become my lullabies

When momma could no longer keep
the slumber from her brain,
then silently I'd beg, I'd weep:
'Wake up and lull me with your curse again!'

THIRTEEN

Eberard's upturned hand lay in front of him on the table. It had the appearance of a dead fish washed up on the beach, its bloated belly facing the sky. He leant forward and picked a brass drawing pin off the desk with his other hand, placing the point against the meat of his thumb, where it bulged into the palm of his hand. The skin indented, growing pale and opaque around the point as the blood was forced away under the pressure. He pushed harder and watched the bloodless area swell. This was where he was caught, he thought sadly: his entire life was situated in that lifeless area where the pressure from the outside had pushed out all of the blood. The passion, the ability to feel, the ability for life itself, had been squeezed out, trapping him in a world of clinical whites and greys. His experience of his own life felt stunted, as if he was cocooned in damp cotton wool. The sounds that reached him were muted. People passed him by as he tried to break free, but the cold dampness weighed him down, inexorably. He could not move with any spontaneity, and so he was unable to control his environment. He was a prop, an inert object.

He lifted the pin; the indentation remained, a purple-black spot marked its centre. The blood was slow to return, gradually colouring the base of his thumb, but leaving a ring of white skin around the puncture mark. He threw the drawing pin at the opposite wall without venom. The nausea of deep-seated depression pushed up against his throat. His mouth felt dry and sour from drinking himself to sleep the night before.

It was early afternoon when he started drinking again, and, after two whiskies, he cancelled his appointment with Doctor Primesh. In a moment of recklessness, he decided instead to go to the club. He was already drunk by the time he arrived that evening. He did not know why he was there; the investigation was closed. But he felt drawn towards the release – maybe the self-destruction – that the place represented for him. This time the muscle-bound bouncer opened the door for him as he approached. The man grinned at him, almost madly, and raised his hand in refusal at the offer of money. Eberard was struck again by the force and pace of the sound that crashed around him as he stepped inside – not really music, but pulsating sound. The dance floor weaved and jammed as before, with even more energy, it seemed. A green laser flashed across the length of the space, forming a tube that invited him further into the lair. Someone bumped against him briefly, gyrating back into the swirling mass, leaving him with a cool, wet patch on his arm. Eberard ran his palm over the moisture. Even though he was dressed more casually this time, he still felt out of place, and his drunken state accentuated his difference, heightening his insecurity rather than diluting it. He was neither black nor white. He was much older than most of the figures on the floor. And he was a policeman.

He lit a cigarette to occupy his hands and moved towards the smaller bar on the opposite side of the club. An attractive woman with high cheekbones and wide eyes nodded towards him in acknowledgement. He was grateful for the ease of her interaction and sat down on a stool at the bar. The couple along-side him were engrossed in each other, their mouths open and moving over one another in long, devouring kisses. The woman had medium-length hair, falling over her eyes, and she wore a loose-flowing shirt buttoned up to her neck. She flexed her body, curving up against her partner, pushing her nipples against the fabric of her shirt. Her partner's cropped hair and tight white vest displayed defined shoulder muscles and an even suntan. They pulled away and cupped their hands together under the woman's nose; a small glass vial nestled in their palms. He watched as she sniffed deeply and laughed loudly, freely and with joy. Her part-ner, feeling the stranger's eyes on them, turned around towards him. Eberard stared for a moment into the smooth-skinned face of a young woman, a teenager with glowing skin and green eyes accentuated by her short hair. She smiled languidly at him. Still half-turned towards him, one eye watching him, she opened her mouth and pushed her tongue out seductively. It glistened pink, and her partner latched onto it with energy, sucking it deeply into her mouth as they rocked backwards and forwards. Eberard turned away, hoping that he had not shown his shock. He heard one of them laugh. The woman behind the bar was still waiting for his order, patient and mildly amused.

'How about a Sinner's Special?' he asked recklessly.

'What's in it?' She looked at him blankly. He mumbled indistinctly and then ordered a double whisky. 'We don't get many whisky drinkers around here,' she said disdainfully, pushing an unopened bottle of cheap blended whisky in front of him. He nodded and watched her pour out two liberal tots.

The whisky tasted sour and acidic. Eberard felt the beginnings of a cramp in his stomach as the cheap liquor swirled down his throat. He turned on his seat to face the floor. To his surprise, Laurent was standing directly behind him, and he nearly spilt his drink as he turned and bumped into the man.

'Mr Februarie. I see you have joined us again. Welcome.' His host's smile was broad and seemed to be genuine. 'I hope you're not drinking the whisky. It really is no good. I apologise.' He said something to the woman behind the bar; the language sounded like a combination of French and an African language. The glass was taken out of Eberard's hand, and within a moment it was replaced with a tumbler of rich, smoky liquid. He sipped it; warm flavours of wood and earth were offset by the sharper taste of mellowed orange and alcohol. Eberard looked at Laurent questioningly.

'Good cognac with a splash of Southern Comfort,' Laurent explained. 'You'll find the two complement each other in a most interesting way. It also has a touch of Cointreau – the tangerine liqueur you enjoy so much in this strange country. It gives it a citrus edge. I recommend it.' Laurent watched Eberard keenly as he took another sip and nodded approvingly. 'Come with me. We can talk in my office.' Eberard stood up reluctantly; he was enjoying the surroundings of the club and did not wish to replace them with a back office full of crates in harsh lighting.

Laurent led him to the other side of the club, close to the door that led to the alley. A small wooden door rested flush with the wall; the painting continued uninterrupted across its surface, making it almost indiscernible in the flashing lighting. Laurent moved a hidden catch and beckoned his guest into a small stairwell, leading up a flight of narrow cement stairs. At the top, he turned left and opened a larger, heavy-wooded door. Eberard followed, stepping into a sumptuous lounge. A huge mirror with a thick brass border faced him; he saw himself full-length, standing in the doorway. Colours and lights reflected back at him, making the room seem larger than it was. He felt his shoes sink into the soft pile of the carpet as he stepped inside.

The walls were painted a deep green, well lit with downlighters and side lights. A long deep-maroon couch covered with scatter cushions ran along the length of the wall immediately to his right. A smaller couch was positioned beneath the mirror in front of him, and a rough whitewashed coffee table occupied the centre of the sitting area. Fresh flowers – white and yellow St Joseph's lilies – were displayed in a pewter vase in the middle of the table, and a small but expensively stocked bar ran against the wall to his left. Two doors led off next to the end of the bar counter. The lighting was more subdued in the corner of the room, and a small lamp cast a yellow glow over the leather surface of a desk, which was empty except for a speaker telephone and a slim pile of documents.

Laurent was already sitting in his chair, rocking back in relaxed amusement. He pulled open a drawer and pushed a balsa-wood cigar box across the desk. He gestured towards the bar. Eberard smiled in amazement and walked slowly across the room, enjoying the soft give of the carpet. There was no music playing, but the tempo of the club could be heard through the walls. The room seemed to be both part of the activity of the club and also somehow set apart – an illicit and exciting chamber.

Eberard approached the bar like a sleepwalker, not noticing the woman standing behind the counter, her lithe body blending into the dark wood behind her. He started when she moved – she seemed like a mannequin that had suddenly come to life – and he grinned nervously. She was topless, her small dark-skinned breasts and even darker nipples pushing out towards him. He felt embarrassed, as if he had walked into her bedroom unannounced; he almost wanted to tell her that she had forgotten to put her top on. Then he squirmed at his own naivety and forced his eyes onto her face, acutely aware of the two shapes in the blurred lower portion of his vision. Her large, dreamy eyes were enrapturing, and, when she smiled, Eberard felt his heart leap. She was holding out a champagne glass. He stepped forward against the counter to reach for it, his eyes falling to her waistline. She was not wearing any clothes at all. He glanced at the sweep of her waist, her hips and the cropped fuzzy outline of her pubic hair, then hurriedly looked back up at her face. She was still smiling, patiently holding out the glass for him. He mumbled his thanks and took his drink to the desk where Laurent was seated.

'Why do we find the female anatomy so fascinating?' his host mused. 'A woman's breast is to us a subject of great and eternal interest. We can spend hours watching the same pair of breasts, how they move, how they bounce and tremble, just how the flesh curves, where the nipples do or do not point. And then, when we are absolutely saturated with that pair, we can move in a heartbeat to another woman, and start all over again.' Laurent swirled the liquid around in his glass. 'Do women spend the same amount of time thinking about us? I don't think so, my policeman friend. Do you?' His eyes sparkled with mischief.

'I asked my students this one year, but they were too young, too inexperienced, to really deal with the question. They wrote only about sex. But I ask you: why, when we talk to a woman, do we struggle to keep our eyes above the level of their chin? Why do we constantly shame ourselves by peeking a look at their chest, hoping to snatch a glimpse of something more? I have caressed the breasts of hundreds of women: small breasts, large, floppy, tight, old, young, and everything in between. And yet, when a new woman walks into the room, I want to know what her bosom is like.' Laurent gestured towards his chest. 'Why is that, Inspector? Why is that?' He gave a little chuckle and sipped his champagne.

Eberard had been thinking almost the same thought. There were times, more often than he would like to concede, when his baser interests took control, when his desire to touch a woman overtook all other urges. He had often wondered why the experience of one woman was never enough. He sat down in front of the desk; the expensive leather cushioned his body.

'It is a debilitation, Inspector. Grotesque. We are trapped, *mon ami*. That's why. We are trapped and tortured by the very society and rules we have created.' Laurent opened the cigar box, and offered it to the policeman. Half the box was filled with neatly stacked cigars wrapped in cellophane. A cigar cutter and silver lighter rested next to them. Then a small square dish filled with a white powder. A tiny shining spoon. Another packet of crystals; some small trapezoid-shaped pink pills. A flat dish with scorch marks. Some hand-rolled cigarettes, perfectly rounded with short tips. The room suddenly seemed very quiet, the air between them filled with exquisite anticipation. Eberard felt a rush of excitement, the need to fulfil his craving. The burn of crack on his tongue, the rush, the sizzle of blood behind the eyes; it was familiar but forbidden territory. His hand hovered like an animal at his side, his fingers rubbing together nervously. He heard a clink of glasses from the naked woman at the bar. The soft light dulled his senses. The champagne bubbled pleasantly in his stomach. He hesitated, and Laurent shrugged, turning the box around. The lid closed with a snap. The moment was over, and Eberard had lost a little more territory.

His host continued as if nothing had happened. 'Consider the following,' he said, sitting back in his chair. 'In the bush, the males are not interested in the females until they come on heat. Then she puts out; the hormonal scents drive the males crazy. Their instincts kick in, and some, like the lion, will mate for days on end. He will force himself upon any female on heat until he is exhausted. And she won't fight him. Why should she? She's brought the turn of events on herself. It would be ridiculous for her to put out a scent and then refuse him. But humans, hah!' he snorted contemptuously. 'Women put out all the time. There is no one time when a woman is especially desirable. No special month or week. Women are taught, from young, to put out all the time. Television, media, advertising – all the parts that make up the civilised world – and their mothers, too, they all tell them this. So we create a world for ourselves where women are constantly on heat. In our eyes.

'But at the same time' – Laurent raised his finger as Eberard tried, through his drunkenness, to understand the point – 'at the same time, we put all kinds of rules in place: monogamy – you can only have sex with one partner. Ages of consent – you can only have sex with a person when they are this old. Consensual sex – you can only have sex with consent.' He took a long gulp of champagne and continued: 'We are torturing ourselves. We have put ourselves in a jail, and we are taunting ourselves with these images of freedom. Consider this, *monsieur*. A male lion walks past a female lion. Do you think he thinks to himself, "Nice nipples, I wonder what it would be like to fuck her"? No, he walks past her and thinks, "Touch my food and die, lady."'

Laurent laughed at his own joke. Eberard found himself smiling, both enthralled and disgusted. His host's manner was totally engaging, almost innocent in its childish enthusiasm. He felt a movement next to him and turned to his side, only to look directly into the dark curled hair of the woman, who was filling up his glass. He felt her body heat for an instant and turned to Laurent, giggling like a schoolboy. The woman stepped around the desk and filled his host's glass; Eberard watched as Laurent ran his hands up her thigh, gently brushing the back of his hand between her legs. His fingers played delicately with her. When his glass was filled, she turned slowly and walked back to the bar.

'The only time the lion looks at her with real juice is when the timing is right. She is ready and she flicks the lever on his hormones and – bang! – it really starts to happen.' Laurent slapped his hand down hard on the table, startling the policeman. 'But until then, it's just about getting on with living in the veld. But with us, with men, we live our lives surrounded by millions of women, all sexual, all the time. Every face, every body, every dress screams at us: "Come and get me!" But the moment you try to respond to the signal ... well, my friend, any man who has lived a little knows what happens – sexism, harassment, rape, abuse, sex without full consent from the kiss to the last drop of semen – these are all outlawed in our world.'

Eberard was nodding, but his head was slumping backwards, relaxed and sleepy. Laurent raised his voice to keep his attention. 'Imagine a room full of lions, Mister Detective. All the females are on heat. But every time the males try and mount them, they get whacked with ... with an electric stun stick. Their balls are shocked with a thousand volts. Now does that sound like the kind of place you want to be if you are a daddy lion? Well, my friend, that is exactly the world in which you live. That is the horrible, taunting, cruel world you lived in ... until you walked in this door.'

The line was dropped without any emphasis. In fact, Laurent's voice had trailed off as he said it, but it was loaded with unspoken possibility. Eberard sat up. He felt some of the fatigue leave him as his interest was piqued. 'What do you mean when you say that that world is left behind when I walk in through this door?' His words were indistinct, and he battled to keep his tongue from slurring over the consonants. 'You said "until you walked in this door". What did you mean?' he tried again.

'Things work differently in my club, Inspector,' Laurent replied. 'Things are not as they seem here. You're already start-ing to learn that, I think. For example: you are a police officer, and I have just offered you a tray of drugs – sufficient to place me behind bars for a while – and yet we understand that, in here, you are not a policeman. You are a man. And I will show you – if you like – that here you can be your own man. But that, *monsieur*, is for another day. You have drunk a lot. And you have a killer to catch. It is time for you to go.' Laurent was suddenly asser-tive. He stood up and started towards the door. Eberard rose unsteadily to his feet. 'I thought I had caught my killer,' he replied. 'Both of them, in fact.'

His host turned to him in a show of great seriousness. 'You must learn not to repeat the same mistakes, Inspector, over and over. It is another fundamental human weakness. We are slow to learn from our mistakes. I have already told you that you are looking in the wrong place. Now it appears that you are not even

looking any more. Don't disappoint me, Mister Detective ...
Eberard ... I am counting on you,' he said earnestly.

Eberard left the club in a whirl of sound and odour. In the fresh
air, the full impact of the alcohol made itself felt. He leant
against the brick wall, and his stomach heaved, the muscles
contracting violently. He vomited heavily onto the pavement.
He remained in the same position, feet astride and retching, for
what seemed an interminable period. He felt unable to move.
Sounds rushed in at him and then receded, fading to a low-
pitched buzz, only to come storming in at him again. Someone
came up to him and poured a bottle of water over his head. He
was incapable of saying anything, but raised his head weakly in
thanks. The water ran down his back and soaked his shirt. He
felt wretched, but the coolness of the water helped him gain his
bearings, and he stood up and felt for his keys. He clutched the
cold metal in his hand for comfort and made his way towards
his car across the street.

Once he was in the car, he considered sleeping on the back
seat. But his bladder was full and he still felt nauseous. He longed
for the cool, clean tiles of his bathroom. He started the engine
and moved unsteadily into the road, oversteering continually
and pulling the car from one side of the road to the other. The
street lights confused him, and on two occasions he had to turn
away from the pavement abruptly, as the front wheels knocked
into the cement kerb. He pulled into the parking area outside the
barracks, taking up two parking bays. He sat in the car, with
the engine off, for several minutes. He considered trying to
park the car in a better position, but decided he did not have the
energy. He lit a cigarette. The smoke made him feel like vomit-
ing again, and he tossed it, still burning, out of the window.

His flat felt bare and lonely. It depressed him that after a
lengthy career in the force he was back at the beginning, living
in police barracks. Living alone. The kitchen sink was piled with
unwashed plates and glasses. He had taken to sleeping in the
small lounge, on a wide sofa, drifting off in front of the television. His blankets were strewn haphazardly on the floor. The

room smelt stale and mildewy. He sighed and closed the door behind him.

He dropped his keys onto the table top beside the door and pressed the message button on the answering machine. The tape whirred as it rewound and clicked onto play. The strident voice of his ex-wife filled the room.

'—rard, the school phoned to say that you haven't paid your share of Christine's fees for the first term. Again. For Christ's sake, it's bad enough when you don't contribute towards the upkeep of the house – but this is your daughter's education … I've had to pay it into the school account. So don't *you* now go and pay the school. You'd better transfer the money straight into my account tomorrow. Don't forget – otherwise my cheque's going to bounce. It's four hundred and fifty rand, in case you've forgotten … write it down, Eberard. Four hundred and fifty rand. Tomorrow. Into my account. Bye.'

Eberard grabbed the slim black machine with one hand and lifted it over his head like a baseball. He threw it fiercely across the room towards the opposite wall. It flew in the air until the electric cable pulled it short, wrenching the socket out of the wall. The machine tumbled onto the coffee table, splitting open. While it was still spinning on the floor, he ran forward and kicked it. His foot caught it squarely on its side. The top panel cracked open and spun away under the sofa, while the body of the machine sailed over the counter and smashed into the drying rack. He heard the sound of glass shattering on the kitchen floor.

Eberard stood motionless, letting his remaining energy drain from his body. He felt his head swirl and his stomach convulse. He closed his eyes and let his body fall backwards, slowly arching in the air and landing with a thump on the sofa. In his mind, he kept falling, tumbling backwards, somersaulting over and over, further and further away. He watched himself disappearing, a tiny turning figure sinking down the length of a dark, deep well. Falling and spinning, smaller and smaller. Until he was nothing at all.

LULLABY

Sing to me a lullaby so I can close my eyes
Rape the dawn of all her lies and we can say
  goodbye
And I don't know myself
I can't love what I don't understand
No, no, no, no
Separate your right from wrong and I can
  sing a different song
Sing to me a lullaby and I can close my mind
Cause I don't know myself
I can't love what I don't understand
No, no, no, no
And I knew the song
Knew the way
And I spoke the truth
I never lied
I don't know myself
I can't love what I don't understand
I can't love what I don't understand
I can't love what I don't understand
No, no, no, no, no

FOURTEEN

THE choice of punishment for the slave-child was the source
of much morbid consideration for Van der Keesel. Although
he was quite capable of ordering the flogging of the girl – he
had done so before in cases of theft – the infliction of physical
pain seemed too simplistic and, in a way, demeaning. The punishment to be brought down on the Boorman family should
be calculated and longer lasting than a mere beating. He spent
some days reflecting on the most appropriate sanction, before
ordering Frederick to bring his daughter before him.

Sanna did not react when she heard Van der Keesel's command; the man stood on the voorstoep of his residence, his thick
hands on his hips and his legs astride like a military general
addressing a foot soldier. She stood with her arms at her side,
staring at him without blinking until he had finished explaining
her task. She was to dig up each vine in the illegal field along the
riverside, individually, without damaging their roots or crushing
the bark around their stems. Then, once the vine was out of the
ground, she would have to carry it in a wet sack along the narrow
path through the bush to the Company fields over the hill, to
the northernmost corner of the tiered field. Van der Keesel had
marked out a stony and unprepared piece of ground. There, she
was to prepare a hole and fill it with clean soil and water, and
plant the vine. Each vine would have to be dug up and carried
separately, one by one, over the rough rocky paths in the sun and
up the mountain slope. Trenches would have to be dug, stones
cleared and holes dug into the hard ground. Van der Keesel addressed his command to Frederick rather than to the child, until
the last statement: 'You will not be allowed any implements,
only your slave hands,' he said coldly, looking straight into her
eyes. Still she did not flinch, returning his stare with an equally
unrelenting gaze. Inside, she felt her heart harden a little more
as the lightness of childhood slipped further away.

It was a mammoth task, and a cruel punishment, given the

size of the illegal vineyard and the ground chosen for transplant-ing. The vines had already rooted, sending out tough tendrils that clasped onto the rocks beneath the soil surface. Sanna broke the soil open with a stick and then dug into the ground with her fingers to ensure that she did not break the young roots. Her fingers were soon cut by the sharp stones and rubbed raw by the grit. Once she had loosened the earth, she teased the vine from the ground, letting the soil shake off as she drew its roots out of the ground. She placed the stump in a wet bag and started the long walk up the hill to the fields. She had to pick her way over the planted vineyard, careful not to damage the plants. The path led down onto the side of the dam, where the clay-like soil was damp and slippery. On the other side of the dam, the ground rose steeply up to where the tiers ended and the raw mountain started. The jagged stones hurt her bare feet, and the short grasses left barbs hanging from her thin legs.

In the new vineyard, Sanna first dug a shallow trench, using the hard trunk of a burnt protea bush. She had prepared a mound of fresh grasses and branches from the riverine scrub to create a small patch of shade; the newly uprooted vine lay in its damp bag under the branches while she dug the hole. If she struck a big rock, or when she tired and the digging took too long, she had to take the bag down to the dam, sliding down the steep slope to the water and scrambling back up on her hands and knees. The area for the hole had to be cleared of stones first; she used her stick to lever the larger rocks out of the ground and rolled them away to the side of the new field. She heaped the small stones in piles before carrying them away in her sack, and, once the surface was cleared, she attacked the soil with the point of the stick, loosening the stones underneath. The stick frequently slipped back in her hand, jabbing into her palms and blistering her thumbs. Sanna worked quietly and with determination, the sweat glistening on her body. Once the stones were cleared from the hole, she cupped handfuls of earth and filled it with loose soil brought up in another sack from the banks of the river. She wrung water from the sack, slowly dampening the earth before making space for the vine's roots. Once the vine was in the hole, she packed small stones and soil around the base, leaving a straight stick in place to tie the stem.

The work was slow and exhausting. Bakka watched her progress in silence. He glided up the slope, and, when she turned, she found him directly behind her, the sun burning around his head, and his dark shadow across her arms. Even when he was not there, she felt her every move was watched.

She returned home at dusk, without having eaten during the day, exhausted, her thin body bruised and aching. She did not speak, for fear of crying in front of her mother, who watched her with wide eyes. She washed her feet in the bucket outside the house and ate her supper in silence, hugging her mother and kissing her father gently on his cheek before collapsing onto her rough mattress.

On the first day of her labour, Frederick had come to the fields to watch her progress; when he saw the nature of her task, he left and did not return again. Now she worked without company, completing fifteen or twenty vines in a day. After the first week, the illegal field seemed no smaller, and the rows of vines stretched through the bush in long, daunting lines.

Van der Keesel visited the field during the day, dismounting and kicking his feet at the newly planted vines. Once or twice, he pulled a transplanted vine out of the ground to check whether its roots had been damaged. Having checked the plant, he dropped it on the ground, without a word to Sanna, who stood watching in anger. One day, during the first week, he sat down in the shade of the bushes and watched her work. He took out his pipe and filled it, unhurriedly stuffing the moist tobacco tightly into the bowl. Bakka stood some distance away, his arms folded and his face shining in the heat. Sanna knelt down to clear the stones, while the acrid smell of pipe tobacco drifted across the field. After a few minutes, she stood up and folded her arms.

'What! You will never finish your work with your arms folded, slave-girl,' Van der Keesel remarked from the comfort of the shade.

'I will not work while you are watching me, Master van der Keesel,' Sanna answered daringly.

'You should watch your mouth, child. It is your large and dirty tongue that got you here in the first place. It can get you into far worse a place if you aren't careful. You'll work when I tell you to. Why should you not?'

The last statement had not been intended as a question, but Sanna, with all the recklessness of a child, answered the man. 'I should not, as I am still only a child, and you are a grown man. It's not proper, I think, that a grown man should sit and watch a child do his work. I will do the work you tell me to ... I have no choice, and I'll finish it, but not while I am being watched.' She stood firm, her arms crossed on her chest.

Van der Keesel stared at her, the flicker of a smile on his lips. 'I have no desire to watch a child doing my work, slave-girl. But I do have an interest in making sure that my work is done properly.' He drew heavily on his pipe as if considering the matter closed, then added, 'So far you have done well – your work is slow but the vines are unbroken and well planted. I will keep checking your work – if it remains of this standard, then I will leave you be. But let me find that you have betrayed me in your work, like your bastard father, and you'll work with me sitting on top of you, if necessary.'

Van der Keesel did not wait for a reply, and none was forthcoming. He tapped his pipe out on the rock and heaved his bulky frame onto his horse. Sanna stood motionless until he had rounded the dam and she could see his figure disappearing, trotting along the path towards the town. Her knees were shaking, both from fear and from untempered rage. The half-burnt ball of tobacco from his pipe lay steaming like a fresh turd on the rocks. Without saying a word, Bakka stepped forward and crushed the smoking ball under his foot. He reached down behind the bush and pulled out a buck-skin flask of water, gesturing to Sanna to take a sip. She drank gratefully, her eyes fixed on the caffer.

It was a while before she returned to her task. But Van der Keesel was true to his word, and he did not return to watch her at work. Once a day, he would arrive, unpredictably, to check the health of the transplanted vines. He said nothing to her and otherwise left her to her gruelling labour. Bakka also left her alone after the incident, although Sanna still turned in fright whenever she heard a noise in the fields.

The following week was parched by the full summer sun. The ground baked in the heat, and the grey stones were scalding to the touch. The sack dried out within a few minutes, and Sanna had to keep returning to the dam to wet the bag and the vine. She squeezed water into the small ditches around the vines planted the previous week and filled the holes with more water than usual. The heat and the continual trips to the dam slowed her down. The ground seemed harder and more unforgiving in the heat, and her hands and feet smarted. Fluid seeped out of her blisters, and her toenails were cracked and warped. On the second day of the heatwave, she slipped while descending the dam wall, skidding on her thigh and grazing the skin off the length of her leg. Her foot struck the cool muddy water with a splash.

She lay on her back with her feet in the water, feeling the sun burn her face and chest. A buzzard circled high in the sky, scanning for rodents or lizards in the clear light. Sanna put her hands flat on the ground and pushed herself a little further down towards the water; it circled around her legs, lapping under her knees. She pushed herself further, her shoulder blades scraping on the earth, rucking her dress up around her thighs. She sat up and looked at her legs lying in the water. A fine layer of silt covered her skin, wafting against her like soft feathers. She rubbed the graze on her leg; the wound hurt but the water was soft and slippery. Lifting herself on her hands, she gently eased herself into the water. A layer of coolness drifted up her thighs, wetting her dress. She felt it trickle around her hips, tickling her bottom. It felt like an embrace from a friend, safe yet exciting. She was wary of deep water, but the earth felt firm and the water beckoned her further. Crawling feet first, she sunk deeper into the river. It washed up her belly, pulling her dress down. She dropped her body, and the water splashed up, covering her small breasts and slopping against her neck and chin. Only her head was out of the water now. She closed her eyes and let her ears sink beneath the surface. There was no sound, only the dull thud of her own heartbeat. She felt calm and transported, taken to a place where heat and hardship could not follow.

Then, through the water she heard another rhythm, a thumping that reached her not by sound, but by feeling – a vibration in the ground itself. She sat up and looked at her hands, orange-brown beneath the surface. Her heels sank into the slimy mud as she stood up, the water pouring from her dress.

Sanna heard the snort of his horse behind her. She knew it was him, but did not turn around. Instead, she leant forward, and cupped the water with her hands, tipping it onto her face and hair. She repeated the process, drenching her hair and streaking her face with silt. The horse stamped its hooves, hot and thirsty. Van der Keesel barked something at the beast. A blue and silver dragonfly flew past her, buzzing noisily just above the surface; then another, with a red abdomen and small wings, its legs almost dragging in the water. She cupped some more liquid and wiped her face before turning to the shore and reaching for the sack. It bubbled in the water as she forced it under and let the fibres soak up the water. The smell of pipe tobacco reached her nostrils. She waited, the sack floating like a body in front of her. She heard him grunt something to himself, and then the clip-clop of the horse being led away. When she finally turned around, he was gone, and she watched him leading his horse slowly towards the other fields, blue-grey smoke drifting behind him.

The following day, she waded into the river next to the field of illegal vines. It was cleaner than the dam, and she could see the rock and weeds on the bottom clearly. She waded into the knee-deep water and sat with her back to the current. Here it was also colder, and, the first time she sat down, the bite of the current made her catch her breath. Although the flow was slow, the water still swirled up against her skin, rising over her arms. She leant backwards, her feet pushing against the rocks, the eddies swirling over her shoulders, running over her neck and chest before slipping away from her. Her confidence grew and she let the water rise around her cheeks. Then she let her face submerge entirely, but the cold water shot up her nose, forcing her to surface, spluttering and coughing.

She swam in the river every day that week, sometimes three or four times. It became an escape from the heat, and her life. On one of her swims, she lay back, feeling the water push against her. She stretched her hands out in front of her and rubbed her palms together. Then, to her left, she saw something move. A flash of yellow and brown broke the surface. She sat up and stared at the spot, a foot away from the bank. It was still again. Nothing moved. She was about to turn away when the surface of the water parted, a little closer to her this time. The head of a large yellow cobra appeared, the length of its body shielded by the glare on the water. The snake curved across the river towards her. She started to move backwards on her hands, but the snake was moving too fast. Stifling a scream, she sank lower into the water, her eyes wide with fear.

The cobra moved with ease, its thin black tongue tasting the air as it advanced. Her muscles tensed as it came level with her feet, but it continued without pausing. Her legs lay directly across its path, but the animal ignored her as it headed for the opposite bank. As it passed, she felt the brush of the current displaced by its body. The tip of its tail sank beneath the surface, and she thought she felt it drag quickly across her skin. She shivered involuntarily, and the snake, sensing her presence for the first time, thrashed in the water, pushing forward onto the river's edge. It slithered up the earthy bank and disappeared into a hole just beneath the line of grass. She waited, her breath short and anxious. After a while, its head reappeared at the entrance to the hole, and it tasted the air with its tongue before retreating.

Sanna stood up gingerly and looked around her. She waded a little way upstream before clambering up the bank and walking carefully back towards the snake hole. She picked up a stick about half her height in length and pushed it firmly into a patch of soft earth just above the entrance. Then she tied some clumps of dried grass in a small bouquet, marking the stick distinctively.

SWEET AND
SOUR LULLABY

There's a lullaby for this feeling
You can find it in dark places
in the woods
sweet and sour
lullaby.

Orange-red will-'o-wisp
follow it
There's relief ahead.
Put off your hood
and listen.

Come to me in this wicked hour
Let senses tie you up
in my web of sweet and sour.
Come to me
and let me feel you
listen to my song.

You can go now
and you mustn't tell a soul
that you heard
this sweet and sour
lullaby.

FIFTEEN

JEREMY Wilder regarded his questioner with arrogance, leaning back in the chair and smiling. Despite his confident manner, Xoliswa noticed that he was fidgeting with a paper clip on his lap. The young man came from a wealthy Cape Town family. His father was the director of various companies, a lawyer by training. The son had grown up on a large estate in an upmarket area of Constantia – an expansive home nestled within sight of the vineyards of Buitenverwachting and Klein Constantia. Three Alsatians guarded the property, barking intimidatingly at anyone who walked up the stone-chip driveway. A full-time domestic-cum-cook had always seen to the family's every need, occupying the small outhouses next to the stables along with her two-child family, a gardener and his elderly wife. Wilder's was a world of entitlement where problems were solved with money and power. His father had studied at Stellenbosch University and had been head student of one of the prestigious residences. It was taken for granted that the son would follow suit: playing rugby for the university and enjoying the freedom of student life while completing a postgraduate LLB degree.

All had not gone strictly to his father's plan. Jeremy was intelligent enough, but not as physically strong or sporty as his father. To compensate, he had joined up with a boisterous group of male students from the residence. His father had had to step in to prevent the boy from being prosecuted for indecent behaviour. After an intervarsity rugby match, the drunken group had been caught urinating on a car displaying a sticker from a rival university. A few weeks after the incident, Wilder senior had had to put a few words in the rector's ear after a disciplinary inquiry into the behaviour of the entire group in a sexual harassment complaint. But at the end of the day, these problems were laughed off by the young man's father as youthful buoyancy playing itself out. The father was a large, overbearing and confident man. His son was less self-assured, and his acute awareness of his physical shortcomings added to his uneasiness. He hid his insecurity behind a fierce wall of sarcastic arrogance. His mother, by contrast, was a simple woman who concentrated on her looks and the material needs of the family. She never challenged her husband or her son and retreated into a world of luncheons, facials and vigorous gymming; to no avail, however, as her husband would flirt openly with young women in his son's presence, winking at him conspiratorially. The wife would smile to herself, keeping her thoughts carefully hidden. In Wilder's father's world, entitlement extended to both possessions and people, and Jeremy was brought up to believe that rejection was not a possibility.

The young man looked at Xoliswa with disdain. 'What do you people think this is about? Do you want me to say: "I did it. Sorry. I won't do it again"? I know my rights: I only spoke to you last time to try to help you. But it seems that nothing will help the police in this country any more. You were given the bastard who killed Melanie. He's dead, she's dead. What more do you want?'

'Are you finished?' Xoliswa asked evenly, keeping her eyes on him. Wilder seemed taken aback by her calm and assertive response. He hesitated, and then narrowed his eyes menacingly. It was such blatant posturing that the constable was not sure if she should laugh out loud or throw something at him. She waited patiently, aware of Eberard sitting in the corner, watching without intervening. Wilder said nothing further, and so she continued: 'You met Melanie through your sister who was a boarder in town?' He nodded and sighed with exasperation. Xoliswa ignored the provocation. 'You dated on a few occasions, but nothing ever came of it?' she went on. 'Did you feel that she wasn't interested in you?'

Wilder's face reddened noticeably. 'For God's sake, what's any of this got to do with you?' He shrugged his shoulders and held up his hand in a gesture of incredulity. 'Yes, we went out. I go out with a lot of girls. Did we have sex? No. Did I want to? Sure, but she's one of many. Do I care? Not at all. I saw her from time to time; campus is a sociable place and we'd sometimes end up drinking at the same pub or whatever. I'm sorry she ended up in the morgue. That's just what this country has come to. You can't even walk home at night without some black taking you into the bushes ...'

He immediately realised his mistake, but Xoliswa did not give him a chance to retract his statement. 'Mr Wilder, your views on the black people of our country aside, your statement here does not accord with the information I have from other witnesses.' She consulted her notes meaningfully, holding the silence in the room for a few moments. Eberard was impressed. 'Firstly, you're probably five years her senior; you're a postgraduate, while she was a matriculant who hadn't been to a single lecture on campus yet. She's from an Afrikaans background; you're from an English one. There's no reason for you to just *happen* to be in her company.' Xoliswa tried to curtail her own sarcasm. 'The information I have, Mr Wilder, is that you were really keen on her.' She paused for effect. 'The information I have is that you would go out of your way to spend time with her. You gave her lifts to wherever she wanted to go; you took her out for supper; you paid for her drinks. Isn't that right, Mr Wilder?'

Wilder gave her a withering look and sat forward in his chair. 'So I liked the girl. What's the big deal? I like lots of girls. Some end up in my bed, some don't. Yes, I liked her. She was a babe, you know. She looked good on my arm,' he said with bravado, his voice becoming shrill. 'I went around with her for a while, okay? It didn't go anywhere.'

'No, Mr Wilder. I'm afraid that's also not quite right.' Xoliswa was unshakeable. The paper clip dropped to the floor, and Eberard noticed the young man's hand trembling. 'You see, as I understand it, the women aren't hanging on your arm, waiting for your next racist comment. Irresistible as you may be, Mr Wilder, the way I hear it, you haven't had a girlfriend for a long time. No one I spoke to could remember the last time you had one. So, you tell me,' she said testily, 'privileged childhood like yours: I presume you get what you want in life. You came to university. Ran with the popular group. How do you react when some schoolgirl five years younger than you rejects you? How do you cope with rejection, Mr Wilder? What was your response when a schoolgirl said "no, thank you"?'

Wilder pushed the chair back and stood up. He held onto the table to stop his hands from shaking. 'This is unfair and you know it!' he said loudly. 'You asked me to come in to clarify my statement. Now you're saying that I'm a suspect? You're just a constable. The Criminal Procedure Act says you can't take a statement from me – you should know that! You're trying to trick me. You haven't even read me my rights. I don't have to tell you anything at all. Are you saying I had something to do with her death or aren't you?' He was trying to shout, but his voice came out in a whine.

'Firstly, Mr Wilder, I am perfectly entitled to take a statement from you. As *you* should know, I can't take a confession from you. If you would like to make a confession, we can arrange for a commissioned officer to be present.' She paused, letting the suggestion sink in. 'Secondly, I haven't called you here as a suspect. We don't regard you as a suspect' – *at this stage*, she wanted to add, but held back – 'I just want you to tell me the truth about what happened that night. I've listened to you go on about your accomplishments with women and your supposed indifference to this young girl. Now I'd like to hear the truth. It's as simple as that.' Xoliswa looked straight into his wide eyes. 'Sit down, Mr Wilder,' she ordered. 'I may be black and you may be white. I may be a woman and you a man. I may be poor and you may be rich. I may even be younger than you. But I'm the police officer who is assisting in the investigation of a murder, and you're the witness who's lying. Keep that in mind when you give me your answers.'

Eberard smiled to himself as Wilder sat down heavily. His young constable had won the day, without losing her calm and without showing any disrespect. Wilder's eyes were cast down and he looked pale and fatigued. Xoliswa placed a clean sheet of paper in front of her and waited. The message to the young man could not have been clearer.

'Melanie used me for her own convenience,' Wilder started, his voice noticeably softer. 'I was ... well, I never got close enough to her to say that I was in love with her. I was infatuated with her, I suppose.' He paused to consider his words, anguished. 'I was useful to her ... sometimes. When she needed me, then she let me be around her. To impress her school friends, to give her a lift somewhere. She'd string me along. She could be very ... you know, suggestive. She was a manipulative person, really. I know what that sounds like, coming from me, but she was. And she's dead and all. Even though she was young, she looked out for herself and only herself. She could be so cold and ... well, dismissive when she didn't need you. She'd string you along until she didn't need you any more, and then she'd cut the string without even bothering to watch how you fell. She could just walk away from you. Without a thought.'

'What happened that night, Jeremy?' Xoliswa asked with more empathy. He looked up at her and acknowledged the change in her tone with a softening of his face.

'I went out drinking with her. She phoned me early in the evening and said that she wanted to go out, so I picked her up from her home. Well, around the corner from her house. She didn't want her father to see me. She told me that he disapproved of our friendship. At least that meant there was something for him to disapprove of,' Wilder half-snorted and looked down at his hands. 'Anyway, I picked her up in my car. She was quiet in the car. She just sat looking out of the window. I tried to talk to her but she didn't listen. We reached the Keg probably around half past eight. Some of her friends were already there. We had supper: hamburger and chips. She had a beer or two. She didn't show any interest in me. I drank quite a lot and talked to one of her friends. Then, at about ten o'clock, she asked me to give her a lift. She didn't say where to; I thought maybe she was tired and wanted to go home. She seemed a bit upset about something.

'So we got in the car, and I started to drive towards her house. I turned onto the main road, and she suddenly started shouting at me, calling me stupid and useless. She said I wasn't worth anything. I don't know what she was so upset about. I mean, she hadn't told me to go anywhere anyway. I told her to calm down and to tell me where she wanted to go. She gave me the name of some street; it's on the industrial side of town. So I turned the car around and drove there. She just sat and sulked with her arms crossed, staring out of the window. I remember she lit a cigarette in the car; she knows I hate that. She did it to spite me, I'm sure. She told me to stop outside this building; it had no signs up and no windows or anything. Just a door in the wall. There were cars parked outside and a few people on the street. It didn't look like ...' Xoliswa motioned to him to slow down. He waited for a few seconds while she caught up with her notes.

'I asked her what was there. She said that I didn't know anything. She was really going out of her way to be nasty. I told her that it didn't look like a very safe area and that I'd come in with her. She laughed, sort of snorted, at me. As if I'd said something really stupid. "You're such an idiot," she said. "You're such an idiot." I got angry and said that she was just using me. Then she kind of sneered at me; she pulled a really ugly face, and I knew what was coming – when I saw her face like that, screwed up like a little rat. She told me to fuck off, that she was going to see a real man. Those were her words: "I'm here to see a real man." She kind of hissed the words at me.' Wilder paused and looked down at his hands, pulling at his fingernails.

'And then?' Xoliswa pressed. 'What happened then, Jeremy?'

'I don't remember what I said. I mumbled something, but she was already getting out of the car. She slammed the door so hard, I think she damaged the seal. I was shaking, so I didn't leave immediately. I watched her go inside; she walked up to the door, and a big black guy standing outside opened it for her. He put his hand on her shoulder as she went in. I noticed that, because it seemed so strange.'

Wilder stopped talking for a moment, and Xoliswa and Eberard waited, watching him carefully, neither of them allowing their interest in his statement to show.

'Then I realised that she was right: I was an idiot. This wasn't her first time at this place. The bouncer at the door knew her. She'd been using me all along and I'd let her. She was right to call me an idiot.' The young man's arrogance was gone, replaced with self-pity and bewilderment. 'Then I drove away. I had no idea … I mean, she told me she was seeing someone there. I didn't think to stay and try to look after her. She didn't want that anyway. She told me to fuck off. So I …' His voice trailed off.

'You're right, Jeremy. It wasn't her first time at the club,' Xoliswa said. 'She'd been there before. We know that much.'

There was a knock on the door, and a uniformed officer looked into the room. He handed Eberard a brown government-issue envelope. Wilder sat hunched in his chair. Eberard gestured to Xoliswa.

'Just give us a minute please, Mr Wilder,' she asked before moving across to her partner. But the young man did not seem to register as he sat with his head in his hands, rubbing his temples distractedly.

Eberard flattened the folded paper for her to read. A covering note to the report had been scrawled in black ballpoint pen.

Inspector, these are the results on the DNA samples from the laboratory. They tested a number of random samples of semen taken internally from the dead girl. They also tested the dress found near the scene. In summary, the results are as follows: all DNA samples of spermatozoa compare positively with the sample taken from the now-deceased suspect. The samples did not indicate the presence of spermatozoa from any other person. Given the statistical probabilities, there can be no doubt that the suspect had intercourse with the deceased shortly before her death. The tests on the dress indicated the presence of seminal fluid.

The conclusion is therefore firstly that the suspect did undoubtedly have intercourse – with penetration and ejaculation – with the deceased shortly before her death and, secondly, that it is likely, given the random sampling, that he was the only person to have had penetrative intercourse with her in a period of approximately 24 hours prior to her death.

Xoliswa raised her eyebrows and looked back at Eberard searchingly. He nodded his head towards the door. Wilder did not look up as they stepped outside the room, his forehead now pressed down on the table, and his arms outstretched at full length.

'I heard from the Attorney-General's office this morning,' Eberard said outside the door. 'They said if the DNA tests are positive they'll regard the docket as closed and they'll provisionally withdraw the charges against Professor du Preez.' Xoliswa frowned in surprise. Eberard continued before she could say anything. 'I know, Xoli, it's a dangerous decision. The press probably won't like it. Apparently the Deputy Attorney-General, Smuts, interviewed Du Preez himself. Du Preez told them that when he confronted the suspect in the cells, the man had tried to attack him. He told them that he shot him in self-defence.'

Eberard looked down at the report. He was trying not to show the disquiet he felt at the turn of events. Du Preez's statement did not accord with what he had told him after the incident, but Eberard had neglected to get a signature on the statement. He had planned to get it signed that day, giving the professor some time to recover after the funeral, but this new, conflicting statement complicated matters.

'Does the AG know about your statement?' Xoliswa was still frowning concernedly.

'When I told them it wasn't signed, they lost interest. Smuts said it was a decision taken by the senior personnel, and that if I didn't like it I could take it up with the Attorney-General himself.'

'Two murders and no one stands trial? I'm surprised that the AG will allow that kind of precedent. I mean, I know that the professor's committee – the KSAK – has all kinds of supporters, the old boys' club from Stellenbosch University. I hope Smuts isn't part of that. This doesn't feel right to me at all.'

'I know,' Eberard replied, grimacing. 'The withdrawal is a provisional one. Maybe there were strings pulled. Maybe there's politics involved. I don't know. He's been through a lot. They'll probably justify it on humanitarian grounds – suggest maybe that they want to give him time to deal with Elsabe.'

Eberard had seen it happen before with these kinds of cases: once everyone had forgotten about it, once some other high-profile murder took up the front page of the news, the file would quietly slip away.

'I'm not going to kick up a fuss unless I've got some basis to complain,' he went on. 'If somebody pulled some strings high up in the AG's office, that won't change unless I've something solid to give them. Let's just keep both dockets with us for now and if we uncover anything more, we can approach the AG again. What do you think?'

Xoliswa nodded her assent, although uncertainly.

'Well done on the witness, by the way,' he added. 'Nicely handled.' He was genuinely impressed with her restraint and assertiveness. She thanked him, smiling, her eyes widening and her smooth skin glowing with pleasure. She looked radiant.

They walked back into the office together. Wilder was sitting upright in the chair. Some of his cockiness seemed to have returned. 'Can I go now?' he asked – rather sarcastically, Eberard thought. He deferred to his partner, who held her hand towards the door.

'Just out of interest, Mr Wilder,' Xoliswa said coldly before the young man stood up. 'Tell me, what exactly was the problem here? That I'm black? Or that I'm a woman? Or that I'm a police officer who you can't order around?' She paused briefly, staring him down. 'Or are all of those things a problem in your world?' She turned her back on him without waiting for a reply.

LULLABY

on candystripe legs spiderman comes
softly through the shadow of the evening sun
stealing past the windows of the blissfully dead
looking for the victim shivering in bed
searching out fear in the gathering gloom and
suddenly!
a movement in the corner of the room!
and there is nothing i can do
when i realise with fright
that the spiderman is having me for dinner tonight

quietly he laughs and shaking his head
creeps closer now closer to the foot of the bed
and softer than shadow and quicker than flies
his arms are all around me and his tongue in my eyes
'be still be calm be quiet now my precious boy
don't struggle like that or i will only love you more
for it's much too late to get away or turn on the light
the spiderman is having you for dinner tonight'

and i feel like i'm being eaten
by a thousand million shivering furry holes
and i know that in the morning i will wake up
in the shivering cold

and the spiderman is always hungry ...

SIXTEEN

THE young woman moved with a litheness that was both languid and energetic. Her body was slim but strong, like that of a dancer. Fluorescent hot pants glowed brightly under the ultraviolet lights, and her white tank top shone against her tanned skin. Her stomach muscles tightened as she arched backwards, arms glistening under the flash of the strobe. Her movements were erotic and inviting; she was confident but innocent, evocative but restrained. Lust lurked about her as she controlled the dance floor, and the gaze of the men and women in the club followed her as she moved.

Laurent was sitting at the short bar playing host to a middle-aged man from the city. Neatly dressed in an expensive jacket and dark pleated trousers, the man's attention was devoted to the figure on the dance floor. He smoothed the greying hair at his temples, an involuntary action repeated over and over again, while he studied the dancer's every movement. His other hand felt blindly along the bar counter for his drink, fingertips touching the glass and closing around it without looking. A barman hovered nearby, replenishing the man's glass as it emptied. Laurent watched his guest seriously, without amusement. The man waited and watched, drinking heavily but distractedly.

Then, almost imperceptibly, he nodded and finished his glass in one gulp. Laurent clicked his fingers at a muscular bouncer standing nearby. The bouncer, dressed in a tight black T-shirt and jeans like the doorman, approached quietly. He touched the arm of the businessman and whispered something in his ear. The man stood up and was escorted politely from the bar. The bouncer lifted the catch on the hidden door leading up to the rooms upstairs, and the two men slipped inside, disappearing from view. The door clicked closed, flush with the walls. The mural figures took shape across the wall, blending across the door. The music increased in tempo, and the dance floor filled with bodies. The dancer still occupied the centre, absorbed in her own erotic display.

Laurent remained motionless, waiting like a predatory animal for the right moment to strike. Then, with the ease and determination of a master, he glided across the floor, somehow separating the figures without disturbing them, until he was standing directly behind the young girl. She spun around and placed her hands on his shoulders with a laugh, enticing him to join her in her dance. He shook his head and leant forward, whispering in her ear. The girl seemed surprised at his suggestion and stepped back, her head inclined thoughtfully. She moved forward again and asked him a question. He shook his head confidently and said something that made her laugh. She nodded her head, agreeing to his suggestion. Then he took her hand and led her off the floor. A girlfriend approached her, curious. They exchanged a few words, and the friend shrugged her shoulders, moving back into the sea of dancers. The couple stepped swiftly past the long bar, and Laurent opened the lock with his key. The door closed slowly behind them, settling into place, only to be disturbed before it could lock by the policeman's boot, shoved forcefully against the frame.

Eberard waited until he heard their footsteps recede. When he heard the sound of the wooden door closing at the top of the stairs, he pushed the door just wide enough to let himself through. He expected to feel the sudden force of a hand on his shoulder as he entered the stairwell, but the door closed behind him, clicking snuggly on its lock. A single naked globe lit the stairs, and he waited for his eyes to adjust to the gloom. Voices from the rooms above him echoed down. Someone – a woman – shouted. A man answered aggressively. Eberard ascended the stairs, leaning into the rough wall, his back scraping against the exposed brickwork. His ears buzzed from the noise of the club, and he had felt drunk even before he had taken the first sip of alcohol. He had no idea what to expect when he pushed the top door open. He was not even sure why he was at the club again, or why he had followed the young woman up the stairs. He felt daring and out of control when he entered into the reckless world of the club. The door moved slowly against the force of his hand.

The sitting room was unchanged, but the mood was very different. The young woman from the dance floor was huddled on the long couch, her face streaked with tears. Her hair was matted against her forehead, and her body glistened with sweat. She screamed as he pushed open the door. Eberard gripped the door handle in an effort not to shout back in fright. There were other men in the room now. They swung around and glared at him angrily.

'Please help me,' the young girl pleaded. 'Please, you must … you must help me!' The bouncer who had escorted the businessman up the stairs leant forward and slapped her hard on the cheek, the smacking sound stinging the air. She shrieked and fell back onto her side, hiding her face with her hands.

A figure moved suddenly in front of him, blocking his path. Laurent assessed him coldly. Eberard saw Laurent's momentary indecision, a vacillation between anger and amusement at the policeman's intrusion. Then his host grinned broadly and stepped towards him, gripping him forcefully by the arm.

'Hah! So you want to see what you're really made of? We'll see if you are ready for this, my friend. We will see. You have come sooner than I expected … but we'll see.' He turned to the young bouncer and issued an order: '*Sortez-la d'ici – dans la salle!*'

The man grabbed hold of the young woman's arm and pulled her to her feet. Her hands dropped from her face, and she looked up at Eberard with an expression of such intense hatred that he had to look away.

Undeterred, the woman managed to drag herself closer to him before hissing, 'Fuck you for not helping me! You're a pig just like the rest of them!' Eberard stood rooted to the spot. Conflicting emotions washed over him, guilt and titillation, disgust and curiosity all vying for dominance. Laurent watched him carefully. He gave another order, irritated that the woman had been able to speak to his uninvited guest. The bouncer tightened his grip on her arm and raised his hand to strike her again. She cowered; her erotic mastery from the dance floor was gone. She had become a frightened schoolgirl, snivelling and crying for help. Her long legs splayed on the floor as she tried to gain a foothold.

Laurent's underling dragged her towards the door on the left of the bar, which already stood slightly ajar. He pushed it further open with his foot and pulled the woman inside. She started screaming again. Eberard caught a glimpse of the businessman sitting in an easy chair, smoking a cigarette, before the door was kicked closed from the inside.

'*La salle des jeux* – the games room.' Laurent raised his eyebrows but did not explain. Eberard started to formulate a question, but his host raised his hand to silence him. The naked barmaid was nowhere to be seen; in her place stood an intimidatingly large man with folded arms, watching the policeman. Eberard looked towards the room where the girl had disappeared. The man behind the bar cleared his throat gutturally, like an animal.

'Sit, Mr Februarie. Please do not concern yourself with matters over which you can have no control. Remember, Eberard, here you are not what you are when you are outside of these walls. Here you are my guest.' Eberard thought of the cigar box of drugs that had been offered to him. And his failure to react to them. He felt the heat of the large man directly behind him, and he flinched, expecting to be grabbed from behind. But when he turned, the man presented him with a glass filled with ice and liquor. He accepted it and sat down, nervous.

'Now, Mr Februarie, I wonder if you can help me. I believe that Mr du Preez is not to be charged with Bullet's murder. Is that right?' There was a threatening undertone to the man's voice.

'The Attorney-General ... the DPP ... has provisionally withdrawn charges,' Eberard answered cautiously. 'The DPP said that if the results ...'

'Just answer the question I put to you.' Laurent cut him short. 'Yes, or *non*? The charges against Du Preez for the murder of Bullet have been dropped?'

'Yes.'

Laurent gave a grunt of disgust, but Eberard continued to explain the DPP's decision. The facts of Bullet's case were clear – the DNA match, the victim's earring in the suspect's room – the Attorney-General was satisfied that the suspect had raped and murdered her. The facts in Du Preez's case were less clear. 'The DPP wants time to assess the situation ... to consider its position,' Eberard explained. 'They don't want a murder charge hanging in the air in the meantime.' He was distracted by a shout of distress from the room within. The man behind the bar cleared his throat again.

'The DPP wants to *assess* the situation?' Laurent turned on him, furious. His forehead was knotted into tight lines, and his eyes raged. 'A man walks into the cells of a police station and executes a prisoner who is being held without probable cause. What does the DPP need to consider? Does your government suggest that this is acceptable? Does your police force condone revenge killings when the victim hasn't even been charged, let alone found guilty? Are you telling me that this is your society?' Eberard stood up, stepping to the side of the chair, unsure of the man's intentions.

'Look, it wasn't my decision. If it was left to me, I'd probably charge the man here and now with mur—'

'Probably!' Laurent interrupted him again. 'What is probably? The man killed an unarmed person who was in custody against his will. He shot him like you'd shoot a diseased dog on the street. You put him there,' he pointed at Eberard accusingly. 'You put him there! You let him be killed like a dog! Now what are you going to do about it?' The woman yelped from the other side of the closed door. Eberard paused and considered his next move.

'What the hell is going on in there?' he shouted back, pointing limply in the direction of the yelps. Laurent raised his eyebrows in surprise as Eberard stumbled over to the door, flinging his weight against it. There was no give. 'Open this door!' he strained, the veins in his neck swelling. He paused, his eyes sweeping over all the faces in the room. 'Somebody open ... somebody open this ...'

'Never mind that, Mister Detective.' Laurent seemed half-amused by the sudden display of bravado. 'Sit down,' he ordered. 'We're talking about Bullet here. Now let me tell you what has happened.' He took his glass and poured a large whisky at the bar. He handed it to Eberard, who took it meekly. 'Bullet had no rights,' his host said more calmly. 'The girl's father had all the power. Bullet was the diseased dog and the father was the avenger. You bring "scientific" proof that Bullet did something to this girl, but you find no real proof. You don't even bother to look for proof. Even the most basic traditional court, out in the middle of nowhere in my home country, even the simplest vigilante tribunal in my home village would want better proof than that. But here, in this wonderful advanced country you call the Republic of South Africa, you can get away with killing a man on no more than the merest whiff of evidence.' Laurent poured his own drink and took a long sip. The alcohol seemed to calm him further. He ignored the ever-quieter pleas and moans emanating from the room next door.

'You see, you never tried to find out anything about Bullet. You knew everything you needed to know. He was not South African, and he didn't have the right papers to be here. That was enough. That made him guilty of any crime you needed to pin onto his chest. Murder. Rape. Whatever. You don't know that he was a hard worker. You don't know that he came to this country to try to escape the madness of his own. You don't know that he sent half his earnings back to his family. You don't know that he was trying to save up to study here. You don't know what it is like to be treated like dirt by Home Affairs in this country. You don't know what it felt like for him to live every day knowing that he could be picked up and thrown in jail, just for being who he is – a black foreigner. You don't know that he had no interest in that woman, a little girl, like your sweet and innocent victim here. Do you think that Bullet travelled across the continent of Africa to be impressed by some *fille à papa*?' Laurent scoffed out loud and downed his drink. 'What do you think? That Bullet was an animal that couldn't resist the temptation of unspoiled flesh? Ha! You have no idea about his needs or desires.

He had his own romantic interests, and your girl was not one of them.'

'Who was then?' Eberard interrupted nervously.

'His real love' – Laurent's eyes narrowed – 'and this is just another thing that you would not know, or didn't bother to find out ... his real interest was a dancer called Clementine. Do you know what a clementine is, Detective?' Again, he did not wait for a reply. 'It's a concentrated fruit of passion – its skin is brighter than an orange, smaller and more compact. It's filled with juices, and the skin is thin, ready to burst at the first cut. Once you have eaten a clementine, you will be slow to return to an ordinary orange. His Clementine was full of the juices of life; she was wild and exotic. She'll take a confused man like you – an indecisive man – and she'll tear your heart out and hand it to you, still beating. She will leave you raw and bleeding just from looking at her.' Laurent brought his face close to Eberard, locking the man's eyes in an intense stare. 'She took an interest in him,' he said more casually as he moved away. 'She liked the way he moved. He was like a dancer too, strong and supple. She made him dance for her sometimes. He got too close to her. She burnt him, deep down and for ever.

'One of these days, when you are ready, and if you wish, I'll introduce you to her. Then, I promise, you'll understand Bullet for the first time. She'll show you things that'll change the way you see the world, Detective.'

The door to the room opened and the bouncer stepped out. A low moaning sound emanated from within. Laurent stepped into the doorway and looked inside, opening the door wide for a moment. Eberard caught sight of the young woman lying on her back at the edge of a bed; a crisp white bottom sheet stretched across the bed. There was no other linen, except for a pile of pillows at the top end of the bed. Her arms were thrown back behind her, and her top was crumpled around her throat. Her breasts pointed up towards the ceiling as the middle-aged man slammed into her, holding her legs wide apart with thick, hairy arms. Laurent glanced at the detective and closed the door. Eberard was both horrified and aroused by the scene: like a pornographic film or car accident, it left him feeling ashamed of his fascination.

'What is your deepest fantasy, Mister Detective?' His host placed his arm on his shoulder and led him back to the bar. His tone was both conciliatory and mischievous. 'Now don't give me some empty, handed-down fantasy. I want to know, when you really let yourself go, when you catch your subconscious libido unawares, as you wake up in the middle of the night, what are you dreaming about then?'

Eberard suddenly felt passionless. He tried to conjure up dark sexual deeds, but he was constrained by stylised pornographic images from illicit films and magazines. He envisaged his ex-wife's cold body lying beneath him, unresponsive and obligatory. He looked back at his host and shook his head uncertainly.

'Well, let me suggest that the ultimate male fantasy, at its truest and darkest, must involve all the elements of masculine sexuality. And those are' – he raised his eyebrows and paused – 'dominance and power, youth ... power over innocence, and of course, performance. If you combine those elements into a single fantasy, into a single act, you have then created the ultimate sexual encounter ... one that contains all the necessary sins to make it forbidden and irresistible: dominance over the subject, the destruction of youth, physical coercion, the corruption of desire. And that is precisely why it is so powerful.'

'What is actually happening in that room?' Eberard asked again, waving his arm towards the door, whisky sloshing over the lip of the glass onto his hand. The groans from behind the door were louder now. He glanced uncertainly at his host; there seemed to be an edge of pleasure in the shouts. Laurent held his look and smiled.

'For a few memorable moments, fantasy becomes reality, and the dream becomes real. How do you create that dark fantasy in a world that has banned each one of its elements? You create your own world, a separate place where there are no rules. You create a space where the unacceptable is allowed, where a man can push away the things that hold him back. Where a man can play out his deepest desires in freedom. It is a place, the only place, where a man can ultimately be free. You may call this place freedom.' Laurent winked rakishly. 'We call this place *la salle des jeux.*'

Eberard sat down on the tall bar stool. The revelation of what he was witnessing was slowly dawning on him, and it took his breath away. The concept of freedom from rules, the idea that you could act out as you wished, free from consequence, was suddenly overwhelmingly desirable. It felt close; he felt he could almost taste the absence of sanction, the lack of boundaries. He looked up at Laurent in amazement. 'Do I understand that this is something that you offer ... that this club somehow creates that space?' He stumbled over his words.

'Let me spell it out for you,' Laurent laughed with genuine merriment. 'The real business of this club takes place up here. This is where I earn my money. There is no money in catering for sweaty, oversexed teenagers. That is what takes place downstairs. Up here, the real men, with the real money, enjoy a service unlike any other in the world. Here, with my assistance, the rules of the outside world are stripped away. Religion teaches that we are all sinners – well, all I do is recognise the truth of that statement and take its consequences to a logical conclusion. Here, men of substance, men of powerful character, discerning men, are given free rein to fulfil their desires. This club, the real club, is an exclusive institution that caters for businessmen. Rich businessmen. Unfortunately, it is only the truly wealthy who can afford the luxury.'

Eberard cocked his head towards the door. The sounds had escalated, a swaying moaning that rose and fell, building even as they spoke.

'Well, my client tonight is enjoying the forging of all the sins into a single event. He's chosen his conquest. She's been delivered to him. She's been dominated. And now, the coup de grâce, she'll give up her portrayal of innocent protest and succumb to the base act of copulating. She'll give up her denial and enter into the world of instinct, where men rut like lions and show their appreciation. The final fragment of his desire plays out; can you hear her? She's not whining now. There's no protest.

Listen to her wallow in her defeat.' Even as his host spoke, the moans and shouts from inside the room lifted in tempo and volume, the undeniable shouts of a woman on the verge of climax. Eberard listened, transfixed. He heard no lower tones from the man, only the higher-pitched yelps from his victim. Then she shrieked and there was silence, but for the discernible panting of someone out of breath.

Eberard inhaled deeply. 'He chose her from the crowd below. You brought her to him. He has forced himself on her and ...' He ran out of words and mouthed indiscernible thoughts.

'He chose her, and we delivered her,' Laurent confirmed. 'He dominated her. He raped her. He conquered her. Her denial turned to lust, and the event is perfect; she confirmed his performance. And so innocence was corrupted.' He opened his hands like a preacher. 'I have given him the space to fulfil his fantasy.' Eberard's head was swimming. He tried to focus on what was being said, clenching his hands in an effort to stop the room from lurching in front of him.

Laurent nodded to the bouncer, who opened the door and entered the room. A few moments later, he led the young woman out, wrapped in a blanket. She looked tired and drawn, and avoided looking at Eberard. The young man led her into the room next door, closing the door behind them.

The lounge, the club, the events Eberard had witnessed, everything around him seemed unreal. He heard himself talking, but it seemed as if he had left his own body, as if he was a spectator watching his own strange reactions to a bizarre situation. Sounds seemed blurred and his head felt empty. Nausea bubbled up threateningly.

'So now tell me, Detective,' he heard Laurent say, 'now that I have revealed all to you. Tell me now, with honesty and courage, what are your real desires? When lust has its tight fist on your balls, and your mind is filled with nothing but fragments of tastes and smells, what would really set you free?' Eberard rubbed his palms across the side of his glass nervously. His host laughed and poured them both another generous quantity of whisky. Comrades in arms tonight.

MEDGAR EVERS LULLABY

Bye, bye, my baby, I'll rock you to sleep,
Sing you a sad song, it might make you weep.
Your daddy is dead, and he'll never come back,
And the reason they killed him because he was black.

I'll tell you a story that you ought to know,
It happened in our town a short while ago.
Your daddy was walking alone for some air,
And a man in the bushes was waiting right there.

That man shot your daddy and laughed while he died.
Your daddy lay dying with tears in his eyes.
He cried for the things that a man leaves undone,
And he cried for the dreams that he had for his son.

What will you do, son, when you are a man?
Will you learn to live lonely and hate all you can?
Will you try to be happy and try not to see
That all men are slaves till their brothers are free?

Bye, bye, my baby, I'll rock you to sleep,
Sing you a sad song, it might make you weep.
Your daddy is dead, and he'll never come back,
And the reason they killed him because he was black.

SEVENTEEN

THE rape of Sanna took place among the spiky grasses that surrounded the field of illegal vines. There was a certain inevitability to the event. It had been foreshadowed in much of what had gone before. Sanna had anticipated it, although not consciously, but in her waking dreams and nightmares. It hovered on the periphery, mosquito-like with high-pitched sound but no definition. Her childish form belied the abuse she had suffered as a matter of course over the years of her slave childhood. She met her torment with resignation, with a sigh of breath that spoke of all the hardships and cruelties meted out to slaves across the colonies. Her particular position in the Cape Colony was an ambivalent one: she was the child of Company slaves, weighed down by the responsibilities of obedience and an absence of rights. But she was property without an owner and lacked the one protection that dominium could offer: the self-interest of a proprietor. She was free, but had been clothed only in the vulnerabilities of freedom. She enjoyed none of its strengths and stood defenceless against the vagaries of authority.

One February morning, Sanna left the house at the usual hour. The rising sun glinted on the rocks and sparkled brightly across the water of the dam. Her naked feet still smarted from the day before. She made her way along the rough path, trying to place her soles between the rocks, looking for the softer sand and fallen leaves to tread on. The sharp edges gouged her skin, making her feet curl like snails retreating into their shells. Her hands, once unblemished, were now covered in blisters and calluses, and flaky scars marked her wrists and forearms. Already the sun made the skin on her shoulders and arms prickle uncomfortably. The ground was still too cool for puffadders and berg adders, but silver-grey skinks and blue and green lizards positioned themselves in the sun's rays. Small rodents crossed her path from time to time, scuttling into the grasses at her approach, and a baboon barked, high up on the face of the mountain. Sanna was surprised to hear its sound; parties of men had scoured the valley and mountain slopes on foot and horseback, killing any form of wildlife that was large enough to eat or intrusive enough to damage the new crops.

She had watched the militiamen open their sacks on the village square, bundling the soft brown corpses out into the dust – small duikers, grey buck, baboons, mongooses, all bleeding in a pile. Her mother had bartered some duck eggs for a small buck, and Sanna had sat in the kitchen and stroked the smooth head, its wide eyes still open, tearless. The militiamen sometimes brought back lion, caracal hyena and larger buck. But soon the larger animals disappeared, shot and killed where they foraged, or driven out of the valley by gunfire and human habitation. Baboons were the biggest threat to the crops, and their troops were hunted mercilessly by the Company men. Sanna stopped and looked up at the mountain, hoping to catch sight of the animal, but it made no further sound.

Renosterbos and fynbos merged along the edges of the fields; small protea trees and restios carpeted the ground, sweeping up to the higher slopes, where bushy ericas and lone mountain cypress trees stood against the grey sheet of rocks leading up to the peaks. Sanna longed to be high up on the mountain, sitting on a jutting ledge and looking down on the fields. The workers would seem like ants, the village like an untidy collection of half-built houses, like a child's wooden blocks scattered across the veld. High above the valley, she would be untouchable. A sunbird twittered past her, its wings and head shining with a brilliant green in the sunshine. It plunged its curved beak into the slender flowers of the erica, sucking up the nectar, its wings beating swiftly. Bees droned noisily among the bright flowers.

She started up the hill again until she came to the field above the tiers. One of the new vines had been torn out of the ground by a passing horse, the soil around the broken stump disturbed by heavy hoof marks. The vine had snapped at its base, and the roots had been stripped by the ground as they pulled out. Sanna tossed the vine into the grasses, watching it circle in the air before bouncing on the hard earth. She dug a fresh hole in the ground, ready for the next vine. The sun beat down on her as she worked. Her day had just begun, but already the gnats circled around her tired eyes.

Sanna was working back in the field of illegal vines, attacking the hard ground with her stick, when she felt movement behind her. She turned to find him standing above her, dismounted already. She knew in that instant what was to happen.

It seemed something of an inevitability to her attacker as well; he did not initiate his violation with great passion or aggression. He seemed distracted, his eyes unfocused and his teeth blackened from too much of the narcotic *sirih*. It almost seemed to be an obligation, a duty to assert his will and his authority.

The sun scorched her face as she lay on her back, his sour breath and rough beard scraping her cheeks. He thrust into her like an animal, pushing at her as if he expected her to respond. She lay passively, whimpering but not trying to fight him. She knew that protest would only result in a beating and so lay still, as if in a faint, or dead. His weight pushed her spine into the stones, bruising her shoulder blades and the small of her back. He made no effort to take any of his weight on his hands or arms, and rested his bulk on her body completely, rocking back and forth. The stony ground left long weals on her back and thigh and an open wound on her buttocks, which Jakoba would need to dress daily for a week. She looked up into the sky, away from his sweating brow, forcing her eyes back until no part of his face intruded upon her vision. High up above her, some swallows were flying in tight circles, diving down, suddenly changing course.

He grunted loudly and pushed up into her, holding still, his eyes also averted from her face. Then he climbed off her, pushing his hand roughly onto her thigh for balance. She felt the sharp puncture of a stick beneath her. Pain and nausea flowed back, enveloping her, and an acute burning sensation stung between her legs. She briefly caught sight of his member, short and thick, glistening with moisture like a dark slug, before he pulled his trousers up and turned away. Something wet – from him? her blood? – trickled down the inside of her leg. She pushed her skirt between her legs.

Van der Keesel rummaged in his saddle bag and sat down heavily in the dappled shade of a protea bush. He filled his pipe, ignoring her presence. Sanna pushed the fabric of her dress further over her legs and sat up. She wrapped her arms tightly around her knees, pulling them into herself, trying to contain the pain that spread up towards her midriff. She stared at him as he stuffed the coarse tobacco into the pipe.

'Why did you do that?' she asked, her voice quivering slightly.

He seemed taken aback as much by the question as by her presence. 'Do not trifle with me, girl,' he replied in irritation, scowling at the dust and stones. But he did not look at her and she sensed an uneasiness in his manner.

'Why did you do that?' she asked again, still staring at him. This time her voice had no quiver; it sounded tired and emotionless.

Now he turned to stare at her, as if seeing her for the first time. The repetition of the question seemed childlike, but her tone was more disinterested than inquisitive. He watched her warily.

'In this world, child, some questions should be asked in expectation of an answer. Some questions should be answered. Some questions have no answers. But some questions should not be asked at all, because it is not your place to ask them. Do not ask me, your master, why I choose to do what I do. The question is irrelevant. It is impudent to ask the question at all. So quiet your mouth, girl, and be thankful that you have not raised my anger once more.' Satisfied with his answer, he turned his attention once again to his pipe. He cleared his throat, spitting a glutinous red mound across the pebbles between his legs.

Sanna blinked slowly, as if she was slightly dazed. There was an edge of defiance to her tone when she spoke again. 'No, Master van der Keesel. It is a question that should be asked and should be answered. In my world, where you have now trespassed, it's a question that needs an answer.' She paused, holding his gaze without turning. 'Why did you do that?'

The viticulturist leapt to his feet in anger. He kicked out at her, spraying dirt and small stones over her. He pointed his finger at her, shaking but silent. She watched him without fear. Then Sanna stood up, knocking the dirt from her dress.

'I am not afraid of you, Master van der Keesel. You are like a man who has fired the shot from his musket, but the ball has missed its mark. Perhaps I am wounded; perhaps you have hurt me somewhere deep inside; but I am still here. You have nothing left to fight me with. The only weapon you had has been used. What can you do now, Master van der Keesel? Strike me? Have me whipped? Have me hanged? Do you think that these will make me fear you now?'

Van der Keesel stood dumbfounded.

'You have all the power in the world, Master van der Keesel,' she went on, 'but only if I fear you. When I stop fearing you, then your power is no more. It dries up faster than the water in that sack you make me carry for the vines. It disappears into the air. It is gone. You think that doing that' – Sanna gestured to the ground where her youth had been broken – 'you think that doing what you did will give you more power. But you're wrong. When you forced yourself on top of me, you gave your power up. You spat it out onto the ground. You have no more authority, Master van der Keesel. I won't work your field. I won't dig up these vines. I won't plant them by the stones next to the dam. I won't wet their roots. I will do no more work for you. And I'm not afraid.'

Sanna did not wait for his response, but turned away from him, leaving him standing alone among the bushes. She walked into the field, hobbling slightly. She seemed in that moment far older, yet more threatening for her lack of youth. Van der Keesel swore at her retreating figure, but it felt no more satisfying than throwing a stone into the empty blue sky.

LOVER'S LULLABY

Lay down now and slumber
Mama's boy is torn asunder
All the fields have gone grey
All the leaves are gone brown

Lay down and don't you wake 'til morning
Close your eyes and helpless through the night
Lay down and dream of love and glory
This is a lover's lullaby

Softly now, close your eyes
Lightly will you fade
The moon was made for wakeful boys
To keep the night away.

EIGHTEEN

Professor du Preez's tone towards Constable Nduku during the short interview was disdainful. Xoliswa could not decide whether the unexpected change was the result of the news that charges had been withdrawn, or because he regarded her as inferior and less worthy of the respect he afforded Eberard. She had read that people in mourning can experience periods of intense anger, often displaced towards those unconnected to the cause of their suffering. Perhaps his manner was a manifestation of his deep-seated grief. But, whatever the reason, his condescension towards her was obvious and offensive. By the end of the short visit, she was glowering at him with ill-disguised loathing.

She had called on the professor at his home to advise him personally of the withdrawal of charges against him. She wanted to be sure that he understood that the withdrawal was temporary and that the authorities could reinstate the charges at any time. It was late in the afternoon, and Du Preez seemed surprised, and less than happy to see her, when he opened the front door. He ushered her into his study unceremoniously, and Xoliswa was again struck by the extensive library and collection of Afrikaner memorabilia lining the walls and shelves. Because the professor remained standing, she did not take the seat offered to her, although Elsabe sat in the easy chair in the corner. The girl looked tired, and fretted with a loose thread on her jersey. The professor walked around his leather-topped desk, placing the dark-wooded piece between himself and the constable. He surveyed her, with his arms folded, before raising his eyebrows impatiently in a gesture for her to begin.

The interview was intended to be a public relations visit, but, faced with Du Preez's arrogance, Xoliswa's own stance towards him changed. He made her feel as if she was being tolerated, rather like a slow child who was endeavouring to state the obvious. He smiled thinly at her, placing his hands together in mock concentration. A tall, thin-stemmed glass of ruby-coloured wine rested on the desk at his side. He lifted it and breathed in the wine's bouquet, before taking a generous gulp. He placed the glass back on the desk carefully, and stopped the constable before she could finish her brief explanation of the withdrawal.

'Quite frankly,' he interjected, 'the police conduct in this matter has been nothing short of inept.' His teeth were stained from the wine, giving him a demonic expression. 'Do I need to explain the meaning of the word, young lady? "Inept", meaning unprofessional or incompetent. There were no statements from witnesses. People who might have seen that bastard with my daughter weren't found. The DNA results took far too long. I mean, if this investigation had been left up to the Stellenbosch police, God knows where we'd be.'

'Sir, police work involves a lot of paperwork,' Xoliswa responded, with a hint of sarcasm. 'In the present case, the delays are understandable, given that two people were murdered within days of one another.' Du Preez's face flushed at her use of the word 'murder'. Elsabe sniffed loudly, reminding her father of her presence. He turned to her and dismissed her with a wave of his hand. She slunk out of the room, looking tearful.

Du Preez's confrontational attitude made Xoliswa defensive, and she found herself emphasising the temporary nature of the withdrawal. 'You need to understand, Professor, that this decision was made by the Attorney-General, not by us. Not by the police, not by Detective Februarie.' The word 'friends' played on her tongue, threatening to slip out into the open. She stopped herself from saying anything more.

'I am perfectly aware at what level the decision was taken, my dear,' he retorted acidly. 'Had the decision been taken by you or your detective, I would have been able to take little comfort from it. It's because it was taken at a much higher level that it means anything at all.'

Xoliswa suddenly regretted having made the effort of meeting him. 'Yes, that may be so,' she pressed on, trying to assert her authority. 'But you need to understand that if circumstances change, if more information comes to light, if policy decisions change, then you can still be charged.'

The professor laughed. 'Miss Nduku, the Attorney-General's office has all the information it could ever possibly hope to receive. *Hulle weet* ... they know who was killed, they know where and how he was killed and they know who did it. Me. And they've decided not to prosecute. I hardly see them changing their minds. Do you?' Xoliswa was about to interject, threatening him with the contents of the unsigned affidavit, but she held back. 'I've been very restrained until now,' the professor continued. 'I've not thrown my weight around and I've let you lot play around at being detectives. But I do have substantial weight to exert, I assure you, and I have grown tired of watching your ... your antics. I come from old Afrikaner stock, and before that French Huguenot stock; my forefathers built up this country to what it is today – or should I say what it was in its heyday.' The professor walked towards Xoliswa, making his way around the desk without taking his eyes off her, burning. The tall glass was cupped in his palms, the wine swilling back and forth.

'We're surrounded by the symbols of that history, Miss Nduku. The wealth of minerals, the history of wars fought and land lost, the development of culture and learning, the taming of the land and its people. My people are committed to protecting this heritage, and so they should. There are challenges and dangers at every turn. And so, with that commitment in my heart, what should I do when some outsider, a heathen, an intruder in my land, my country, stalks across my life and takes that which is most precious to me? Do you think that I'll just sit back and accept it? No, Miss Nduku, no.' Du Preez placed the wine glass on the table and took a step towards her. 'I come from a breed of proud men who are prepared to fight to protect their families and their heritage. And men like me understand that. So, thank you for your little visit. It wasn't necessary. As you can see, I'm well aware of my position and I don't need your assistance, however well meaning. So, if that is all you came to say, thank you and let me show you out.'

Xoliswa chose not to respond to the professor's diatribe. By the end of his speech, he was standing directly in front of her, breathing hard. The subliminal threat in his words was underscored by a lack of respect for her personal space. She felt deeply disturbed, not only by what he had said but also by the flash of irrationality she had seen in him. He seemed subtly unhinged, as if his internal fight to maintain control was wavering. Xoliswa stepped out into the clear sunlight with relief. Large oak trees cast welcome shade across the broad driveway. A slight figure was waiting outside, slouched against the side of the police car. Du Preez escorted her across the driveway to the vehicle.

'For God's sake, Elsabe, why are you loitering around the car? She'll think you want to steal it or something. *Gaan binne in die huis, meisiekind,*' he scolded her. '*Ek sal later met jou praat. Weg is jy!*' Xoliswa tried to catch the girl's eye, but Elsabe ran off too quickly. The constable started the car and drove off without bidding the professor farewell, pensively drumming her fingers on the steering wheel.

When Xoliswa returned to the office, she tried to explain the nuances of the meeting to Eberard. He pretended to listen to her, but his eyes were glazed and his breath smelt of alcohol and stale cigarettes. His body slumped forward and his eyes rolled. He looked as if he was still intoxicated, and Xoliswa shook her head in annoyance. She was aware of his drinking; it had been getting worse during the course of the investigation. On several occasions he had arrived late, and more often than not she would smell alcohol on his breath. Eventually, Xoliswa gave up and walked to the door, half-expecting him to call her back and apologise. She turned in time to see his head slide listlessly onto the desk; his right eyebrow pushed against the wood, skewing his face and making him look demented. She closed the plywood door, pulling on the handle and slamming the boards into their frame. The resultant bang was unsatisfying, and she strode down the passage in frustration.

An hour later, Xoliswa returned to the office, black coffee and filterless cigarettes in hand. Eberard was sitting up in his chair, rubbing the red indentation on the side of his face. A dark patch of drool marked the desk where he had fallen asleep. He mouthed a silent apology and accepted the coffee gratefully. It had a thin, burnt taste, like boiled acorns or badly made *moer koffie*. Xoliswa pulled up a chair in front of the desk, the bare metal legs dragging noisily on the floor. The yellowed stuffing pushed out from the holes in the faded and dirty-blue fabric of the cushion.

'You're destroying your career,' she said straightforwardly. 'Whatever you've managed to build up – and it must be something, because they gave you this case – you're destroying it with booze and stupidity. You may be my superior officer, but you're messing things up. And I don't want to be dragged down by you.' A wave of anger passed across Eberard's face, but his partner was undeterred. 'My career is just beginning. When I've finished my degree, I want to enter the force. I have plans about transforming it, about contributing to something more important than my own needs. There are things that need to be done.' Xoliswa looked around the room as though she expected to begin cleaning it. 'I don't know what has happened in your life, Eberard.' It was the first time she had used his first name. It felt out of place in the confines of his office, and yet strangely affectionate, despite her angry tone. 'But I won't allow some drunk to mess that up for me. I won't let that happen.' She kept eye contact with him until he looked away.

'So what do you want?' He tried to sound cutting and cynical, but he came across as petulant instead. She eyed him distrustfully.

'Either you commit yourself to making this investigation into something worthwhile ... you be professional, or you cut me loose and let me carry on elsewhere. I'll probably ask for a transfer from the station anyway. It's your decision. Make no mistake, I'd like to work with an experienced detective like you. But I'm not prepared to become a victim of your personal crisis.'

'What fucking investigation?' Eberard raised his voice. 'The Du Preez girl was raped and murdered by the Burundian bastard. The Burundian bastard was killed by the Du Preez girl's racist father. My killer has been killed. The killer of my killer has been set free. The father has wangled some kind of indemnity – God knows how – from the DPP's office. My files are closed and, for the rest, I'm free to do what I like!' He shouted the last few words aggressively, feeling close to tears. The confrontation angered and frightened him.

'Your investigation is not over.' Xoliswa was unmoved. 'You're hiding behind racist assumptions to avoid doing your job properly. There's every chance that Melanie's killer is still out there. Wilder's still not in the clear in my books. She had other suitors who might have felt aggrieved. There are plenty of gangsters around town, cruising the streets and looking for easy prey. The DNA test has given you a convenient reason to close your file and soothe your misgivings and guilt in booze. You know as well as I do that we had no case against the Burundian – not yet, anyway. And until you can look me in the eyes and tell me that he was the only possible killer, until then, your investigation is not over.'

Eberard felt cornered behind his desk, trying to distinguish between depression and fatigue, but the one flowed into the other. There seemed no way to fight the lack of motivation: alcohol, medication, depression, a wall of exhaustion. He wanted to explode with anger at his junior officer, but he could not muster the energy. And in his heart he knew she was right. His last visit to the club had raised many new possibilities. But there were also fears that he found difficult to articulate. He stared at his partner, but felt unable to confide in her.

'Are we working together, or am I asking for a transfer?' Xoliswa asked, finally breaking the silence. Eberard sighed and nodded his head. 'What?' she asked, irritated. 'Say it.'

He felt like a child being chastised at school. 'Yes, okay. You're right,' he said, smiling, despite his depression. 'Yes, we're going to work together and make sure that the Burundian was the one. Are you satisfied with that?' He looked up at her and was surprised to see her smiling back, triumphantly. 'And now will you please leave me and my hangover alone?'

'Well, Detective Inspector,' she said, emphasising his title grandly, 'in that case, perhaps you should take a closer look at this.' She pushed a handwritten statement across the desk towards him. It was the statement of Constable de Bruin, the officer who had searched the Burundian's room. The writing was dense and deliberate, the naive handwriting of an ill-educated police officer. Eberard had read it before. He shrugged his shoulders.

'Look at paragraph six; look at the wording of that paragraph,' Xoliswa said boldly. 'Read it carefully,' she added. Eberard felt a twinge of irritation, but said nothing. He read the short paragraph slowly.

> I found a mans clothing and property by the bed. I found one womans earing by the table next to the bed. It was shape of half moon and silver in color. I placed earing in a plastic bag. On my return to the station it was put into the register under 13/223. I was then told that the earing was identified by Mr. Du Prez as belonging to daughter, the deceased.

'Well, apart from no grammar, bad spelling and getting Professor du Preez's name and title wrong, what's the point?'

'What does he mean "by the table next to the bed"?' Xoliswa asked. 'We took it to mean on the floor somewhere around the side table. But it could mean *on* the table, couldn't it? It's just bad English.' She paused, watching Eberard's reactions. He frowned at her impatiently. 'Okay, so I asked De Bruin,' she confessed. 'He told me that he found the earring on the side table, next to some magazines and an alarm clock.'

It took them ten minutes to reach the industrial area. When they pulled up outside the back of the warehouse, the street was empty. A heavy haze of diesel fumes from the neighbouring industries polluted the air. The gutters smelt of urine. It seemed a world away from the excitement of the club. Two pied crows cawed loudly, picking at something stuck to the tarred road. The door to the passage leading to Bullet's room was unlocked, and they walked quickly down to the last room. Someone had nailed a small posy of veld flowers to the door. Eberard felt a pang of disquiet. The door was closed but not locked, and it opened into the room where he had arrested Bullet a week before. It seemed a long time ago now.

The room had been turned upside down in the search; the officers had broken furniture and left piles of clothes and books lying in the middle of the room. The mattress had been cut open and handfuls of grey stuffing hung out in thick ugly bulges. The bedside table remained in position, a small pile of magazines resting on one side. The alarm clock had been smashed open on the floor, its wires and display hanging out like a crushed rodent.

Eberard dropped to his knees and started running his hand under the bed. His fingers felt along the wooden skirting. There was a small gap between the roughly lain floor and the skirting and walls. The gap widened as he ran his index finger away from the bed and under the table. He sat on his haunches and pulled the table back from the wall. A glint of silver immediately caught his eye. He pulled on a hook of wire, and the small silver half-moon earring emerged from beneath the skirting board.

Xoliswa sat down on the bed. He tossed the earring to her. It landed with a light plop on the dishevelled sheets. She picked it up and rubbed the face of the half-moon with her fingers, staring at it in her hands for a while.

'She removed both her earrings herself, didn't she?' the constable asked rhetorically.

LULLABY

Under the cover,
Knees to my nose—
The wind huffs like my mother's breath
Outside the womb.
Chest heaving,
Limbs askew
I squeeze like the hunter's prey
In a hole too small.

NINETEEN

L AURENT sat alone in his office in the upstairs lounge. The fan in the laptop computer hummed quietly; the screen slowly scrolled down as he pushed his finger against the mouse. One of his feet rested, sidelong, on the desk, and a tall glass of vodka and lime juice, filled with crushed ice and slices of lemon, stood half-drunk at his elbow. Music from a Congolese band poured out from the sound system, mournful lyrics about the hardships of a people caught up in war and poverty.

Pourquoi les habitants d'Afrique doivent-ils souffrir autant?
Pourquoi la vie au paradis doit-elle être si difficile?

Why must life in paradise be so hard, Laurent mused. He scrolled down further, murmuring as he read. The news from Rutshuru was still not good. The refugee camps had fanned out across the countryside; the camps were like hungry holes, sucking in the local people, destroying their land and polluting the rivers. Even those villages that were able to sustain themselves eventually succumbed to the promises of handouts and protection. The villagers had no reason to believe that they were at risk, but the pervasive aid propaganda, the flood of people moving across the land towards the camps, created an unsettling fear that slowly pulled at them, like the incessant tugging of a child. Stories of tragedies abounded: villages destroyed by foreigners, mysterious plagues, aid workers. The elders were insecure, not wishing to lead their communities back into devastation. Eventually, the livestock was untethered, the crops collected, and people made their way to the camps – their animals disappeared into a swirling mass of famine, their crops finished within a day. Fields lay wasted and pathways grew closed. The villages lay open, their people already dependent on the trucks of water and grain.

Laurent's brothers had fled south and were trying to establish themselves again. The refugee agencies were tired of the relentless political intransigence; the politicians were tired of the continual incursions from the camps in Rwanda and Uganda. The United Nations peacekeepers had been moved further north to cope with rebel insurgents, and the camps were at the mercy of bandits. His beautiful town was falling apart. His school had closed, his students scattered. His land was being eaten by parasites. Soon, only the external shell would remain. The forests would collapse, the balance between people and nature overturned.

'*Pourquoi la vie au paradis doit-elle être si difficile?*' the singer pleaded. Laurent shook his head sadly.

His melancholy was disturbed by his manager, who opened the door without knocking. Laurent looked up angrily, but before he could shout at him, the man blurted out, 'There's trouble downstairs.'

Laurent swung his foot off the desk and cleared the screen on the laptop. He walked swiftly down the stairs and out into the club. The music had stopped and the general lights were turned on, making the space seem inappropriately still. The light destroyed the ultraviolet effects on the walls, showing up the drab paint, and spilt drinks reflected in puddles on the floor. The middle of the dance area had cleared, the dancers standing around in a circle. In the centre, the bulky doorman was holding a man down on the floor, roughly pushing his arms behind his back. The man writhed like a lizard in an attempt to break free. A young teenage girl stood beside them, crying, and being comforted by one of the barmaids.

Laurent approached the two men. The doorman grabbed hold of the struggling man's chin and turned his face into the light. Laurent could see that Eberard was very drunk; the policeman's eyes rolled wildly and his face was wet with sweat.

'Take him upstairs,' Laurent said coldly. 'And get the lights off and the music back on.' Then he turned to the barmaid. 'What happened?' The young woman in her arms sniffed and blew her nose on a paper napkin.

'That guy made some kind of move on her,' the barmaid said. 'I didn't see anything, so I don't really know.'

The young girl turned to Laurent, her eyes red and puffy. 'He started dancing with me,' she whined. 'I saw him earlier, watching me, like a real creep.' Her hair was matted with cold sweat against her forehead, and Laurent felt a wave of distaste. His face remained expressionless. 'Then he came onto the floor and tried to dance with me. He was drunk. He tried to touch me, trying to hold my waist. I brushed him off and went to dance on the other side. He just followed me. Then he grabbed my breast. I screamed at him to fuck off and leave me alone.' Tears started to run down her face again. Her nose was running too. Laurent's eyes bore into her unrelentingly. 'He said ... he said he was a friend of the owner of the club.' She looked at Laurent uncertainly, but he nodded for her to continue. 'He said that if he chose me, then he could have me. He said that he could do anything he wanted to me. He said ... some really disgusting things. Then he tried to grab me again and I started screaming and hitting him. Then the man from the front door came and helped me.'

Laurent took out his own cotton handkerchief and handed it to her. She looked up at him, surprised, and smiled nervously. He did not smile back.

'I'll deal with him,' he said firmly. 'He's very drunk and obviously doesn't know what he's talking about. You go with this lady; she'll clean you up, and after that you can have drinks on the house for the rest of the night. If you have any more problems, you let this lady know. All right?' The girl nodded and turned away. He watched her being escorted to the toilets at the back of the club. The music started up, and the white lights suddenly dimmed, the mural figures leaping out from the walls under the ultraviolet. He stood for a moment, watching the dancers thread back onto the floor. The scene was so far removed from his thoughts of home. One of his waitresses passed him with a small tray of clear shooters. He raised his eyebrows at her enquiringly.

'Tequila,' she responded. He took one and downed it without relish.

When he returned to the upstairs room, Eberard was prostrate on the long couch, groaning. Laurent laughed mercilessly when he saw him.

'You fucking idiot. You are the stupidest man that ever lived.

Do you know that? I've never met anyone stupider than you. And I've never met anyone who allows his own life to be so dictated to ... and destroyed ... by his own prejudice.'

'What are you talking about?' Eberard moaned. His head swirled and he felt nauseous. His body ached as if he had been beaten, but he could not remember anyone hitting him. He closed his eyes, but the darkness rushed in at him like a wild animal. He opened them again with a start.

'What's the colour of evil? The colour of all that's forbidden? It's the colour of night, and darkness. Isn't that right, Inspector Detective?' Laurent did not wait for a reply. 'Your life and your reactions to people are ruled by your noble belief that white is rational and predictable while black is unknowable and untame-able.' Eberard was too drunk to argue. Laurent chuckled throatily to himself and walked across to the bar. 'What an arsehole you are,' he said. He poured himself a whisky and purposefully twisted the cap closed without offering Eberard any. '*Imbécile*. You think that you've entered some voodoo world, a world of black magic where the normal principles for white people are suspended. You think that businessmen can come down here into our dark world and behave like animals, like us, and then leave and return to their civilised homes.'

'But that's what you told me,' Eberard managed to blurt out in protest.

'Bullshit! *Crétin!*' Laurent turned around angrily. 'I told you that I offer the elite an opportunity to fulfil their fantasies and desires. It's an exclusive service that I offer. Do you think that this is actually how I live my life? Do you think that when I go back to my home town, I can grab any woman off the street and rape her and cast her aside? Is that how you imagine my society works? Of course you do, otherwise you wouldn't behave like such an idiot!' Eberard tried to sit upright, but slumped back down against the back of the couch.

'I'm embarrassed for you. I really am. You're an embarrass-ment to your gender and your bastard race. I can feel my toes curling backwards just thinking about how stupid you are. God, what an idiot!'

Eberard pulled himself upright in anger. 'Stop insulting me! I don't know what the hell you're talking about. Either tell me what you're on about or leave me alone!' He sounded like a petulant schoolchild.

'Okay, okay, since you're too foolish to understand, I'll spell it out for you. It seems that you believe that you can walk into my club – my house – and choose any young girl from the dance floor. You think that because this is my club, run by foreigners, you can choose this girl and bring her up here and rape her. Then you can walk out and somehow, miraculously, it'll all be taken care of for you.' Laurent clicked his fingers to illustrate his point. Eberard eyed him warily. 'I told you that I offer a service,' Laurent continued. 'Men come here to play out their fantasies and I help them. I have a group of hand-picked girls. My clients choose their favourite from the list of possibilities. They tell me their fantasy. The simulation is put in place and choreographed by me and my staff. The chosen woman performs for him on the dance floor. He pretends to choose her afresh. She's lured off the floor and brought upstairs. Here she's subdued and subjected to my client's chosen whims. It is a dance. It's a game. My clients are successful businessmen, professionals, judges, people who are used to being in control. Dominance sex is the usual request. The rules are clear, though: simulated violence only; no accessories – whips, sticks, none of those.' Eberard covered his face with his hands as the truth began to sink in. The women – well some of them – were Laurent's workers, his elite staff. And they were trained – was it possible? – in the art of simulation: simulated protest and submission; simulated anger and interest.

'The best simulated climax you've ever heard,' Laurent explained. 'I offer the oldest service in the world, my friend. All I do is tailor the play to the audience.' Eberard thought back to the sounds emanating from the games room three nights ago. Had he been completely duped? Laurent laughed again at the policeman's misery. 'You thought it was the real thing, didn't you? You didn't listen to what I was telling you, not properly, because everything I told you was filtered to fit into your skewed view of the world.'

Laurent watched him quietly for a while. Then he sat down beside him on the couch, holding the glass of whisky within Eberard's reach. 'Do you know that there are over two hundred languages in Congo-Zaire, my friend?' Eberard looked at him blankly, still trying to make sense of his blunder. 'That's a lot of speaking, *non*? But in the north-east of the Kivu province lies the Ituri Forest. There you'll find the Mbuti pygmy women. They wear ritual *murumba* – painted cloth made from bark. They'll tell you that when everyone has stopped talking, there's silence.' Laurent paused, closed his eyes and held up his hand dramatically. 'But for them, silence is not a lack of sound, because the trees and the land will still be talking to them. Silence is the absence of noise, the end of disruption and disharmony. Quiet – *ekimi* – is the presence of harmony. You need to stop talking. You need to be quiet and listen, my friend. *Ekimi.*'

Laurent considered his statement and repeated it softly to himself before continuing. 'It is tragic, don't you think, that our supposedly boundless capacity for new thought should be so restricted by useless boundaries we have learned? Look how it's hampered you in your own work. You can't view any facts clearly. And your beliefs caused you to reach three conclusions, each one more bizarre than the next.

'First, you decided that my man, my friend – Bullet – raped and killed the Du Preez girl. Then – and I saw it in your eyes when we spoke, so don't deny it – you decided that the dead girl must have been "chosen" at this club. That somehow her death was tied up with the service that I offered here. And thirdly, and it's the worst for you, my friend, the policeman, you decided – yes, you were drunk – but you still came to the conclusion that you could come into my club and that I'd help you force yourself onto any woman you chose. I told you, when I first met you, that you were looking in the wrong places. Rather than listen to what I was saying, you buried your head even deeper in the trough, ignoring any real evidence. You followed that track until you ran into the bank on the other side. And now you find that you have nowhere else to look.' Eberard still could not react.

'Your head was filled with noise, the pounding noise of society.' Laurent tapped the side of his temple. 'How could you think? *Ekimi* – quietness, without that you cannot have a clear thought. You should try it sometime, Detective. Especially if the thoughts you have end up with one person being killed and the killer being set free.'

Eberard took the glass out of his host's hand and downed its contents. He wiped his mouth with the back of his hand and looked at Laurent with heavy-lidded eyes. 'I have been an idiot, you're right. I'll leave and I won't bother you again. My days in the police force are over. Not because of tonight. I've had enough of the boredom, enough of all the crap of my job, enough of myself.' He rallied slightly. 'I just want you to know that I did look elsewhere. I told you that we found an earring in Bullet's room ... well, I went back and found the other one. She took her earrings off and placed them next to the bed. The one must have been knocked off and fallen behind the table. That's why we didn't find it. You may have been right. I don't know. But I did look.'

'Of course I'm right.' Laurent did not intend relenting. 'You tell me that the DNA test proves that Bullet and Melanie du Preez had sex before she died. There's no witness to this event, but your science tells you that what you want to be, is. Let us suppose that your science is not subject to the same prejudice. Let us just suppose that, and it is a big assumption, my friend. So then you tell me that this result shows that she was raped by him. But there's no logic in that. If Bullet had sex with that girl, then it was because they both wanted to. If you'd asked the right questions, if you'd bothered, you would've found out that any sex between clients and my staff takes place with a condom. It's one of the unbreakable rules, and it's respected by both sides. If you had asked, you would've realised that, if your victim had been chosen by one of my clients, there would've been no trace of semen. But you didn't ask, because the question never occurred to you.'

Eberard didn't understand. If their sex had been consensual, did that mean that she, Melanie du Preez, had actually had a relationship with him, the Burundian? 'Was this just a one-night thing?' he asked, shaking his head. 'Don't tell me for the investigation, just tell me what you know for myself, so that I can ...' His voice trailed off weakly.

'There's only one person who can answer that question for you. I don't believe that you're ready to meet her, not in your present state anyway, but your ridiculous antics tonight leave me with little choice. The time has come for me to introduce you to Clementine, and then you must leave my club and not return. Do you understand that?' Eberard nodded uncertainly. 'I don't want you back here. Ever.'

Eberard tried to stand up, but his feet slipped out from underneath him. He fell back onto the couch and watched as his host walked across to the right-hand door, knocking gently. A voice beckoned from within. Laurent opened the door and stepped into the room. Eberard heard a soft conversation in French. 'She'll be with us shortly,' Laurent announced as he closed the door again.

'She was in the room all the time?' Eberard asked incredulously. Laurent raised his finger to his lips and smiled.

'Perhaps, as a final favour, I can give you a last drink. If you kill yourself when you drive away from here, it's not on my conscience. *La vie au paradis doit-elle être si difficile.*'

Laurent smiled to himself as he poured a large quantity of amber whisky over ice. He brought the drink to Eberard, but remained standing. The door to the bedroom opened, and a tall black woman, her hair bunched on her head in a high bun, walked into the lounge. Eberard had not seen her before. She was completely naked, save for a series of thick gold bracelets around both wrists and ankles. She was carrying a plastic folder delicately in front of her. Eberard was captivated by her grace. She moved fluidly, her breasts flat against her chest, her long legs stretching out in front of her. She was both utterly feminine and wholly androgynous. He lifted himself up on one hand, but she was looming above him before he could stand.

The woman bent forward, her dark eyes searing into Eberard's. Her muscular body stretched endlessly towards him, and Eberard noticed the taut muscles in her arms as she placed the folder in his lap. His eyes were drawn to her face, and her lips broke into a sardonic smile. She held his gaze for a moment, then turned and walked gracefully away from him, a smile still pulling at her lips. Her feet padded luxuriously across the carpet. Eberard watched, transfixed, as she closed the door behind her with a gentle click. He turned to Laurent, who was leaning against the bar, chuckling. His host nodded his head towards the folder, gesturing for Eberard to look down.

Eberard placed the folder in front of him on the table and opened it. The pictures took his breath away: the figure was erotic and suggestive, yet innocent at the same time. In all the pictures, the subject was looking directly into the camera, eyes wide open and alluring. In one picture, she was kneeling in a crawling position on a concrete floor, her belly stretching out of focus between her taut breasts. In another, she was arched backwards, staring upside down out of the page, her slim body extended. In another photo, she sat on a rough wooden chair, her elbows on her knees, staring and laughing, enticing. She was half-dressed or naked in all of the images, presenting her body to the viewer without emphasising any particular aspect.

It was a powerful advertisement, more subtle than simple pornography. She did not touch herself; she did not push any part of her body forward for the viewer's delectation. It was as if the viewer was irrelevant to her, as if she was caught unawares, innocently but seductively at play. Except for her eyes: they bore into the viewer with a ferociousness that was startling. They seemed hungry and predatory, giving the photographs an uneasy and captivating edge.

Eberard looked up at Laurent in confused surprise.

'I introduce you to Clementine,' the Congolese man said dramatically, his arms extended and his eyes wide. 'Physically adventurous beyond any fantasy. Young, pretty, sexual. Rebellious and tough. A penchant for strong black men. Speaks passable French. The mistress of the games room. The most requested employee of Laurent Kitsire's exclusive club. His most valuable possession. His most highly paid madame. And the terror of Bullet's poor heart.'

The young girl's eyes seemed to follow Eberard as he moved the page, daring him, admonishing him. Melanie du Preez – as he could never have imagined her – pouted seductively up at him.

'And now perhaps, Inspector, the doors of your perception have been opened just a little more, *non*?'

COLDSLEEP LULLABY

Sleep, my darling, sleep
Say good-bye to Mother Earth
No more tears to weep
As we leave the planet of our birth

Sleep, beloved, sleep
Say your prayers then close your eyes
We've promises to keep
Brand new lives to build beneath new skies

   We've shed the dust of Terra – broken free
   Enclosed ourselves in ice to sleep the years
   And when we rise our eyes will finally see
   A new dawn shining bright through all our fears

So sleep, my darling, sleep
Years will pass before we wake
We ride upon the deep
Our star-born legacy to finally take

   This parting of the ways was long ordained
   We know not where we'll end up or how far
   But no regrets, no cares, will bar our way
   As we spread ourselves like dust throughout the stars

So sleep, my darling, sleep
Say good-bye to Mother Earth
No more tears to weep

TWENTY

SANNA kept her word and did not return to work in the sun-baked fields. Each morning, she kissed her father goodbye as he made his way along the dusty track towards the sheds to collect the spades and hoes. And each morning, Frederick's eyes locked with those of his daughter, searching anxiously for some sign that her wilfulness had been exhausted. Instead, he saw his wife's determination in Sanna's firm jawline and direct gaze. He would turn from her, his heart heavy with worry, and walk out into the bright sun, muttering soft prayers for his family.

It tore at Sanna to see her father's misery, but she did not waver in her decision. She avoided Van der Keesel's fields, taking care not to walk in the open and keeping off the main paths into the town. She kept to herself, preparing and waiting; she was wary of the man's anger, and she understood that her visible insubordination would invite retaliation. Adult slaves would never have defied their masters in this manner; even inadvertent slackness was met with whipping. Open defiance was akin to revolt. It justified execution. But Sanna was at an age where the rules were still unclear; even men like Van der Keesel recognised that young girls could not be seen to be treated with the same roughness as adult slaves.

However, her unexplained absence from the fields would have been noticed by all the workforce. They would speak of her defiance; the viticulturist would notice the hushed whispers, the way Frederick was being isolated, and the watchful silences of the field-workers as he passed. Van der Keesel had no way of knowing whether Sanna would speak of the events and whether her defiance of him would remain a secret. All he knew was that he would not take the risk of being humiliated by a child.

After a few days of Sanna's absence, Frederick returned from the fields, dirt smeared across his arms, and took his daughter to one side; Van der Keesel had enquired as to her whereabouts, he told her. He urged her to reconsider her position, to go to the viticulturist and promise to return to the fields the next day. Jakoba heard her husband's pleading tone.

'Leave her alone, Frederick,' she interrupted. 'What do you want her to do? If she goes to him, she will no longer be a child. You know what will happen if she goes to him. It will be a sign. Leave it be.' Tears started up in Frederick's eyes, weathered and pinched from years of working in the sun's glare.

'Papa,' Sanna said softly, 'tell him that if he wants to speak to me, he will have to come to me. I will not go to him.' Frederick moaned, but said nothing to contradict her. Jakoba nodded approvingly. 'Tell him, Papa,' Sanna added, 'that if he has something to say to me, he'll find me at the river every afternoon, when I have my swim.'

Jakoba looked up in alarm. 'Sanna, what are you playing at? Don't play games with this man, do you understand? Be strong, stand up for yourself, but don't try to humiliate him. He can still hurt you.'

'I'm not playing games.' She held her mother's gaze, until Jakoba clicked her tongue and turned away. Sanna turned to Frederick; he took her hands in his and rubbed them distractedly. 'Will you give him that message, Papa? Just tell him that I'll be at the river in the afternoon, every afternoon, behind the field where he found the illegal vines. Will you tell him that?'

Frederick nodded his head uncertainly, looking at his wife for assistance. Jakoba shrugged her shoulders and ignored his pleading looks. Sanna turned her father's hands over, wrinkled and dusty like soft leather, and rubbed her fingers across his knuckles.

'You mustn't worry, Papa. He won't hurt me again, I promise.' She smiled at him, willing him to accept her assurances. His eyes were still brimming with tears, but he nodded, more firmly this time. They sat together while the dying sun cast its glow across the veld, and listened to the sounds of the approaching evening. A spotted eagle owl flew noiselessly between the thorn trees, swooping up to land on a waiting bough. Frederick felt Sanna's heartbeat pulsing through her wrists: still a child, for tonight, he thought, perhaps for the last night of her life. He hoped only that when he touched her wrist again, he would still feel the rhythm in her flesh.

The following day, Van der Keesel rode across the dusty field that was to be prepared for the new vines. Frederick, terrified of his master, had conveyed his daughter's message with trepidation to Bakka. He had expected to be abused, perhaps even struck, by the overseer. But Bakka simply looked at him, staring at his face as if searching for something. When Van der Keesel arrived, Bakka turned and walked to the man as he trotted on horseback between the rows of vines.

Van der Keesel's reaction was subdued. He pinched his chin thoughtfully when he heard the news. 'Swimming at the river? I must go to her?' He did not appear to be speaking to Bakka, and the overseer did not answer him. Without saying anything further, he rode off back across the field.

That afternoon, the sun burned down. The river was just deep enough for Sanna to lie flat on her back and submerge beneath the surface. The water was cool and ran swiftly over her body, tugging at her arms and pulling the skin on her bare legs. The end of her simple cotton shirt flapped in the current and clung tightly to her body as her stomach and chest emerged above the water. Small platannas and tadpoles skirted about her as she drifted in the current, motionless like a drowned body.

Sanna heard his horse snort from behind the bushes that obscured the stream from the fields. She pushed herself further upstream with her feet and elbows, surveying the riverbank. Then she let her body settle down onto the stones on the river bed, her eyes closed, her nose above the water line, breathing quietly. A waft of stale tobacco and putrid leather reached her. She could feel his presence watching her. Her fingers stroked the smooth stones on the bottom, feeling their weight. She turned her head slightly and opened her eyes. He was standing in his riding boots, smeared with mud, staring down at her.

'Sit down on the bank,' she said simply, watching him. He stared back, uncertainly; she arched her back slightly, her chest breaking the surface of the water. She saw the lust flare in his eyes. He obeyed and sat down on the slope, leaning back onto his hands.

'Good,' she said, keeping control of the situation. She let herself submerge again, blocking out all sound, and the heavy smell of him. She let her hands drift over her face, smoothing the cloth down against her young breasts, touching her thighs. Her heels pushed against the rocks to stop her being pulled along with the current. She came up for air and sank down again. She came up again, and down, over and over again, each time subtly more suggestive than the last. Then she pushed herself up on her elbows, her torso clear and dripping. She turned to him once more; his left hand was on his groin, his face ruddy and infused. His right hand pushed back into the bank just in front of the tassels of dried grass on the stick that Sanna had stuck into the earth two weeks earlier.

Van der Keesel shifted his weight in an effort to get up, to come to her in the water. His hand brushed past the snake hole and touched against something small and warm, hanging delicately from a thin branch stuck into the soil. He started and sat up. Turning quickly to his right, he saw the half-dead mouse hanging by its tail, twitching. A small drop of bright-red blood was forming at the tip of the rodent's nose, and a dull-yellow incisor protruded from its crushed mouth.

'What's this?' he asked, his voice rising in accusation. The mouse swayed on its noose from the touch of his hand.

'It's just a mouse, Master van der Keesel. It's only a mouse.' Sanna paused, waiting, her eyes focused on the swinging mouse. 'From my kitchen ...' Her voice trailed off innocently.

Van der Keesel looked at her in confusion. He stared back at the mouse and his face darkened. But he could not move; the sleek head of the speckled yellow snake was already out of its hole, within striking distance of his hand. The cobra's head swayed slightly as it watched the mouse, coiling its body behind it in preparation for the strike. Van der Keesel looked back at Sanna in horror. His weight pushed down on his arm, and the muscles in his back burned from the effort of keeping still. The fields were quiet; a locust flew past, its wings thudding through the motionless air. The river gurgled quietly to itself. A hadeda flew overhead, screeching loudly. Neither of them moved.

Then Van der Keesel, straining, looked sideways at the snake. The heel of his boot lost its grip on the bank and he slipped forward. The cobra reared in alarm at the sudden movement, hissing. Van der Keesel tried to hold the swaying mouse still, and his hand clutched at the ground directly in front of the reptile. Sanna watched as the cobra lunged forward and sank its fangs into the man's swarthy arm. Its mouth was wide, pink and black inside. Van der Keesel roared with pain, thrashing out at the snake. This only alarmed the reptile further; it struck out at his flailing arms again, pulled short, and then rose to its full height, hissing and flattening out its hood. Van der Keesel was shouting, in pain or in anger, and clutching his arm. He pulled his boots in underneath him and his body toppled forward, rolling down the bank.

Sanna was still sitting in the water when he plunged in next to her, splashing water over her head. She leapt to her feet and scrambled further downstream.

Van der Keesel stood up unsteadily. 'You brought me here to that snake!' he screamed. 'You knew that snake was there. You murdering whore! I'll have you hanged! I'll have you and your family burned and hanged.' He lurched towards Sanna, intent on strangling her. But his boots were thick, and their soles smeared with mud; he found no grip on the smooth rocks and tumbled forward into the water. He stood up again, blood now mixed with the water running down his face. Sanna kept a safe distance from him, retreating steadily down the river.

'Go and get me help, you slave-whore! Why are you standing there, get me help!'

'No, *Master* van der Keesel' – Sanna stressed the man's title – 'I'm not going to get you help. You've been bitten by an African cobra. You will die in a little while. There's nothing that can help you. The more you try to get away, the faster it will get to your heart and your brain. The poison is inside you now. There's nothing more to be done.'

Van der Keesel stood gaping at her while she spoke. Then he erupted, storming after her like a madman, his fist swinging out uncontrollably. She turned and fled, plunging down the river bed. The water surged around them as they lifted their legs high, trying to avoid hidden potholes and the edges of sharp rocks. His heavy boots smashed down, twisting against the uneven rocks under the water. Sanna's toes wedged between the stones, her feet torn by the pebbles and sticks. Her ankle twisted, causing her to cry out and grab her leg in pain, and he lunged forward and managed to hook his fingers around the bottom of her dress. She pulled forward with all her weight and he stumbled, falling headlong beside her into a shallow pool. Off-balance and with no arm to break his fall, Van der Keesel's head hit a rock just beneath the water. Sanna heard the crack of his skull – a sound of bone giving way; a sound both hard and soft, like an over-boiled egg cracking on the fire.

She stood up and turned, panting and half-weeping. Van der Keesel lay half-submerged in the water, and the pool stained with pink. A red blossom surged around his head, swirling about his ears. He lay still, buoyed by the current, his feet dragging against the rocks. She watched and waited, her chest heaving. Then, in a gesture way beyond her years, she spat at his body.

LULLABY

Shall I stay or go
Through the door
Will the pen to flow
Watch the stars
Sleep's a chore

The moon is growing cold
It hangs like a sliver of tin
How do our dreams unfold
And why are my bones feeling thin

I watch my pen as though
My fingers could shatter like icicles
And before my eyes
Lie glittering and useless on a field of snow

TWENTY-ONE

A fly buzzed noisily against the window. Eberard thought he could hear its bulging eyes banging against the pane. He imagined his own eyes, protruding, knocking heavily against the glass, leaving streaks of tears. The vision disturbed him, and he opened his lids with a shudder. The noise of traffic outside escalated, and he thought he heard shouts in the charge office below. The air in the office was warm and stale. Unsorted statements lay scattered across the desktop and floor – piles of dockets waiting, rotting, for his attention. He stared at them dully, uninterested in the lives and traumas between the brown cardboard folders.

He closed his eyes again, remembering the feeling of raw emotion that had once filled him, overpowering his thoughts. The pain of feeling too acutely could crush you in its tight hand, he thought. The burden of witnessing the horror of daily life had overwhelmed him: children of drug abusers, left unfed and snivelling in their soiled clothes; children who were drug addicts themselves, their eyes hollowed out, escaping into the backs of their skulls; children who were sold to drug abusers, cynical, hardened by a lack of care; people who destroyed their lives; people who were willing to decimate any other life. It was a world without compassion, a world of immediate need and no consequences. Soon, small events jarred and every contact started to leave its mark on him – a hundred faces haunted him at night, and he was washed in the tears of others, suffocating, clawing for space to breathe again. Towards the end, Eberard had stopped being able to separate that world from his relationship with his wife, or from Christine. The barriers crashed down and his life was swamped with abuse. He had become aggressive and fearful, lashing out at those around him. Once, he had thrown a plate at his wife when she had nagged him about some household chore, and, when she'd tried to comfort him because of the ensuing guilt, he had pushed her, hard, against the kitchen sink. His need for escape drove him inexorably, he felt, towards the very source itself: first, he sought the cleansing power of cocaine; then the dulling numbness of crack; and finally the otherworldliness of heroin. But still the pain seeped through the closed doors, tormenting him at every turn. His collapse had been a relief in the end.

Now the feelings had gone, hammered into dust by medication and hours of loneliness and inaction, weeks of staring at the bare windows of the rehabilitation centre. What was left was worse, perhaps – a gnawing barrenness, the absence of feeling. But sometimes he felt a twinge, a stab of real emotion that slipped through the defences. He had felt it in the church, of course, staring at the cold wooden coffin. And he had felt it again that morning, unexpectedly this time. He was walking across Mill Street when he caught sight of Elsabe, walking on her own. He had called out to her and invited her to have a cup of coffee with him.

At first she seemed wary of him, as if she felt their meeting had been planned. She looked out at Eberard from under her fringe and hesitated in her answer. He gestured towards a nearby coffee shop with tables and chairs scattered in the shade of a large oak tree.

'Okay,' she said eventually, a little reluctantly. They walked across the street in silence, and she sat down awkwardly in the metal chair, pulling her dress over her knees. A brown oak leaf drifted down from the branches above them, landing gently on the tablecloth between them. A young waitress took their order. Eberard ordered a filter coffee. Elsabe shook her head at the waitress.

'Please, Elsabe, have something.' Eberard tried to look concerned, fatherly. She stared back at him for a moment and then nodded to the waitress.

'Just an orange juice, please.' In that moment, with her child's body, gangly legs sticking out over the metal rim of the chair, her arms folded insecurely across her chest, her bottom lip protruding, waiting for her juice to come, a wave of familiar pain overwhelmed Eberard. He felt the gaping loss of Christine in his life. Memories of times spent playing with her, chasing her in her grubby dress and leather sandals across the park, the feel of her sticky hands on his neck as he had picked her up. She had had the same pouting expression when she tried to be grown-up, chastising him for something he had done, or had forgotten to do, hiding the little girl underneath.

'What did you want to say to me?' Elsabe broke his thoughts in a thin, wavering voice. Her hands left her chest and started fiddling with a sugar sachet. She kept her eyes down, not looking at him.

'Well, first of all, I wanted to know how you were doing.' He paused, waiting for her to respond. She sat sullenly, picking at the corners of the sachet. Eberard let out a small sigh and proceeded. 'Secondly, I wanted to know what you knew about Melanie's boyfriend, from the club. She may have mentioned something. You may have heard something from her friends, or one of your friends.' The waitress brought their drinks, and he waited until the woman had walked away. Elsabe leant forward and took the glass of juice in both hands, slurping quietly. A small piece of fruit was left on her upper lip when she put the half-empty glass down.

Eberard was about to try again when, to his surprise, she responded, looking up at him directly. 'I know who you're talking about. You're talking about the black who was shot by Daddy ... by my father. You want to know if I knew that he was my sister's boyfriend, don't you?' Her tone was accusing and Eberard said nothing, waiting. 'Well, I knew that she was seeing someone. Melanie didn't tell me anything. But I heard two of her friends talking. Someone had seen her at the club, and she was with a black man. I didn't know if they had just started seeing each other or what. I didn't know anything. But I knew that she was ... fucking a black man.' The word was incongruous in her childlike mouth, and she had to force it out, perhaps in a deliberate effort to shock Eberard, or to try to sound grown-up. He sat unmoved, frowning intently back at her.

Elsabe hesitated, unnerved by the lack of reaction. 'I knew she was seeing a black man,' she continued more softly. 'And I knew that Daddy would never approve of that. So I didn't say anything, not to her and certainly not to my dad. I didn't know it was that man at the club. I only realised that afterwards.'

'Tell me a little about your father. Why would he not have approved?' Eberard tried to sound casual, but he immediately saw that he was asking too much of her. She stared at him with sudden loathing, shaking her head slightly from side to side. Then she took her glass and finished the juice.

'No, I'm sorry, but I can't talk to you about my father.' Her face was flushed, and Eberard thought he saw a tear gather in the corner of her eye. But her expression was angry when she looked up at him.

'Can't or won't, Elsabe?' He met her stare, and she looked away, her face turning an even deeper red. She stood up, slung her bag over her shoulder and walked away without thanking him.

Eberard had sat sipping his coffee for a long while, surprised by the mixture of emotion he was feeling. The smell of coffee had reached him, and he remained under the tree, savouring it.

The aroma had soon dissipated, though, and now, as he sat slouched in his office, the pervasive disinfectant had taken hold again. The inside of his nose prickled at the chemical astringency. And then, almost imperceptibly, a hint of something warmer reached his nostrils – the smell of a warm summer field hovering on the edges. He tried to identify the fragrance. It was a bit like earth itself, but not fetid or cloying – cleaner, brighter. He opened his eyes slightly and a tall figure came into focus. Xoliswa was standing in front of his desk, arms folded, watching him.

Eberard could not ignore the lightening he felt in his heart. More and more, he sought out her presence. He turned to her to listen, not to talk; to watch, not to be seen. Perhaps she was his solace, he thought. Solace was different from escape or comfort. Comfort was like a cold stone in the hands of a dying man. Comfort was the structured faith of religion. Comfort was the canonised phrases and rituals that formed a barricade around despair; while solace was faith in a god. Xoliswa's presence gave him meaning; it lifted his faith in other people; it showed him what could be. But it was uncompromising and allowed him no escape. Her presence was fresh but also direct and unrelenting. It unnerved him. It was easier when his senses were dulled or restricted. Drunkenness and hallucinations blunted his emotions, but heightened other unanticipated scars. He closed his eyes again, shutting off the visual world.

He became aware of the scratching of her foot on the floor, a persistent grating sound of grains of sand and dirt being shifted across the wood. She was still looking at him, as if he had never shut her out.

'Don't think that you can escape me by closing your eyes,' the constable said evenly, reading his thoughts. 'You're like a father with a hangover. You're the man who has been out drinking and womanising all night, home and in bed for only a few hours. Now you must face the day: you must face your wife and children.'

Eberard could see the scene: the nauseating smell of pap on the stove; the foul-tasting water and sour tea; the family buzzing around him.

'You close your eyes and hope that it'll all go away,' Xoliswa went on, 'that your family will leave you alone out of sympathy and respect. But you've lost their respect.'

She was right, Eberard thought. It was a good comparison. She had no more sympathy for his suffering and would carry on pulling at him, beating at his sore skull like a demanding family. There was no way out of this hell, the prison of his own making.

'Now, are you going to stay inside, hoping that they'll leave you alone, knowing they won't, or are you going to open the door, walk outside and look straight up into the sun and take your punishment?' Xoliswa stood with her hands on her hips, half-enjoying the speech.

'The sunlight will burn my eyes to their stalks.' Eberard smiled wanly. He knew it was weak, but it was his best shot. 'What if the sun is so intense that I burst into flames as the light touches me?'

'Do you think that the sun ever sets?' Xoliswa retaliated. 'The sun is always there; it's always midday. Time stands still while you're inside your hole. You know that, Eberard. Nothing's resolved, nothing changes, nothing moves while you hide away. Whether you open the door today or in a week's time, it'll be just the same.'

'Why can't I wait for tomorrow, then?' The words sounded pathetic even as he spoke them. He hated himself for being so weak.

But Xoliswa did not chastise him, not directly. 'When you grow up like I did,' she confessed, 'with nothing, and your only hope of getting anything is what you can scrounge out of the dirt – when you grow up like that, you learn to live each and every moment with its full offering. You don't wait for tomorrow.'

It was the first time that she had said anything about her background to him. He had sensed that she had come from another place, another time, but he had never really understood what her childhood or family had been like. Her comments and behaviour had always been utterly professional. She had answered questions politely, but with little elaboration. He felt his curiosity rise.

'Rich people have the same idea,' she went on, feeding his interest, '"live each moment to its fullest"; "live every minute as if it were your last". But they don't know; they think this means that you must cram every moment with as many things as possible. They become desperate to fill the space. How can you enjoy the moment unless you're in the very fanciest car that money can buy? How can you enjoy it unless you're also drinking the most expensive wine? They rush from one moment to the next, chasing a dream.' Xoliswa's body shook slightly, and Eberard sat up in his chair, his whole being focused on the woman in front of him.

'When my father smoked his pipe, nothing else came into the moment. He drew the smoke in with all of his soul. He tasted everything that the tobacco could give him.'

Xoliswa walked to the window and looked out onto the court-yard. She spoke tenderly, painting a picture of a man sitting in the red dust outside his hut in the hills above Peddie, content, unconcerned about what he had to do next, about who could be waiting for him, or what he might need in the following moment. 'He didn't also need to be driving at two hundred kilometres an hour in a fast car. He didn't need the best music system in the world. He didn't want to be in the most exotic place on earth.' She shook her head and walked back to the desk.

Her story transported Eberard, and for a while he felt removed from the dockets and ink stains of his festering office.

'And my mother,' she continued, 'when my mother sat in front of her radio and listened to the drama show, she didn't worry about what she was wearing. She lived the world of the play completely. Because in the next moment, her radio could break, and there was no money to fix it.

'Where I come from' – she lifted her chin in an expression of pride – 'you take from the moment what you can. If you don't, you're never ready to die because you're never able to stand still. If you have lived this moment properly, death in the next is not a terrible thought. If this moment is just a breath in a race towards the next, death is unthinkable.'

The words sounded judgemental, even arrogant. But Xoliswa's demeanour was simple and open. Her skin glowed under the office lights. She was breathing harder from the effort, the enthusiasm, of her speech. Eberard watched her, almost in awe, feeling strange and conflicting emotions tugging at him: warmth, fear, comfort, dismay. He did not want her to stop; he wanted to know more. He wondered about her life, about her childhood, her mother, the books she'd read, her waking dreams. 'And your father?' he asked hesitantly. 'Is he … I mean, what happened to him?' He had heard her mention him on a few occasions, but this was the first time she had ever spoken about him so openly.

Her father had died several years ago, she told him. She described the scene of his funeral. It had rained, and the valley was green and wet that day, covered in a cool mist that hung in the air like silk. The clumps of earth were filled with the promise of better crops. Xoliswa told him how she had wept unashamedly, placing her father's clay pipe on the top of the pinewood coffin, the stem towards his head. 'So that he would not have to hunt for it in the afterlife,' she explained, smiling. Eberard was absorbed by the scene, listening with intense concentration. She described the thud of the warm earth striking the lid of the coffin, reverberating in the valley. 'It's a sound I'll never forget,' she confessed. 'I went back to him sometimes, to try to talk to him. But the spirit world is a difficult and complex place.'

She was still standing in front of Eberard, her stance at odds with the intimate nature of her speech, imbuing it with an almost theatrical quality, as though she was giving a school oral or playing a part in a drama. He wanted to ask her to sit down, but feared that the interruption would end her unveiling.

'I miss him; I miss the smell of his pipe and the way he laughed. He taught me to sit still. Sometimes I wish he was here to teach me again.' Xoliswa smiled to herself, and Eberard noticed a tear running down her cheek. He felt fervently in his pocket for a tissue, but she wiped it away with the back of her hand. He wanted to stand up and hold her against his own body, but stayed rooted to his chair.

'But when you' – Xoliswa pointed at him – 'feel upset about the death of a young girl like Melanie du Preez, you're thinking about what she could have achieved. You're thinking about her as a grown woman, with children, grandchildren for her father. You're thinking of your own loss, you're sad for what you haven't achieved yourself. But what does any of that matter to her? Why is her death sad for you? She won't be a lecturer at the university. She won't get married and have children. Why does that matter to you or to anyone else? She can't regret it.

'I'm sorry that she's dead, not because of her future that has been cut short, but because of her past. Her poetry, the collection she kept, is full of pain and unhappiness. I doubt that she enjoyed many happy moments in her life. Perhaps before her mother died. But after that? She wasn't given the opportunity or ability to enjoy life. That's the sadness of her death.'

Xoliswa lifted up her hands and shrugged her shoulders, as if to show that she had said all that she could.

They looked at each other, neither moving nor speaking. Eberard smiled at her – a full, open smile of affection. He felt something in him shift. It was not only overt emotion; it was a deeper movement of years of desperation, a shifting of layers over layers, an aligning of thoughts. He wanted the moment to be held, suspended. Xoliswa looked back at him, her eyes wide and questioning, searching his face for a sign of his meaning.

The office door screeched open, startling them, and the office cleaner, Majiet, sloped into the room, dragging a heavy-bristled broom behind him. Grey curls pushed out from beneath his tight-fitting cap. He grunted towards the constable before dropping some post onto Eberard's desk. The top envelope had no stamp on it; childish, upright block letters addressed the envelope to him as Captain Februarie.

'Jiet, where did this come from?' he asked. 'It wasn't posted.' The cleaner shrugged his shoulders in disinterest and traipsed out of the office without answering.

The moment between Eberard and Xoliswa was gone, and the constable, back in professional mode, leant over the desk to see what had arrived. Eberard slipped a ballpoint pen into the envelope, tore the paper across the top, and pulled out a thickly folded piece of purple paper. The colour was familiar, but he did not immediately identify the source. Only as he started to unfold the page did he recognise it.

'It's from Melanie's collection, from her scrapbook,' he said, although Xoliswa had already made the connection. The edges were roughly torn and spiked. 'It must be one of the pages that was torn out.'

Eberard flattened the paper on his desk, running the back of his finger against the creases. The writing was in black pen, strong letters that flowed at an uncaring angle across the page. The letters were poorly formed, and the pen had dug into the paper, scoring it and pulling up fine threads of fibre. The title had been written over repeatedly, thick black capital letters marking the words 'Sweet Lullaby'. The rest of the writing was in small letters, scrawled heavily and quickly.

Eberard read the short piece to himself, feeling the blood drain from his face.

SWEET LULLABY

He touched my cheek, gazed into my eyes,
Twirled my hair around his finger.
'Close your eyes and let me into your soul,'
'Hush my baby, sweet lullaby.'
Hands crept, minds deceived,
'Hush my baby, sweet lullaby.'
Brittle caresses, innocent tears,
'Yes, my baby, let me in ...'
Jagged edges, a scarred heart,
'That's my girl, sweet child.'
Drowning in deception,
He took with him my locks of innocence,
'Hush my baby, sweet lullaby.'

TWENTY-TWO

He took with him my locks of innocence
'Hush my baby, sweet lullaby.'

SUSAN Primesh stopped reading and looked up at them. Her face seemed slightly anguished. Eberard sat, expressionless, waiting for her to finish reading through the collection in its entirety. She paged back again, turning the thick purple page slowly, her fingers holding each page at the corner before letting it fall. Dust particles swept out from the book, filtering down a beam of light from the window. A telephone rang mutedly in an adjacent room.

Time is deceptive in this office, Eberard thought. During a session, it seemed immaterial; the outside world would stand still as he delved into his emotions. Time was an inappropriate concern when he was trying to come to terms with his spiralling depression. Yet it was always there, watching him. He was always surprised when he looked up and saw the small clock, placed inconspicuously, but obviously, on the desk behind her. Time rushed while he spoke, using the opportunity to speed along while he wasn't watching. And time always won, dictating how far he could progress. No matter how deep the emotion, no matter how poignant the memory, the clock was always in control, and the moment was ended. He had the same feeling now: that the languidness of the moment belied the silent rushing of time beneath. While they waited, breathing easily, the seconds hurtled breathlessly by.

Primesh was frowning again, her fingers running along the riffled edges of the torn paper. Her eyes flicked across the surface of the page, looking for meaning. Eberard watched her, intrigued.

He had been nervous about approaching her at first, finding the idea exposing. And he had been surprised at his feelings of vulnerability. Primesh was not his personal psychiatrist; she had been appointed by his superiors to assess him. She was the perfect person to help him interpret Melanie's actions.

Earlier that day, he had been wrestling with his discomfort when Xoliswa had walked into the office.

'I've been thinking about that lullaby and ...' Xoliswa's voice tailed off as she saw the look of intensity on Eberard's face. 'What is it?' she asked, inclining her head. He realised then why he felt disconcerted about approaching Dr Primesh. It had nothing to do with his relationship with the psychiatrist. There would be no blurring of boundaries, and, if there was, it did not concern him. His anxiety did not arise from her knowledge of his darkness. It had to do with his constable, standing here before him, and her perception of him. It was her knowledge, and her judgement, that he feared. He looked up at her; already his heart had quickened. Her hair was braided tightly off her forehead today, lifting the line of her eyebrows and accentuating her eyes.

She had stood before him, unblinking, her body motionless as she waited for him to speak. Eberard had felt flustered, uncertain of his footing, but he managed to return her gaze.

'Xoli,' he started, deliberately, seeking out her compassion. 'I think I know someone who can help us with this. But I need to explain something to you first.' Inexplicably, he felt tears welling up in his eyes, and he frowned, almost out of irritation. 'You know that I've had a difficult past. Some of my history you know, some of it you don't. Things ... in my life ... things have not worked out the way they might have.' His voice was full of emotion, thick and uneven. She put her hand against the door and gently pushed it closed. The simple gesture held the promise of acceptance rather than judgement, and Eberard smiled appreciatively.

'Well, as you know only too well, I'm still quite a mess.' His nervous laughter sounded feigned in the room. 'And I'm not getting any better. But anyway, one of the conditions of my appointment here is that I undergo a kind of assessment, a monitoring with a local ... psychiatrist.'

Xoliswa was looking at him with such kindness that he stopped talking. Their closeness in the room, the closed door, the glint of tears in her eyes, all overwhelmed him. He sighed and wiped his eyes with the back of his hand.

'I think she could help us ...' He forced the words out in a single breath, his hand still covering his eyes, but stopped short when he felt Xoliswa's touch. She drew his hand away from his face, and Eberard felt her breath, warm on his cheek. He looked up into her eyes and felt a tear tickle as it ran down the side of his nose. He sniffed and brought his free hand to his nose.

'I'm sorry,' he said, half-laughing as he tried to wipe the trail away.

'Don't be.' She took her hands and gently drew his head towards her stomach. Her skin was warm through the cotton fabric. At first, he resisted, trying to keep the lightest of touches with her body. But she held him firmly, and he let himself rest against her. Then the tears streamed down his face, wetting her shirt. Bubbles of spit pushed out from his mouth, popping on his lips, and his chest heaved as he wrestled for air. She said nothing, holding him, waiting. He managed to stem his breaths, and his body slowly stopped quivering. But still she pulled him against her. He heard her stomach gurgle – a gentle sound. It did not worry her if he cried on her, if his nose ran, if he heard the sounds inside her. She was not trying to be anything other than human. It was her peaceful confidence, her lack of pretence, her imperfection, that calmed him. He knew then that he had fallen for her. Not the surface sting of lust. Not the temporary bruising of infatuation. But the deep bite of love, in all its impractical exigencies.

Eberard sat hunched against her frame for what seemed like hours. She did nothing to move him, said nothing to distract him. And even when his face was dry and his breathing was slow and easy, she kept her hands on him. He let the feelings flow through his body, a sensation he thought he had lost. It did not really matter whether she loved him back, he realised. All that was important was that he had found feeling again. Wave upon wave of emotion, painful but not destructive, unnerving but unmistakeably real. Like a man who has regained his sight, it's not important what he sees first, only that he can see it.

'It doesn't matter, does it?' he finally asked, lifting his head.

'No,' Xoliswa replied, her hands brushing over his hair. 'No, it doesn't matter.'

Now her quiet presence felt reassuring as she sat alongside him, with her hands folded in her lap, waiting for Primesh to finish reading. His head felt clear and uncluttered. It was a refreshing feeling, and for the first time in a long while he was able to concentrate fully. Strange, he thought, that the turmoil of emotion should result in clarity, while its absence had been so confusing and stultifying. He looked up as Primesh lowered the book, clearing her throat.

'The collection is quite fascinating,' she started. 'There's a slow progression, as you pointed out, from innocent, old-fashioned lullabies towards quite sad and even shocking poetry. They suggest that she was a sad young girl ... even disturbed as she got older. As a child, she chooses naive songs that her mother would have sung to her. Then you see her exploration, collecting lesser-known works, reflecting her independence. And then the choices of an adolescent girl – a young woman – calling out for help. Towards the end, she's chosen poems about being trapped and feeling alone. Given her terrible history, that's quite understandable.

'The last one – the one that was torn out – is the culmination of this process. It's the last in the series, but its message is also the finale. Its position makes it important, as does its content. But having said that, on its own, I'm not sure what I'd make of it,' Primesh said carefully, looking directly at Eberard. 'I'm not sure what you want me to make of it, Inspector.'

Eberard appreciated her formality. Since agreeing to talk to them, Primesh had been careful to keep a professional distance between them, avoiding using his first name, and not mentioning any aspect of their history or the missed sessions. He leant forward in his chair eagerly. 'Go on. Please. This is helpful.'

'Well, it's a lullaby about a young girl,' she continued, 'an innocent girl, whose innocence has been taken from her by a man. She's been deceived by someone close to her. You notice the marks – quotation marks – indicating his speech. He's singing a lullaby to her and using the soothing nature of the song to beguile her. On its own, I couldn't take it any further than that: it could be a boyfriend, a family member.'

'Add to that' – Xoliswa spoke up – 'the fact that someone, possibly the dead girl or her sister, tore that page out before we could find it. Someone didn't want us to find that poem. And that same person has now decided to send it to us. That must make it important.'

The psychiatrist nodded. 'You're right: someone didn't want it to be seen. But it wasn't destroyed, so it wasn't the case that it should never be seen – only that it shouldn't be seen at the time. Any number of things could've prompted it being torn out. Then the return of the page – and directly to you – is even more telling. It's meant to be some kind of message. But the fact that the page, or the poem, is important to someone, doesn't itself suggest what meaning can be given to it. What we can surmise is that it resonated very strongly with Melanie du Preez – strongly enough to have been the last entry in the collection. There's a message from Melanie in the poem. There's also a message – perhaps a different message – from the person who returned it. But you'll need to look further to find out what those messages are.'

Eberard sat back in the chair. It was true: they didn't know if the message was related to Melanie's death. The fact that she felt deceived by somebody didn't necessarily cast any light on her murder. It may have been a separate, unrelated incident. 'We've done some extra work since we got the letter, but we haven't found anything really helpful,' he explained. 'Melanie and the Burundian seem to have had a relationship, but she dominated, not him. He's still our main suspect. But he doesn't fit the profile of the man in the lullaby. There are other possibilities – an older lecturer, for example ...' Eberard caught himself thinking out loud, divulging details that were still unverified.

'There's another, unrelated aspect,' Xoliswa said after a moment, 'which we'd like to ask you about, if that would be all right?'

Primesh nodded, a little uncertainly. 'Okay, if you think I might be able to help.'

Xoliswa explained about Professor du Preez's prior conviction. Although it was a fairly minor charge, it had concerned her when the charges were dropped for the killing of the Burundian. 'I retrieved the docket in the case, and he pleaded guilty to hitting the driver of the car that was involved in a collision with him.'

Eberard continued, picking up the thread from his partner. 'Du Preez's wife – Melanie's mother – died in the accident. Du Preez was driving, and he punched the driver of the other car on the scene. He told me … at least, we were led to believe that the other driver was reckless, and Du Preez had been so incensed that he couldn't control himself. The assault wasn't very serious, fortunately, so no one took the conviction too seriously. But Xoliswa … Constable Nduku … had a look at the inquest docket arising from his wife's death.' Eberard paused, waiting for his partner to continue.

'Well, there's no finding,' Xoliswa explained. 'It seems that the inquest wasn't pursued. The docket must've been filed away without it ever reaching an inquest magistrate. But there was a short statement from the policeman who attended the scene. He said that both drivers appeared to be under the influence of alcohol. He says that Du Preez was aggressive and that his breath smelt strongly of alcohol.' Xoliswa looked across at Eberard. He lowered his head for her to continue. 'There's also a statement from an eyewitness who was at the traffic light on the other side of the intersection. He says that the light was red for his own car when the accident happened, and that he'd stopped at the intersection waiting for it to change. I went to look at it this morning. It's a standard two-lane intersection. When the robots are red for cars in one direction, they're red for those going the opposite way. If the robot was red for the eyewitness, the robot must've been red for Du Preez.'

'Du Preez had been drinking. He drove through a red robot. His wife is injured in the accident and dies. But Du Preez attacks the other driver?' Eberard inflected his voice into a query.

'Well, we all have different reactions to trauma,' Primesh said calmly. 'The most common and immediate response is denial. It's a natural defence mechanism in order to cope with shock.' She stood up and opened the window, letting in a gentle breeze. Eberard could smell the resin of freshly cut pine trees and the diesel from a passing truck.

'However,' she continued, 'in a complicated situation, particularly where guilt may also be an active emotion, denial won't necessarily take a simple form. Rationalisation is very common where there's guilt; we rationalise our conduct, or the situation that we're facing, in order to reduce our feelings of guilt. So we try to take away our own emotional reaction by using our cognitive functions of logic and reasoning, even if it's false reasoning. Another more complex defence is that of reaction-formation. In simple situations, it involves transferring the cause of the guilt onto others in order to elevate our own position. So, to use an example, someone who's racially prejudiced will often be the first to point a finger at others and accuse them of racism. This makes them feel better about their own position; the act of accusing is a form of denial, as it presupposes that they aren't racist.

'Professor du Preez's reaction is a complex and more extreme combination of these defence mechanisms,' she went on. 'When he climbs out of the car and is faced with the accident that he's perhaps caused, his reaction is to transfer the blame onto the other driver. In order to prove – or at least confirm – his own lack of culpability in the event, he accuses the other driver and then assaults the man in a fit of rage. To those present, and probably in his own mind as well, he's the wronged person rather than the perpetrator.'

'Is it a calculated decision to try to create the impression of innocence?' Xoliswa asked.

'No ... although that's difficult to say,' Primesh answered cautiously. 'These reactions are formulated in our subconscious, and they are immediate. We can reflect on them and analyse our reactions, but it's often hard for us to appreciate the basis of our reaction in the moment. In Professor du Preez's case, it's unlikely that he had the time or insight to premeditate his response. His anger would've overwhelmed him, and his reaction would've been spontaneous. He would've felt real anger, fury, towards the other driver.'

Eberard reached forward for his glass of water and pressed the cold rim against his lower lip. 'He does seem to have trouble dealing with anger. The press reported that he was attacked by the Burundian in the cells. That's not what he told me. He told me that the man insulted him – or his daughter – and that he lost control and shot him.'

Primesh frowned but said nothing.

'I think we should bring this prior statement to the attention of the Public Prosecutor's office,' he concluded. 'They may see the shooting of the Burundian differently.' Xoliswa nodded in agreement.

Eberard looked at the clock. They had already taken up a considerable amount of Primesh's time, with no real results. It was probably best, as she had suggested, for them to look for more clues and for him to tell the authorities about Du Preez's other statement. He caught Xoliswa's eye and gestured towards the door. He was about to thank the psychiatrist when she lifted her hand, indicating that she had not yet finished.

'Yes, but his decision to put himself in that position was premeditated,' she explained. 'His decision to fool the policemen on duty. The decision to take a weapon. They aren't the work of the subconscious. And when the man insulted his daughter … well, his reaction isn't based on transference. The anger is directed at the appropriate subject.'

'Except that we know that the Burundian probably didn't kill Melanie,' Xoliswa interjected, sitting back into her seat. 'So why would he talk about her like that? By all accounts he was in love with her alter ego.'

'And I never heard him speak a word of English,' Eberard added, his voice rising again. 'Even when we caught him off-guard in his room, and when I had him in the interrogation room, he never once broke into English. Maybe that was a pretence, but it does make Professor du Preez's account even more of a problem.' He looked up at Primesh expectantly.

The psychiatrist sat quietly for a moment, mulling over the information. It seemed unlikely that Bullet had raped Melanie; although Du Preez would not have known that. If the Burundian was in fact innocent, how did Du Preez's account of what happened in the cells tie in with events? The doctor pursed her lips in concentration.

'You mentioned,' she said finally, 'that Melanie used the name Clementine when working at the club.'

Eberard nodded. 'The club owner told me that she used it because of the French word for fruit. You know, layers of sweet and sour. That kind of thing.'

'Yes,' the psychiatrist interrupted, again raising her hand, 'but it's also the title of a song, a lullaby, to be correct. Now I don't see that song in her collection.' She paged through the book once more, shaking her head, then put it down. 'But I seem to remember that there's something in the words of that poem – everyone knows the refrain, maybe the first verse or two. But there's a full version. I remember reading it in my days at university. There was something about that song that was strange.' She stood up and walked to the door – almost in a daze, Eberard thought.

'Give me a moment while I have a look for it. I think I have it here; it's in an anthology by Burgess ...' Her voice trailed off as she left the room. Neither Eberard nor Xoliswa spoke, waiting for her to return. The constable gently rubbed her thumb against the raised crease of her trousers, and Eberard looked up again at the clock. Primesh returned after some minutes, an open book in her hands. The anthology was covered in old plastic wrapping, the corners of the cover frayed. She was mouthing the words quietly to herself, tapping the page with her finger.

'Yes, here it is. In the last verse. It's really a rather strange version. I can't remember what its origin is; I doubt Melanie would have known about it from an anthology like this. But then you'd probably come across it on the Internet these days. Everything seems to end up there.'

Susan Primesh's face was flushed, and she seemed uncharacteristically unsure of herself. She held out the book, opened, for Eberard to read. 'It's a bit ... well, I think you'd better read it yourself, Inspector.'

CLEMENTINE

In a cavern, in a canyon
Excavating for a mine
Lived a miner, forty-niner
And his daughter, Clementine
Oh, my darling, oh, my darling
Oh, my darling Clementine
You are lost and gone forever
Dreadful sorry, Clementine.

Light she was and like a fairy
And her shoes were number nine
Herring boxes without topses
Sandals were for Clementine
Oh, my darling, oh, my darling
Oh, my darling Clementine
You are lost and gone forever
Dreadful sorry, Clementine.

Drove she ducklings to the water
Every morning just at nine
Hit her foot against a splinter
Fell into the foaming brine
Oh, my darling, oh, my darling
Oh, my darling Clementine
You are lost and gone forever
Dreadful sorry, Clementine.

Ruby lips above the water
Blowing bubbles soft and fine
But alas, I was no swimmer
So I lost my Clementine
Oh, my darling, oh, my darling
Oh, my darling Clementine
You are lost and gone forever
Dreadful sorry, Clementine.

How I missed her, how I missed her
How I missed my Clementine
Till I kissed her little sister
And forgot my Clementine
Oh, my darling, oh, my darling
Oh, my darling Clementine
You are lost and gone forever
Dreadful sorry, Clementine

TWENTY-THREE

S ANNA carried her unbidden child inside her, parasitic and yet somehow fulfilling, exciting. She never spoke of its father. Van der Keesel had been found the day after his death, floating face down in the river. His body was drained of blood; it had swirled away down the river. Governor van der Stel instructed the Company's medical officer to conduct an autopsy the same day; he found the puncture marks from the snake, the blow on the right side of the temple, the side on which he had been found in the river. The explanation for these wounds was clear, but the officer was puzzled by the fracture of the skull on the left side, behind the ear. It had obviously been caused by considerable force; the skull had caved in around the point of impact, and fragments of bone were embedded in the man's brain. After some deliberation, the officer declared that Van der Keesel must have been bitten and, in a panic, fallen on his left side, sustaining the blow to the head. Although a massive injury, he must have had the strength to stand up momentarily, before falling again onto his right, sustaining the lesser injury. The explanation was hardly satisfying, but the Governor had little choice but to accept the finding of death by misadventure. Van der Keesel was given a Company funeral; the gunners from the naval ship fired a seven-gun salute into the bay, the harsh crack of cannon fire echoing off the grey cliffs of Table Mountain. His body was laid to rest in the small Company cemetery in Constantia.

Sanna's parents knew that she carried his child. Jakoba had bathed her daughter's wounds and washed the blood from her thighs; she knew what had happened in the fields, even before Sanna had run into the house sobbing. But they could not know what had taken place in the river on the day of Van der Keesel's death. Sanna had walked into the house that afternoon, dazed but strangely quiet. Her feet were cut and her knees had deep bruises that were turning purple and blue. The deep wound on her thigh started bleeding again. Jakoba rubbed oil into her torn skin, stroking her daughter's battered young body. She did not ask, but saw something in Sanna's eyes that drove fear into her heart. Frederick sat outside in the sun, smoking a half-lit pipe, distractedly pulling on the stubborn tobacco. He stared in front of him without seeing.

The following morning, the news was brought to them: Master van der Keesel's body had been found in the river. This time, Jakoba did not look into her daughter's eyes. Sanna stood up and walked to her bed on the floor, curled up on the straw and pulled a blanket over her head. Jakoba and Frederick sat outside, holding hands, not talking, watching the wind blowing eddies of dust across the fields. None of the slaves went into the fields. Even though no one had laid a hand on the viticulturist, the slaves and burghers feared retribution. Jakoba and Frederick sat all morning, silent, trembling now and again, each trapped in their separate anguish for Sanna. Van der Keesel's name was not mentioned in the house again.

Sanna did not return to the fields. She remained at home, tending to the vegetable garden, cooking for her parents and cleaning the small house. She did not venture into town or leave the area around the river. Sometimes she would return to the water, but not to swim, just to sit and watch the river flowing past. She dreamed of pink-tinged water, of stones that blossomed with red blood, but when she sat on the bank, the water was clear and clean. In her mind, she saw his body, large and bloated like a drowned buffalo, pushed by the current. But the river was filled only with rocks and boulders when she returned to it.

The girl's belly pushed out, swollen and taut, distorting her thin, childlike physique. When she was nearly at term, she started to bleed – at first, just a small spotting of dark red on her blanket in the morning. She washed it in the river, rubbing the stain with coarse sand. But one morning, a week after the first spotting, she awoke early, before the hens had started to stir, and noted a trickle of dark, red-blue blood coursing across her thigh. She called Jakoba softly, but it was Frederick who woke up from his shallow sleep. He brought a candle to the side of her bed and knelt down.

'What is it, Sanna?' he asked worriedly. She smiled at her father and reached out to touch his face. Her fingers were stained with blood, half-dried and sticky.

Frederick pulled the blanket back and saw the wet straw, the small pool of coagulating blood on the underblanket. He turned his head, so that she would not see his shock, and stood up.

'Wait, my child. Wait for me.' Without saying anything further, he ran to his neighbours and returned with a cart and two horses. He picked Sanna up in his arms and carried her to the back of the cart, wrapping her in all the blankets in the house. Jakoba stood at the door, silent, her hands over her mouth.

The journey was a long one, each bump of the wheels of the cart making Sanna moan with pain. It felt as if the baby was trying to slice its way out of her body. When she cried out, her father pushed the horses even harder, and by the time they arrived at Van der Stel's residence, they were exhausted. The Governor's housekeeper, an intimidating Dutch woman, was not impressed by the unannounced arrival. But before Frederick could plead their case, her sullen reception was overshadowed by an unexpected ally. Bakka appeared, moving silently out of the shadows. Frederick drew back, fearful, as Bakka strode to the cart and pulled back the blanket. The man took in Sanna's broken body for a moment, before turning his wrath on the housekeeper. He spoke a dialect to her that Frederick could not understand, but the words were harsh and spoken forcefully. The housekeeper dropped her eyes.

'The Governor is out on business in the colony,' Bakka said, turning to Frederick. 'But Her Ladyship is here. You have a brave daughter, Boorman. I've watched her. I've seen what she has done. Now I will do this for her.' The housekeeper mumbled something in a hushed voice before disappearing inside. Bakka did not wait for her return, scooping Sanna up in his arms. He was already at the large door when the housekeeper returned with two footmen. Bakka's massive form brushed past them as he carried Sanna inside.

Constance received Frederick with sympathy. She remembered his quiet politeness and her husband's praise for his skills as an artisan. She touched Sanna's brow with her hand. It was clear that the girl was critically ill and in danger of losing her life and that of her baby. She ordered the men to carry the patient into one of the spare bedrooms. Bakka grunted at them dismissively and carried her himself, laying her down on the clean white sheets. Sanna had never rested on a bed so soft: the fabric was smooth and light and smelt of fresh soap. It felt as though she was back in the dam, with soft layers of mud falling on her skin. She drifted into the water, letting the silt cover her face, dropping on her eyelids like gentle rain.

Constance, pacing restlessly in the room while waiting for the midwife from the estate, watched the girl drift in and out of consciousness. The chambermaids had prepared hot water and towels. A wire hook and steel surgical knife had been boiled, and glinted on the towels in anticipation. Still the midwife did not arrive. Sanna moaned lightly and her colour paled.

'There's no more blood, my lady,' the chambermaid announced nervously, dropping the sheets back over the child's wan body. Constance put her fingers against the thin neck.

'She's leaving us. Come,' she beckoned, 'we cannot wait any longer.' The two chambermaids drew around the bed anxiously, uncertain. Constance summoned up her resolve, before gripping the sharp-ended wire hook. She inserted it into the vagina, prodding upwards until she felt Sanna's tiny cervix, unripe and closed. Constance pushed a little harder, trying to catch the membrane. A flow of warm, bloody water spread out across the bed, and Sanna wrenched awake with pain.

Constance approached her in a whisper. 'The father, my dear, who is the father of your child?'

At first Sanna shook her head, but, in her delirium, she could not withhold his name: 'Keesel. Keesel,' she moaned. The chambermaids looked at each other, frowning, unable to discern her meaning. But fury crossed over Constance's face. She put her finger on Sanna's lips to quieten her.

There was no more pain. Sanna felt cool, as if a breeze was blowing gently across her chest. She saw the river, flowing past their small house; the water was clear, bubbling with iridescent bubbles. She could see all the way to the bottom, even in the deeper pools, where the river bed was sandy and soft underfoot. Coolness enveloped her, floating her away, downstream.

But the baby was still trapped inside her dying body. Constance stroked the girl's damp hair, feeling her heartbeat fade, softer and softer, drifting gently away. And then, when it was still, Constance nodded to the chambermaid. With a shaking hand, her servant handed the Governor's wife the scalpel.

In a last act of violence, Constance sliced Sanna's body open from above her navel, dragging a deep cut across the full length of her belly. The skin and thin layer of muscle pulled back over the swollen uterus, now almost bloodless. Again she dragged the knife, more carefully now, and pulled out Sanna's son from his still-warm lair. He left his mother's lifeless, mutilated body, lying on the cold white sheets.

Van der Stel returned home that evening, filled with tales from his latest expedition into the hinterland; he was eager to share them with his wife and looked forward to her enthusiastic response. He was met instead by her anger. He tried to subdue her, but, by the time she had taken him into the bedroom, Constance had worked herself into a rage. Sanna's body, bloodied, lay beneath a single sheet, the white cotton blotted with dark stains. The Governor was taken aback and felt a flush of annoyance.

'My fair lady,' he began, frowning at the outline of the body in the soiled bed, keeping one eye on his wife.

'Don't you "fair lady" me,' she retorted. 'This is the handiwork of your chosen employee. This is how he goes about his work.' The Governor's frown deepened. 'Van der Keesel!' she shouted. 'The man you allowed to act as master of your slaves. The man who passed orders for the Company as if he were the governor of this godforsaken rubbish pit. The man who passed out commands, who punished the slaves without consulting you.' Constance turned a cold eye on her husband. 'The man who, it appears, enjoyed himself by taking forcible advantage of young girls.' She walked up to the bed and pulled the sheet back. Van der Stel blanched and stepped away.

'For God's sake, Constance, you can't have some dead slave girl in our house ...' His voice trailed off as his wife approached him.

'Yes, I am Constance,' she declared. 'Let us not forget that I am Constance; the *"groote"* Constance, the butt of his cheap liquor-house jokes; Constance who married the mixed-race bastard; fair-skinned Constance with her dark-skinned Governor.' Van der Stel reddened with surprise and tried to deny the accusation, but she would not hear his protestations. 'I know what is said behind my back, as do you, Simon. But I set no score by what he said. He was a philanderer and a scoundrel. He was rude and objectionable, and I never liked the man. He showed nothing but disrespect towards me and my position as wife of the Governor of the colony. Now I find he has abused the innocence of a child and taken her by force. If he were alive, I would see him driven from the colony, back to Holland, where I understand that similar charges await him.'

Van der Stel sighed, nodding his head resignedly. 'You're right, Constance, you're right. What more do you want me to say?' He shrugged his shoulders and headed for the door. But his wife was not finished.

'You told me that his work in the colony is important to us; I wasn't aware that the impregnation of children was a matter which the colony held dear.' The Governor winced but made no attempt to interrupt. 'But be that as it may, I am almost sorry that he's dead; my choice would have been to send him back across the sea, preferably dangling on a long rope behind the slowest supply ship. Now that he's dead, I am of a mind to have his body exhumed from the estate's cemetery and have him buried with the slaves.' Van der Stel's eyes widened in horror at the suggestion.

'However, I'm mindful of your own position in this disastrous matter. Here are my conditions.' She paused and stared at him evenly. 'And I shall not be swayed, Simon.' The threatening tone of her voice left the Governor in no doubt of this. 'Master van der Keesel's estate shall be retained by the Company,' she continued in low tones, 'under my personal control, to be used to provide financially for every need of his new son. Once his estate is depleted, the Company will continue to do so in his place. The child will be placed into foster care. No mention is to be made of his parenthood or the circumstances under which he was conceived.'

Van der Stel could see that his wife was in no mood to be challenged, but he could not help but cautiously ask: 'Foster care, my dear? Who do you have in mind to care for a bastard child in these ... unfortunate circumstances?'

Constance snorted at his choice of words. 'Rather more unfortunate for that child lying dead in that bed than it is for you, sir.' She stared at him, but then softened her voice. 'As it happens, I've already sent word to the person I have in mind. Mrs du Preez recently lost her husband. She's still young enough to look after a newborn child. She has no children of her own, and she needs something to keep her occupied.' The Governor wanted to protest his wife's decision, but her mood had softened and he was reluctant to endure any more abuse. He let her continue.

'I anticipate that Mrs du Preez will be only too delighted to take the child in and nurse it as her own. The child is light of complexion. He will take her name, and perhaps in time we will all be none the wiser.'

And so it was decided. Van der Stel raised no further objection, nor could he, and the following day he made the necessary arrangements for Mrs du Preez to receive a grant from the Company, delicately recorded in the books of account as 'repairs to the estate'.

The tiers of new vines were left unattended; some of the plants were stolen and planted in backyards and along river plantations, in defiance of the Governor's orders. Weeds wrapped themselves around the stems and smothered the abandoned shoots. Rain and wind gnawed at the tiered steps, slowly breaking down the construction. Within a few years, the mountain had reclaimed its slopes, and all signs of the viticulturist's dream were erased. It would be another two hundred years before the dream would be pursued again.

LOOKING-GLASS RIVER

Smooth it slides upon its travel,
Here a wimple, there a gleam –
O the clean gravel!
O the smooth stream!

Sailing blossoms, silver fishes,
Paven pools as clear as air –
How a child wishes
To live down there!

TWENTY-FOUR

THE Du Preez home looked quiet from the outside, and there was no answer at the front door. Eberard banged the brass knocker again, harder and with more determination. A dog barked from a neighbouring garden, but the house was still.

Sunlight filtered through the leaves of the oak trees, making dappled puzzle pieces on the brick driveway. Two brown house sparrows picked at the grass seeds caught in the cracks. As Eberard walked back to the car, he detected the smell of cut grass, fresh but soured by petrol fumes from the mower. Two domestic workers, kitchen scarves tied tightly around their heads, walked past the house and fell into whispers at the sight of the police vehicle blocking the driveway.

'*Molo, sisi,*' Eberard heard the one say softly to Xoliswa as they passed.

'*Molo, mama.*'

'*Kunjani wena?*'

'*Philile, ma.*' Soft, warm voices, like summer raindrops falling onto the dust of the land.

Eberard and Xoliswa had just arrived from the clinic in town. Earlier that morning, Eberard had obtained a warrant for Melanie's hospital records on grounds of searching for any history of abuse. He had strode into the magistrate's office and casually handed him the request form.

'I thought this case was closed,' the magistrate said gruffly. Eberard shrugged his shoulders and looked out of the window distractedly. The magistrate skimmed over the request, raising his eyebrows when he saw Professor du Preez's name, and looking up at Eberard in surprise. Eberard stared back at him blankly, giving nothing away. The magistrate pursed his lips in concentration, now reading through the request in its entirety, before grunting in resignation and signing the warrant without commenting further.

Xoliswa had waited outside, sitting in the car. She looked up at Eberard as he opened the door, an uncharacteristic hint of anxiety in her eyes. He nodded, and she smiled broadly before starting the engine. They drove to the clinic in silence.

The hospital records recording Melanie's details were stacked in a buff-coloured folder with a faded white sticker. Because she was Du Preez's dependant, Melanie's history was filed together with her father's. Eberard and Xoliswa had sat down on the fake-leather seats in the waiting room, reading through the description of each consultation slowly. The thin pile of papers recorded a few visits to the clinic: for Du Preez, a laceration of the foot that needed stitching, a haemorrhoid operation several years before; in the case of Melanie, a recurring urinary tract infection, a reference to a possible stress-related spastic colon, counselling for insomnia. In themselves, perhaps only signs of a stressed teenager.

'It's not enough,' Eberard said disappointedly. Xoliswa gestured to him to keep reading.

And then, from the middle of the pharmacy printouts, Eberard picked up a single-page consent to operate. Although the operation had been performed by the professor's private urologist, the clinic had provided the operating room, and the professor had had to sign a consent form. At the bottom of the page, in fading but unmistakeable print, was the description of the surgery.

Eberard stared wordlessly at the form as its significance struck home.

Xoliswa now stood next to the open passenger door, with the radio turned right down. Eberard's own hand radio hummed noiselessly, clipped into the straps of his bulletproof vest. His hand closed over the butt of his pistol. The familiarity of the smooth metal in the palm of his hand, and the weight of the loaded firearm, were comforting. He felt some of his old omnipotence again. As a young trainee he had rushed into situations, oblivious to his own vulnerability. He had relied on the authority that his uniform established, the unseen army that stood behind him, the unstated power that his confidence conveyed. As well as the spoken threat – his right to carry, and use, his firearm. But slowly that confidence had been eroded; situations had disintegrated and were governed by irrationality, fear, humiliation. His authority was illusory; the army behind him was disinterested, debased. His firearm was his impediment, the source of the danger, the weapon that turned.

Eberard crouched down at the corner of the house. The brickwork felt warm and rough against his cheek. He rested, leaning low against the wall. The study window was closed. Underneath the sill he could see the tight yellowish balls of a spider's web, held together with gossamer strands. The dried husks of moths and flies hung like dark leaves. Butterfly pupae dotted along the surface of the wall – some cracked open and empty, others still holding their cargo. Inside, the telephone was ringing. It echoed distantly in the quiet house. The display on Eberard's cellphone was illuminated. Tiny globes along the edge of the glass cover lit up like stage lights. No one moved in the house. His knees felt stiff, and he tried to adjust his position. His toes pushed into the front of his shoes, tingling with pins and needles.

Eberard moved his thumb to disconnect the call. Then he heard a soft click on the other side. The ringing had stopped. No one spoke. Again he heard a faint sound.

'Professor, it's Inspector Februarie,' he said slowly. He held the phone closely to his ear. He thought he could hear someone breathing on the other side – breaths coming in short, staggered hisses. It could have been interference in the reception. No other noises. 'Professor?' he tried again. Just a crackle. 'Professor, this is the police,' he said more assertively. Then he heard a noise, the distinctive sound of someone stifling a gasp for air. He was on the other side of the telephone line, waiting. They were perhaps only a few metres apart, Eberard deduced, standing on either side of a thin wall, but connected by telephone lines and signals that spanned hundreds of kilometres, the sound of their every breath racing across time and space.

'Professor, this is Inspector Februarie. You need to tell me where your daughter is. Where's your daughter, sir?'

'My daughter's dead.' The voice sounded so clear and close that Eberard started involuntarily and looked to his side nervously, half-expecting the speaker to be leaning against the wall behind him. He turned his back to the wall and let his body slide down until he felt the ground supporting him. The back of the over-sized bulletproof scraped noisily against the rough brickwork. '*Julle het haar vermoor,*' the voice hissed at him.

'No, Professor. Not Melanie.' Eberard paused. The man on the other side was silent. 'Where's Elsabe?'

'Elsabe is safe. With me. Why do you want her?' The professor's voice was menacing. 'Do you want to take her away from me as well? *Nie weer nie, nie weer nie.*'

'Professor, what have you done with Elsabe? Is she all right?' Eberard's throat felt dry and scratchy. His buttocks pressed painfully into the stones on the ground.

'What have *I* done with her?' The man's reply was immediate and angry. Eberard thought he saw a shadow pass along the closed window, and he pulled back behind the corner. '*I* have done nothing, Inspector. *Jy's die een!* You let that bastard *swarte* take Melanie from me. And now you want to do the same to Elsabe!' He was shouting uncontrollably now, the words flowing in a thick stream. 'I won't let you anywhere near her. If I see you, so help me, I'll shoot you like a dog in the street. I'll shoot you, you bloody bastard! Do you understand me! *Ek skiet jou dood, polisieman! Hoor jy vir my? Dood!*'

Du Preez was shouting so loudly that Eberard pulled the cellphone away, only to hear the man's voice clearly through the closed window from the room inside. He tried, unsuccessfully, to interrupt the tirade. Finally, when the voice on the other side paused, he cut in loudly: 'Professor, I know what happened. Do you understand that?' Eberard raised his voice. 'I know what happened to Melanie.' The response was a dead-tone ring as Du Preez put the phone down. Eberard waited for a short while and then called again. He heard the phone ringing and the sound of someone moving about, heavily, inside the study. The receiver was picked up after nearly ten rings. Again no one spoke; there was only the heavy breathing of the listener.

'Professor. I want you to hear what I have to say. Listen carefully, please,' Eberard implored. He took the silence as acquiescence and continued. 'I've just come from the clinic in town. I went there with a warrant for Melanie's hospital records.'

'We know about the operation, Professor.' Eberard waited for a response. None was forthcoming, but he heard, almost felt, the man bump into something as he started to move around the room.

'Sir, your wife had been dead for six years. There was no other relationship in your life. In fact, Elsabe told my partner that you hadn't had any romantic interests since the death of your wife. So why did you need to have a vasectomy, Professor?' The breath on the other side hissed like a snake. But still Du Preez did not say anything. Eberard continued with more confidence.

'You only have a vasectomy if you're sexually active. Were you sexually active, Professor? And why a vasectomy? To leave no trace? To be free from ...'

'*Fok jou, my maat*,' the voice interrupted harshly. '*Jy is 'n dooie man wat praat, verstaan jy?* I'll kill you. I'll shoot holes in your stupid *kroeskop* head. Go to hell with your smutty ... dirty questions. Step into my house and I'll kill you!'

The man's anger was heated and confused. Eberard felt his own rage welling up in him, cold and focused. 'No, sir, that's where you're wrong: if I have to, I will kill *you*.'

Eberard pressed the button to end the call. The phone was sweaty against his palm. He stood up with difficulty, the edge of the vest pushing down on his thighs as he tried to rise. Xoliswa was still standing by the car, frowning questioningly.

'I think he's got her in there with him,' Eberard said breathlessly as he walked back towards her. 'Even though they dropped the charges, they still haven't given him his firearm back. But that doesn't mean he's not armed. It's easy enough for him to get a gun. He threatened to kill me on the phone just now. And he sounds quite deranged, very angry.' He dropped the cellphone onto the passenger seat, freeing his hands, and bent down and picked up the R5 automatic rifle. The cold steel gun was heavy in his hands. 'Call backup from the station and tell control to get the negotiating team down here. I'm not going to wait for them. If he's got her, we'll need to move on him now. When you've made the calls, come in through the side door that leads into the kitchen. I'll be at the door to the study ... and Xoli, wear a vest.'

Xoliswa put out her hand and took him by the arm. 'Personal is one thing. Stupid is another. Please be careful. You have a future, you know.'

He looked at her appreciatively. His future had only started to come into focus again because of her. It was only through her eyes that he had started to see a life again.

'Thank you, Xoli,' he replied simply. There was no need to say anything more. He touched her hand gently, before edging back towards the house.

The kitchen door was made from thick, rough wood – an old stable door. Eberard rattled the brass handle gently; the top half moved against the frame, unlocked, but the bottom half was on a latch. He tested the latch by pushing his heel against the wood. It gave a little, and then stuck fast. He listened for noise from the other side. A clock chimed somewhere in the house. He pushed harder with his heel. The door moved slightly further, a dull cracking sound emanating from the frame. He put his shoulder against the lower door and pushed his weight inwards. He could now see a glimmer of light from the kitchen as the door came away from the frame. Halfway down the door he could make out a small steel latch; the two screws into the base were pulling out of the wood. He pushed again and the screws came out with a small puff of dust. The door swung open and Eberard jumped back, the rifle against his shoulder and his finger on the trigger. Nothing moved on the other side. A mottled-brown linoleum floor and unpainted pine cupboards gave the kitchen a simple, unpretentious feel. He was surprised at the unsophisticated furniture, in contrast to the leather-bound opulence of the front rooms of the house.

Eberard stepped up into the kitchen, the butt of the rifle pushed firmly into his shoulder. He moved a cat's plastic bowl of milk to one side with his foot; the soured contents splashed over the side, leaving a thin trail on the floor. A box of cornflakes next to the kettle and a few unwashed plates in the sink were the only signs of life. The motor of the fridge hummed quietly.

Eberard moved through the open doorway into the passage. The front door appeared at the end of it, and a little light came down its length, sucked up by the dark carpets and wooden doors. He held his breath, straining to hear any sound. The house seemed unrelenting in its stillness. Exhaling slowly, he pushed the rifle back up as his arms sagged with its weight. Then he heard the sound of a chair being moved; it came from behind the closed study door. As he approached the door, edging down the passage with his back against the wall, the smell of chemicals greeted him. The air was overpowered with a sharp and biting odour. He dropped the rifle into the crook of his arm, and his hand felt for the cool, round knob. The door was unlocked and opened a fraction towards him with a loud crack of its hinges. The smell immediately grew stronger.

'Don't move, or I'll shoot you as you stand there!' The professor's voice boomed across from the other end of the study. Eberard could only make out the closed window in the narrow space between the door and the edge of the frame. He leant back against the wall, the rifle still cradled in his arms. The smell made his head feel light, as if he had stood up too fast. His nose started to water as the chemicals irritated his eyes. He drew the back of his hand across his eyelids.

'Professor, is Elsabe in there with you?' There was no answer. 'You must tell me where she is; otherwise I'm going to have to come in to look for her.'

A high-pitched laugh was the only reply.

'For God's sake, Professor, you must tell me: where is she?'

'My daughter is where she belongs,' was the sinister reply. 'With me. Now leave. *Gaan weg, boesman.*'

Eberard took a deep breath, trying to stay calm. Then he tried a new tack. 'When did you discover that Melanie's boyfriend was black?' It was more a statement of knowledge than a question. He paused while he waited for the comment to sink in. 'When Melanie shouted at him that her father would kill him, it wasn't him she was frightened of. It was you. When you discovered that she was seeing a black man, she knew you'd be furious. That's what she meant, Professor, isn't it? That you would be angry? Or did she know that you would actually go so far as to kill him?

Did she really mean "he will *kill* you"? I think she knew what you were capable of, Professor. I think she knew only too well.'

There was some movement from behind the door. Eberard stepped back from the wall and raised the rifle level with his eyes. The square sights stood up like a castle on a hill, topped with a luminous white marker. The end point on the barrel nestled between the battlements, concentrated on the door. The sound of footsteps receded to the other side of the room. He lowered the rifle again.

'You know absolutely nothing about my daughter, *klonkie*. Leave, or I'll tear you apart. You're a drunkard like the rest of your slave kind. A thief and a drunkard. I'm part of the builders of this land. You're part of its destroyer. You're no more than the rubbish in the gutters. You're the filth on the bottom of my shoes. Now get out of my house! *Voertsek!*'

The professor's attempts to intimidate him only increased Eberard's resolve. He did not fear the man's blustering insults. He realised, perhaps for the first time, how powerful a weapon knowledge could be.

'You're the slave, Professor, not me. You'll never be free, not physically free. You're going to jail for a long time for what you've done. You will most likely die there. But you could free yourself from your burden by letting go your hatred, by letting the world know what you've done. By telling me. I can liberate you, because I know what happened.' The professor gave no response, just the slow panting of a man trapped.

'You can't hide it from me, Professor. You had sexual relations with Melanie. Not just on that night, but for months, for years, before that. You're the man in the lullaby. You're the hunter your daughter feared. You're the one who took her locks of innocence. You're the spiderman on candy-striped legs. You are her coldsleep lullaby.' Eberard felt his own voice constrict with anger. He stopped speaking, letting the rifle butt rest on the floor, feeling sudden exhaustion. Du Preez's silence was his admission of guilt.

'You'll get no confession from me.' The voice from the study also sounded tired now. Eberard persevered, angry again.

'This is your confession, Professor,' he seethed. 'This is your confession. You found out that Melanie was having a relationship with Bullet; she was *fucking* a black man.' He spat the words out. 'Not just any black man, but an illegal Burundian immigrant. Had she rejected you by then? Told you what she thought of you? Taunted you? She chose him over you, and she chose him carefully. She chose him to hurt you. And it worked, didn't it? Maybe she threatened to tell your secret. Maybe she wanted to protect Elsabe. You'd started to abuse Elsabe as well, hadn't you? Maybe she told you she'd go to the police. Maybe she just rejected you. Maybe that was enough. It doesn't really matter, Professor, does it?'

Eberard stopped and waited, then let his next words fall one by one, like solid marbles on the floor.

'*You* raped Melanie that night, didn't you? You lost control. Not just control of your temper – you lost control of years of guilt. It exploded inside you in that one terrible moment. You raped your child, Professor. But she fought back this time, screamed at you, scratched you. So you hit her with the first thing that came to hand. Just to subdue her. Just to make her stop. You crushed her skull with a brick. You thought that you'd killed her, Professor, didn't you? So you stripped off her clothes and put her body into the river.'

The sounds in the study were increasing, the noises of a caged animal pacing, hissing.

'We didn't pick up your DNA on the test, because there was only seminal fluid from you. So, we found the DNA of your daughter's lover instead. We could've tested the body later, of course, if we'd had any doubts. But you had her cremated. I wondered about that at the time: cremating a young girl's body. It seemed so quick. And killing the Burundian to secure your innocence. That was a bold move, Professor. You risked a lot doing that, but then you had a lot to play for. Playing one murder against the other: one the moral reaction of a wounded father; the other the actions of a sick man.'

Du Preez roared at him from the other side of the door – a scream of retribution and fury. As the sound reached him,

Eberard kicked the side of the door hard and leapt into the doorway, the rifle aimed at the opposite end of the room.

The professor was standing behind the desk, his mouth still open in a hideous, deformed scream. His clothes were dishevelled and he was unshaven. He clutched a cheap white paraffin candle in his hand, holding it out towards Eberard as if it were a crucifix warding off advancing demons. Elsabe sat slumped in a chair positioned between them, but closer to the window. Her legs sprawled awkwardly to one side, and her neck was bent unnaturally towards her left shoulder. The flame of the candle sputtered as Eberard closed the door gently behind him.

'As you can smell, Detective, the room is doused.' The professor spoke calmly now, but pointed his chin at Eberard in defiance. His voice was thin and strained, hoarse from the scream. 'My fate and that of my daughter … it's in my hands now.'

Their eyes remained locked. Then Eberard took a single, deliberate step into the room, placing his front foot firmly onto the damp carpet. The professor frowned slightly but said nothing. Eberard spoke evenly: 'What you can't understand is that I welcome it.'

He stepped to the side, his feet squelching on the flooded floor. He kept his eyes on the man holding the candle, stretching out a hand towards the figure on the chair. Her skin was still warm, but the blood flow beneath the surface was barely detectable. Eberard could not be sure if he'd found a pulse. His face flushed with anger as he squeezed her limp wrist.

'No one is innocent, Detective,' the professor explained. 'Not you. Least of all you. Not me, not her.' Du Preez stretched out his arm and pointed the candle threateningly towards his daughter. Eberard noticed that the arm of the chair was soaked in petrol.

In one swift motion, Eberard dropped the girl's hand and raised the gun to his shoulder. His antagonist was nothing but an outlined figure in the sights of the rifle. He could have been a target on a firing range or a criminal fugitive. The room seemed quiet and unusually bright. The flame of the candle danced to one side of the front sights, weaving as the professor's hand shook slightly. Eberard stopped thinking. Just for a second, he felt serene and in control. Then he squeezed the trigger.

A short blast of air blew over his face, and a spinning brass shell turned slowly across the room. He squeezed again, and again. And again. Objects moved in front of him, entering and leaving his field of vision without sound, turning and falling. The candle, the shell casings, a flash of red blood, all slowly spinning, knocking against the furniture, popping on the wooden desk, staining the wall, bouncing on the carpet, rolling on the floor, lying still, silent.

Eberard had fired six rounds before the falling flame reached the dense layer of flammable fumes within a foot of the ground. As the seventh tipped bullet left the muzzle, the room exploded. Fire immediately filled every possible space of air in the study, sucking the oxygen into the explosion. The burst of pure heat and energy tore the desk apart, scattering pieces of wood still untainted by the fire itself through the windows and cracking the frames. Outside, the newly arrived policemen threw themselves to the ground to avoid the splintering shards of glass. There was no air inside the room; everything in front of them, everything around them, inside them, was plasma. It hit the professor with a solid force that stopped his last breath in the second that it erupted; it hit him like a sheet of metal, crushing him against the blood-splattered wall. He breathed in fire itself, and the heat scoured every part of his body.

Elsabe's chair was overturned, and the explosion sent her sprawling towards the door.

Eberard could not feel the heat. He was in a cold place, one abandoned by blood and feeling. Streams of red and orange and blue played and danced in front of him. He watched the air burn at the edges of his eyelids, savage and pretty, all the colours of the rainbow. It swirled and leapt, the shapes of fierce animals and desert landscapes forming and disintegrating like clouds. He felt cold, but comforted. The fire was cleansing. It would take his enemy away from him. It would punish the man and exonerate his pursuer in pure bursting heat. It was an ending. He gave himself up to it without any resistance.

The conflagration roared at him like a demon, howling and tearing. Its force threw him back against the door. His trousers and the front of his bulletproof vest exploded into flame, and the blast tore the rifle from his grasp. As his back hit the wooden door behind him, he felt it give, and he tumbled backwards. A hand grabbed the neck of the vest, lifting him, arching backwards, into the passage. His eyes felt seared and his skin burned painfully. Patterns played before his eyes, bright and dark. The door was kicked closed, but the force of the explosion threw it open again. He felt himself being dragged across the carpets, the sound of footsteps running hard alongside him. He tried to open his eyes, but could see nothing; they were filled with fluid. His lungs heaved, scarred and burnt from breathing in the first blast of fire. His body shook with pain before darkness enveloped him.

Eberard lay on his side on the brick paving. Hacking coughs wracked his whole body. Cool water trickled out of the end of a hosepipe, running across his eyes and face. His trousers were still smouldering. The melted polyester stuck to his calves and pulled painfully every time he tried to move. He turned his face upwards and let the water splash over his cheeks. He imagined lying in a clear rock pool, in cool mud with frogs and dragonflies darting about, looking up towards the top of a thin waterfall. He traced the separate drops as they came over the rocky edge and first started their fall, all the way through the clear air, splashing onto his skin. He felt calmed by the waterfall, and his breathing came more easily as he let his body relax.

Xoliswa had not left him since grabbing him out of the room of the inferno and dragging him down the passage. Her hands felt soft on his face, stroking his wet cheek. He smiled as she ran her thumb gently along the line of his lips. Her eyes did not leave his face. The air was fresh, filled with the smell of pine needles. And the unique, indefinable scent of another person.

ROCK-A-BYE-BABY

Rock-a-bye baby, on the tree top
When the wind blows, the cradle will rock
When the bough breaks, the cradle will fall
And down will come baby, cradle and all

EPILOGUE

THE Eerste River bubbled across the smooth stones of its bed, coursing between the banks of grass and twisted roots of trees. The river water was almost amber, the colour of weak rooibos tea. It threaded through the town, a marker on its long journey to the open sea. People walked their dogs, throwing sticks for them across the open expanses of mown grass alongside the banks. Couples sat with their hands intertwined, basking in the late afternoon sun and listening to the water gurgle and splutter as it passed. Upstream, two children bent over, concentrating, as they took aim, skimming flat stones across the weir. The distant roar of a council truck was borne by the wind. A small group of workmen, dressed in blue overalls, was loading alien wattle bush onto the back of the yellow van. A grey-headed heron paced in the shallows, stirring up the mud with its open feet, picking at the fleeing beetles and larvae.

Dappled light played across Elsabe's face as she walked beneath the trees. Her companion walked beside her, matching her every step, close enough to support her, but without touching. Elsabe walked slowly, still weak and unsteady on her feet. She could have reached out to the person next to her, held on to an arm, asked for a rest, but instead she went on, clutching a small wooden pot with both hands determinedly, her eyes surveying the ground in front of her.

'Perhaps there, where the water goes over the weir,' Elsabe said, pointing ahead into the light.

'We can take our shoes off and stand in the water,' Xoliswa suggested, her voice soft but clear.

'Yes,' Elsabe replied.

They walked down the gentle slope to the concrete weir; water poured over the edge in a constant stream, cutting a wide hole into the riverbed before drifting out into a large pool. The heron strutted off further upstream as they approached. They sat together, untying their laces and pulling off their socks in silence.

They moved their toes about, almost involuntarily, enjoying the feeling of being barefoot in public.

At the river's edge, they sunk their feet into the flowing water gingerly, but the water was warm and the current gentle. The flow caressed their ankles and tickled the top of their feet.

'We should take our shoes off more often,' Xoliswa said, laughing lightly. Elsabe said nothing, but looked up at her. Her eyes were bordered by dark rings, and she looked tired, but there was the suggestion of a smile. Xoliswa smiled back. 'Come on, let's go out into the middle,' she said, gently putting a flat hand against the young girl's shoulder.

Once they had edged out to the middle of the weir, they turned to face downstream. Elsabe removed the top of the wooden pot and crouched down onto her haunches, the water splashing up against the curve of her jeans.

'Ready?' Xoliswa asked, bending down next to her charge. But Elsabe had already started to tip the pot towards the water. A slow trickle of powdery ash began to run in a line, fluttering out across the water's surface. The patch of water discoloured slightly and then cleared as the ash was sucked over the edge of the weir. Elsabe tipped the pot further and the contents rushed out towards the river.

They stood for a while, watching the stream absorb the last flecks of grey. Only a slight dusty residue remained on the water's surface, for a while bouncing up and down on the ripples, catching the sunlight, and then disappearing for ever.

Elsabe's eyes were dry, but her voice was filled with emotion when she spoke at last: 'Melanie would have wanted to come here, in the end.'

Xoliswa put her arm around the young girl's waist and squeezed her. They turned together, pushing their toes through the warm brackish water before making their way back towards their shoes on the bank.

ACKNOWLEDGEMENTS

Thanks to Terence Chua (www.khaosworks.org) for permission to reproduce his lullaby and the title, and to Robert Plummer, Helen Moffett and my editor, Martha Evans, for their guidance and enthusiasm. Thanks also to Lindy Solomon for generously sharing her time and ideas, and as always to Patti for her tireless support and encouragement.

LIST OF SOURCES

'O skoonheid van die lyf, jy slaat' (p. ix) – NP van Wyk Louw, *Raka*, © 1978, reproduced with permission of Tafelberg Publishers

Hush, Little Baby (p. 8) – traditional

Sleep Baby Sleep (p. 22) – traditional

Golden Slumbers (p. 33) – Thomas Dekker, seventeenth century

Toora, Loora, Loora (p. 44) – traditional

Lavender's Blue (Dilly Dilly) (p. 53) – traditional

Brahms Lullaby (Lullaby and Good Night) (p. 69) – Johannes Brahms, nineteenth century

All Through the Night (p. 83) – traditional

Suo Gan (p. 91) – traditional Welsh lullaby

Lullaby ('I shall find for you shells and stars') (p. 106) – Gian Carlo Menotti, *The Consul*, copyright © 1950 (renewed) by G. Schirmer, Inc. (ASCAP). International copyright secured. All rights reserved. Used by permission

A Lover's Lullaby (p. 118) – George Gascoigne, sixteenth century

Lullaby ('The light is losing all its charms') (p. 127) – © Martha Evans 2005

'Lay your sleeping head, my love' (pp. 128–30) – copyright © WH Auden, reproduced with permission of Faber & Faber Ltd

My Childhood (p. 141) – © Dora Teitelboim, from *All My Yesterdays Were Steps: The Selected Poems of Dora Teitelboim* (Jersey City, NJ: KTAV Publishing House, 1995), reproduced with kind permission of the Dora Teitelboim Centre for Yiddish Culture

Lullaby ('Sing to me a lullaby so I can close my eyes') (p. 152) – © Danny le Pelley/Guarana 2001

Sweet and Sour Lullaby (p. 160) – © gembolding, from the website Paradox Poetry, www.paradoxpoetry.com, 2004

Lullaby ('on candystripe legs spiderman comes') (p. 170) – The Cure, from *Disintegration*, lyrics by Robert Smith, reproduced with permission of Universal Music Publishing (South Africa)

Medgar Evers Lullaby (p. 181) – © Richard Weissman 1964, reproduced with permission of the David Gresham Entertainment Group (Pty) Ltd

Lover's Lullaby (p. 187) – © Janis Ian 1975, from *Between the Lines*, reproduced with permission of EMI Music Publishing South Africa

Lullaby ('Under the cover') (p. 196) – © Cathy Dekker, from the website 'College Poetry', http://hal.ucr.edu/~cathy/index.html

Coldsleep Lullaby (p. 207) – © Terence Chua 2000, from the website 'Khaosworks.org', www.khaosworks.org, reproduced with kind permission

Lullaby ('Shall I stay or go') (p. 214) – © Joe Jackson 1994, from *Night Music*, reproduced with permission of Sonya TV Music Publishing

Sweet Lullaby (p. 224) – © Tammy (surname unknown), from the website 'Tammy's Castle on a Cloud', http://home.ptd.net/~martian/poems.html, June 1998

Clementine (p. 234) – traditional

Looking Glass River (p. 243) – Robert Louis Stevenson, nineteenth century

Rock-a-Bye-Baby (p. 256) – traditional

The author and publisher gratefully acknowledge the permission granted to reproduce copyright material in this book. Every effort has been made to trace copyright holders and to obtain their permission for the use of this material. The publisher apologises for any errors or omissions, and would be grateful if notified of any corrections that should be incorporated in future reprints or editions of this book.

Bᵀ
6/19/14

BALDWIN PUBLIC LIBRARY

3 1115 00642 4898

MYS
FIC   Brown, Andrew (Andrew
Brown   David)

         Coldsleep lullaby.

$24.99

DATE			

NO LONGER THE PROPERTY OF
BALDWIN PUBLIC LIBRARY

BALDWIN PUBLIC LIBRARY
2385 GRAND AVE
BALDWIN, NY 11510-3289
(516) 223-6228

BAKER & TAYLOR